RAGE OF GODS AND DRAGONS

THE ORIGINS OF CYLLA
BOOK FOUR

HARLEIGH ROSE KNIGHT

Rage of Gods and Dragons
Copyright © 2025 by Harleigh Rose Knight
All rights reserved.
This is a work of fiction. Names, characters, places, and incidents either are
the product of the author's imagination or are used fictitiously.
Any resemblance to actual persons, living or dead, events, or locations is
entirely coincidental.
No part of this book may be reproduced in any form or any electronic or
mechanical means, including information storage and retrieval systems,
without written permission from the author, except for the use of brief
quotations in a book review.
Published by Harleigh Rose Knight

Formatted by Vanessa Mena, Inkspark Digital
Cover Design © 2024 by INKBookDesign
Edited by K.F. Starfell
Map Design by Danni of DandyFantasyDesigns

Identifiers
ISBN: 978-1-963934-08-3 (eBook)
ISBN: 978-1-963934-09-0 (paperback)

TRIGGER WARNING

This book may discuss topics that are not suitable for everyone and may be difficult for some readers. This book includes mentions of parental neglect, emotional abuse, torture, grief, self-worth trouble, gore, violence, memory loss, violation, coercive dynamics, infant death, dismemberment, physical abuse, panic attacks, forced infertility, child death, and attempted sexual assault. This is a story about deities with loose inspiration from mythology. If topics of violence and death are too much for you, put the book aside and take care of your mental health first.

May the odds be in your favorite character's favor

CYLLA
OURANOS
BRONTIDE
ORKST
ASHBELL
ELOWEN
EDUR
SEPHTIS
SEA OF ERENDIS
EREBUS
DAXON
BRISA
ELD
MIDORI
SELMOR
SOLARIS
MOIRA

CHAPTER ONE

THE BEGINNING OF THE END

SAGE

I wasn't sure if I watched Nikola in horror or wonder. His presence was so strong that I felt like he might swallow me whole. I stood inside a castle with walls so high I couldn't have reached them if I'd wanted to, yet I felt as though I'd been placed in a small maze. Compressed and unable to pick the right path to walk.

Most of my life had been spent unable to commit to one feeling or another. I'd wanted to be a guild leader, but couldn't commit to being at center stage in conflicts. I'd wanted to be with Vespera, but couldn't commit to leaving Onyx behind. I'd wanted so badly to be able to stand tall and confident in a decision. The pressure of seeing it through to failure was unbearable enough that I backed out any time I moved too close to certainty.

It seemed that none of those things mattered in the end. My wants, my wishes. They hadn't stopped life from moving. Dreams hadn't kept anyone by my side.

Onyx had left me behind as though we were strangers. Vespera hadn't made an effort to see or speak to me. Nikola and Sahir told me to forget about her. They claimed that she was a waste of my time, but I would have been lying if I'd insisted that I didn't miss her.

I'd wanted to seek her out when I was alone, but I couldn't shake the feeling that something terrible had happened to her. When Nikola was near, I would forget about her. He carried such a strong aura that nothing ran through my mind when he was close. The air around him seemed to thicken, pressing against my thoughts until they scattered like leaves in wind.

I felt nothing for Nikola until he was within touching distance.

When he was within reach, my body was on fire for him. I would have killed for Nikola to touch me. The intensity of it stole my breath. I felt so strongly that his touch was worth killing for. I was ashamed and terrified to admit how willing I was to do anything he wanted in exchange for one touch. The thought alone made my pulse quicken and my hands tremble.

I hadn't enjoyed fighting as much as I should have for the job I'd picked. I did what I had to do to pay for what I needed. With Nikola close, it was different. I craved to hurt someone just for him to smile in my direction. The desire was sharp and foreign, cutting through my usual reluctance like a blade.

Nikola called the high fae of his court to the gathering hall. The halls of Nikola's court were unlike anything I'd seen in any other land. Hooded statues lined the front of each column on the way to his throne like a guarded hallway, their carved faces hidden in shadow. The scent of old stone and something metallic, blood, perhaps, hung heavy in the air. The throne was the disappointment of the room. The colors were vibrant, golds and reds, and each column held its own swirled designs from top to bottom, but the throne was nothing.

An oversized chair, simple and hardly padded. He must not have planned to ever use it. I couldn't imagine Nikola being satisfied with it any other way. He never would have called something so simple his own.

Voices were raised, and the sound echoed off the walls around us like thunder trapped in stone. Nikola took his place in front of the throne, and Sahir took his right side. There was only one place for me to stand, but it felt wrong to place myself in it.

I didn't fully understand why I was beside him. Why was I important enough to have a conversation with, let alone be one of the closest people to his side? I knew that I should feel honored, but I felt as if I were making all of the wrong choices again. I was a simple woman with a simple goal. Maybe I should have been happy to stand beside such power. If there was anyone who had the means to help me make the kind of difference that I wanted to make, it was Nikola.

But would he help?

Our differences seemed so vast that it was hard to imagine him standing aside so that I could live quietly, spending my afternoons in a bookstore. The image felt impossibly far away now, like a dream half-remembered upon waking.

"My loyal subjects," Nikola's voice boomed out, each word striking the stone walls and reverberating through my chest. "Today is a day that will be remembered for an eternity. It will be etched in stone and paper for generations. Today, we start at the beginning of the end. New ideas and life will blossom, and we will create the kind of world we want to live in. Under one god, under one set of rules, we will ensure those that want to cause us or our families harm with their opposition will be eradicated. Peace will be ours if we are willing to fight for it."

Fae roared in response. Their fists pounded at the sky as if Nikola had spoken every word their hearts needed to hear. Sometimes I thought it was more his presence that pulled people in than the words he spoke. There was something about him that was melodic, hypnotic in its cadence.

"Today, I will grant all of you the ability to not only be

loyal members of my court but defend those you love against the threat that is upon us from the skies. There are gods among us who wish to not just harm us but to kill us. They wish to see us turned into dust so that they may mold a world without us. They think that they're better than us. We won't let that happen!" Nikola's voice was like a hammer of steel striking an anvil.

The Fae didn't ask any questions. They didn't ask who the enemy was. They never pressed for more. They drank him in like water in the desert, parched for his every word.

I wanted to ask. I hadn't seen a single deity lash out or hurt anyone. I'd seen chaos at Nikola's request.

"It is time we move out of the Age of Starlight and enter the Age of Darkness. It is after that light will shine on a new world." Nikola finished his sentence with a rumble of a laugh that made my spine tingle.

Nikola parted his lips, and out came a tune that would haunt me. Darkly beautiful and smooth was the sound, like honey laced with poison. It felt as if the notes tried to strangle me, wrapping around my throat like invisible fingers. They did strangle the Fae. Black notes wrapped around their arms, legs, and throats until they were spread by all four limbs, wider than should have been allowed. The life-like notes entered their mouths, and from the Fae's core to limb grew a layer of black mold that pulsed with unnatural life.

The notes tightened until the sound of ripped flesh was louder than the melody that Nikola still sang out. The wet, tearing sounds made my stomach lurch. Fae bodies crashed to the ground, covered in fuzzed mold as only torsos. Their arms and legs landed separately with sickening thuds against stone.

Screams of pain mixed in with the song until they also hummed the cold tune back to Nikola, their voices creating a twisted chorus. As many legs as a spider released from where their limbs had once been, and the same number of arms grew from the stumps left on them, black and chitinous and wrong.

There was a familiarity to watching someone allow spiders to leave their body. The sight tugged at something buried deep in my memory.

Their mouths poured a neon orange liquid that foamed like rabid hounds at dinner. The drops from their lips caused the ground to sizzle beneath them, stone hissing and bubbling where the acid touched.

Nikola had turned the Fae into monsters.

Was that what he considered a gift of great power? Sure, they would be able to defend their loved ones from a common thief. He hadn't lied in that regard.

Their loved ones would never see them the same way again. They would never be seen as noble guardians with great power and the king's favor. They'd be seen as monsters. The weight of that realization settled heavy in my chest.

Nikola closed his lips and stopped the tune. I felt like I could take my first deep breath in minutes. I took my breaths rapidly enough that I became light-headed, the cool air rushing into my lungs like salvation.

Nikola turned to me and smiled. The look sent shivers of fear and desire equally through me. He'd done it again. I was scared of him, but I enjoyed being scared of him and being close to him. I wanted to act out until he looked at me with that same intensity.

I needed him to look at me with approval. I craved it like I craved air.

"Go, my loyal subjects. Protect our new home while I lay the foundation on which we will build our future." Nikola called.

The group of creatures roared in response. They moved with such speed and so many legs that I felt my lips turn down in disgust. The sight was something I could have only dreamt up on my worst nights of sleep. Never would I have imagined seeing such a thing, the stuff of nightmares made flesh.

"Come, let me show you something else." Nikola held his arm out, his voice gentle as if he hadn't just ruined the Fae's future.

He talked to me as if he hadn't just destroyed lives. He spoke softly, his features even and calm. The hardened jaw he kept clenched tight sat casually with a slight smile playing at the corners. If I were a woman who enjoyed betting, then I would bet that he was using some sort of magic on me.

I took his arm because if he were using magic on me, it worked. I was entranced by him, caught in his web like a willing fly.

I needed him.

He stopped our walk in front of a plain wall. He pointed to the wall, and in a snap of his fingertips, a mirror of water surrounded by vines and flowers appeared like a hidden door. He moved us through it together. I was sure I would come out the other side soaking wet, but I was dry as a bone in the hot summer sun. I was as dry as the grass at Nikola's feet. It wilted and died under his steps, turning brown and brittle with each footfall.

Another shiver ran through my mind. I felt like I'd seen it before, too. It was always only a fleeting feeling, like trying to grasp smoke.

The land was shining white. Bright enough that my eyes scrunched shut against the glare. The reflected sunlight was too much at first. I needed time to adjust my eyes. Nikola took my arm and placed it in Sahir's instead, his touch lingering just long enough to make my skin burn where he'd touched.

Nikola left the two of us and moved ahead to knock down walls. The land was a compound, pathway after pathway leading into room after room. White and silver colored every detail, and the white was tarnished quicker than if it had been any other color. The grass beneath him turned black and brown, and the walls turned crimson with the color of gods being thrown around beneath Nikola's mercy. The metallic scent of blood filled the air, thick and cloying.

The sight informed me that we hadn't come for peace. We'd come to take over. He hadn't brought me with him to show me something special. He'd dragged me along his path of destruction like I were an accessory on his belt loop. The realization stung more than I cared to admit.

"This reminds me of the past." Sahir smiled, her eyes gleaming with something that looked like nostalgia. "A friend and I once did something similar."

"You have friends?" I asked, genuinely surprised.

Sahir shot me a side-eyed glance before she spoke again. "I have many friends, and if I didn't, it wouldn't matter. Daddy is all I need in the end."

The words that left her lips made my head throb with familiarity, like an echo I couldn't quite place.

"I had a friend once who stuck by my side no matter what I did. I could have told her to kill her own sister, and I'm sure that she would have simply done so to prove she was loyal to me. She wanted to save me. As if I need saving." Sahir's laugh was sharp and bitter. "She turned against her friends and family to stay with me. She killed her sister's people to keep me happy. She was a fool, and even while I was gone, even after she nearly stood on two solid feet, in the end, she didn't brighten up any."

Why was the story important to me? The words twisted in my stomach like a knife.

Nikola motioned us forward. He tore down the towering cathedral in front of us and erected his own rubble-built hall. Dust didn't need to be fully clear before I saw him forming his own throne of the bodies of the gods he'd thrown around moments earlier. A smaller seat was placed beside his, made of carefully placed marble from the walls he'd crashed down.

Sahir moved ahead of me with pride, stepping carefully

around the running forms of others trying to flee the destruction. Nikola stopped her and moved her to the side without offering her a seat. He took my hand, walked me to the marble seat, and helped me sit to his left. The marble was cold against my legs, and I could smell the dust and death that clung to everything around us.

Sahir's tanned skin looked sun-kissed with how flushed red she became, her jaw clenching tight with obvious anger.

"Go get her," Nikola demanded of Sahir.

Sahir stormed off, pulling the bottom of her dress in such a rage I thought it might tear the fabric.

"Do you like it?" Nikola asked me, his voice soft and intimate despite the carnage surrounding us.

"Yes," I breathed. My heartbeat quickened.

I didn't like the sight of death, but I liked anything he gave me. I'd answered him so quickly that even my own mind hadn't caught up with my lips.

"I'll make you something better once we have settled in. For now, I hope it makes you feel like a queen." Nikola murmured.

A queen? My heart skipped again, warmth flooding through me at the promise in his words.

Sahir came out, dragging a woman who was hardly keeping on her feet. Her brown eyes looked up at me as if she'd seen a ghost. I might have missed it beneath her matted orange hair if not for the way her entire body went rigid. Sahir tossed her to the ground with a smile. Not a smirk, a smile so wide I saw her canine teeth gleaming.

"Yumi. I was surprised and elated to hear that you were still alive. I thought for sure the sisters would have killed you as soon as they learned the truth. Imagine how shocked I was when I discovered that you managed to keep so many things to yourself. I did not give you enough credit." Nikola crossed one leg over the other and clapped in mockery, the sound sharp in the dusty air. "I didn't give you enough credit." His jaw clenched. "I want to become close again, Yumi. We were good together once. If you hadn't betrayed me, we could have skipped so much of the middle ground we've been floating through."

"Me?" The woman coughed with her laugh, blood speckling her lips. "You betrayed me!"

"Your jealousy is what betrayed you. It led you down a path against me. If you could have shared me, we could have also shared in the spoils of the realm. You could have sat beside me like these girls are now." He nodded in the direction of Sahir and me.

"Do you think Dahlia will let you keep her?" Yumi shook her head, her voice hoarse. "She will sooner skin you alive."

"I have spies that tell me Dahlia has no magic. How tragic is that? She's now joined the useless siblings." He leaned forward on his seat, his eyes glittering with cruel amusement. "Here is my offer. I won't punish you further as long as you agree that the throne and the realms are mine to control. You will assist me willingly from this day forward, and I won't doubt your loyalty."

"Should I refuse?" Yumi asked from her knees, her voice barely above a whisper.

"Then I will eat you whole where you kneel and become a master of starlight as well. I think that I have a strong enough body now to hold two primordial positions. Don't you?" His face was unmoving while he spoke, carved from stone and just as cold.

Yumi looked at me for several long moments that made my stomach turn before she relented. "Fine."

Sahir crossed her arms tightly around her chest with a frown. She used her foot and shoved the woman forward with unnecessary force. Nikola snapped his fingers and broke the glowing chains that were wrapped around Yumi. After several rolls across the dusty ground, she unwound the chains that had bound her, her movements weak and pained.

"Who is she?" I asked Nikola in a whisper, leaning close enough to catch his scent. Something dark and intoxicating.

"She is the once mighty Goddess of Starlight." He whispered back with a smile that made my pulse race. "Even original deities bow to your future husband."

My stomach shuddered, but my heart quickened at his words. Future husband. The promise of it both thrilled and terrified me.

CHAPTER TWO
THE AGE OF DARKNESS KNOWS NO PEACE

Nikola had created a collar of bone for the Goddess of Starlight. To me, it was no way to form an alliance. The Goddess had already tried to remove it, and she held the blackened wounds around her throat to prove it. She smelled of rotting flesh and looked just as close to death's door. The stench made my eyes water when the wind shifted in her direction.

Nikola had her tasked with pulling Gods from the stars in the sky. I'd never imagined that's where our deities came from. The idea of being locked away, only able to watch the world age and people die while you had to wait patiently to be allowed to be born, sounded terrifying. The idea that something we gazed at and talked about as beautiful in our night sky held waiting souls made my skin crawl.

It was a chilling thought.

Did they dream? Would they remember everything they'd watched while they sat in the sky? Could they speak to each other? The questions circled my mind like vultures.

Why did Nikola want so many born at once? Did he think

they would help him in the war he wanted to fight? How could he have been so sure that he wasn't creating his own force of opposition?

I wasn't convinced that there needed to be a war. No one contested him being king of Cylla. Wasn't that enough? No one so much as stood strongly in front of him when he took over the realm of the Gods.

I didn't agree with what he was doing, but I wanted to be near him. The conflict tore at me from the inside.

So I stayed silent while I watched the Goddess of Starlight slowly rot around her throat and push herself until her fingers bled to pull souls from the sky. She did it surrounded by a lush garden. A sickening contrast, beauty thriving while she withered.

I couldn't pick a side. Maybe what Nikola was doing was wrong, but who was I to judge whether it was any better or worse than other Gods? There had to be something I didn't know. If I thought about it hard enough, there would be many reasons the other gods were wrong, too. They'd watched us starve and never lifted a finger.

Maybe both sides were wrong, and I would do better not to pick a side. The thought brought little comfort.

"She looks like she's happy and treated well."

"Who are you?" I asked with a jolt, spinning around to face the newcomer.

One red eye and one black eye looked down on me. "I am Deimos, God of Dreams."

"Do you know her?" I pointed to Yumi, who was bent over her work, shoulders shaking with exhaustion.

"I know her very well." He answered, his voice carrying an edge of something I couldn't identify.

"Does she deserve this?" I asked, then held my breath waiting for his response.

I studied his face for the answer he might not give. He searched my eyes with pity, and the look made my chest tighten. Deimos was the first one to look at me as if I were a disappointment since I'd stood at Nikola's side. His brows pressed together for a brief moment before he settled his expression back to neutrality.

"She deserves a lot more than what she's getting. She has done a lot, even if many have forgotten it. Do you feel bad for her?" His mismatched eyes examined me with his words.

Did I feel bad for her? Or did I feel bad that I had to witness her treatment? The distinction felt important, though I couldn't say why.

"If she did something wrong, she should pay for it, right?" The words came out as a question, uncertainty bleeding through every syllable.

"Should she? Or should she get a second chance?" Deimos countered with another question.

Our conversation made my head throb. It wasn't his words that hurt my ears; it was his voice that shook my mind like an earthquake. I felt as if it might explode. I grabbed my skull and bit my lip hard enough to taste copper. He started to feel familiar to me, like a half-remembered dream.

"It seems easier to reset you than I thought," Deimos mumbled, more to himself than to me.

"Deimos, stop confusing my toy," Nikola declared as he entered the garden, his presence immediately commanding attention.

I groaned at the ache in my temples. "Toy?"

He hushed me, but lingered his gaze on me for a second longer than necessary.

"I don't think that she should be allowed here." Deimos snapped at Nikola, his voice rising with each word.

"Should I decide your opinion is needed, then I will ask for it. Until then, we should settle on how nice it is that I did not ask what you thought," Nikola replied, his tone deadly calm.

"If you keep her here, they will come!" Deimos' voice became increasingly louder, desperation creeping in.

"Don't be so emotional, Deimos. That is exactly what I want. They will be drawn to her like a magnet. If they are coming to me on my time, then there will be no problems." Nikola nodded with satisfaction. "Why would I want to go to them?"

My mind cleared, and the aching stopped as fast as it had started. I exhaled slowly, relief flooding through me.

"I will excuse myself," I offered, attempting to bow and leave.

Nikola stopped me by gripping my arm, his fingers firm against my skin. "No, Deimos was leaving. It's in his best interest. We don't want a reset at a time like this."

Deimos looked at me with his two-tone eyes for several moments too long, and I shifted beneath his intense gaze. He relented under Nikola's glare and left, but he held his chin high still, defiant to the end.

"What was that?" I asked, rubbing my temples where the pain had been. "His words sent my mind spiraling. Like a chisel to ice. I thought my skull would break apart."

Nikola nodded, his shaggy white hair moving around his forehead with the motion. "I wouldn't worry about your mind. I will make sure it's stable. As for his presence, he carries a bit of anger."

"Anger?" I furrowed my brows, wanting to understand.

"I haven't bothered to ingest what the mortals are tossing around as teachings these days, but I'll assume it's inaccurate to the truth. Deimos is the God of Dreams. Her son." He pointed at Yumi, who hadn't looked up from her work. "She is the Goddess of Starlight. One of the original beings. After the originals came the seasons. After the seasons, there was Justice, Protection, and Space. Then there were the sisters. Four of them were created. Creation, growth, life, death. Without them, life didn't exist correctly; through them, our world flourishes. Once, Deimos was tasked with capturing the sisters for his mother. He failed, and now he is failing again." Nikola's tone held mockery and satisfaction in equal measure.

"Again? The sisters are here? Is that what the war is about?" I shook my head, trying to process it all. "Why would anyone need control of them? No, how would anyone control something like that?"

"What if one day they decided to cleanse the realm because they didn't like it anymore? Who would stop them?" He asked, his eyes boring into mine. "Uncontrolled power in the hands of a few girls seems foolish and irresponsible. Does it not? As for the how, that's what the false deities are for. Four perfectly shaped bodies, primed and ready to be filled with the power of the sisters and left in the hands of those better suited to wield it."

"What if the one controlling them decided the same?" I challenged, surprised by my own boldness.

Nikola smirked before he lifted his arm for me to take. "That's enough for now. We have other things to get to."

I was disappointed with the answer. I wanted to know more, and I wanted to see the sisters. I wasn't interested in the gods before, but if I was going to help him, if I was going to be part of something that would likely kill many, then I needed to know what it was all for. I needed to know why we were doing so many questionable things. The weight of not knowing pressed against my chest.

He guided me to another room that had once been nothing but white and silver. A table long enough to seat an army was still intact in the middle of the room. Nikola had turned the rest into dust-covered rubble. I ran my finger over the thick layer of dust on the surface of the table, leaving a clean trail in my wake.

White was so easy to stain.

I took my seat at the nearest corner to Nikola. There were already so many faces scattered around the room. Angels stood with golden wings tucked and faces scrunched in the furthest corner of the room. They whispered to each other, their voices like wind through feathers.

I'd heard of Gods having a mortal form and a form they used in their own realm. It had to have been true because some of the beings sitting around were larger than anything in Cylla. They had tails of snakes or horns on their heads, their otherworldly nature impossible to ignore.

I realized after a few moments that Nikola's creatures were hunched on the other side of the room as if they were guards. One gazed down at its own orange drool dripping onto the ground and burning a hole through the tile with a steady hiss.

"If everyone is ready to start talks, my ears are open," Nikola announced, settling back in his chair with the casual confidence of someone who knew he held all the power.

"You can not just enter Semper and turn it to ruins!" one man with horns yelled.

He'd been waiting for the go-ahead to speak, his words tumbling out in a rush.

It told me more than anything he could have added. His words screamed in opposition, but his body still gave Nikola enough respect to wait for permission to voice it. He spoke out, but he still feared Nikola. The contradiction was written in every line of his posture.

"Turn it to ruins and then claim charge!" Another yelled in agreement, emboldened by the first.

The candles in the middle of the table flickered with their heated breath. I glanced at Nikola; I tried to move only my eyes. His face was stone still, like always, but I saw the darkening of his eyes. His eyes were already black, but they'd held life to them. The more voices yelled, the less life he held. It was like watching light being snuffed out, one flame at a time.

I sat up straighter and pulled my shoulders back in anticipation of Nikola's response to the group that was clearly unhappy with him.

My heart beat in my throat like a caged bird.

He motioned for his creature to move to the table. It trudged itself to a cart on wheels and passed out silver chalices to everyone at the table, its many legs clicking against stone with each step.

"I think we should start with lowering our voices. No progress was made while overcome with such anger." Nikola observed, his voice cutting through the tension like a blade.

He lifted his own glass and took a drink. I watched his throat bob with the swallow, but I still didn't trust my own cup. I hadn't felt thirsty before, but with the thought in front of me, my mouth felt parched as desert sand.

I was not the only apprehensive one in the room. Not a single hand touched their cup.

"Come now. Do you think I'd poison you? Do you consider me so uncreative? I may consider you rude if you deny my offer of friendship." Nikola's words carried a warning wrapped in silk.

His voice was still smooth as the tabletop, and his eyes as dark as an abyss. Eyes shifted around and searched for who would be first to take a drink. I didn't know why I did it. There was nothing circling my mind. There was not a single warning to stop, and there was no good reason to proceed.

I lifted my cup and took a drink. The cold cherry wine took the dryness from my mouth, and I set the cup back with too much force. The sound rang out like a bell in the tense silence.

The liquid washed away my dry mouth, but it did nothing for the still air I silently breathed.

"Good girl." Nikola hummed, and the praise sent warmth flooding through my veins. "If she can do it, so can the rest of you."

My body lit up like an evening sky during a festival at his words. He was proud of me. The feeling was intoxicating, better than any wine.

The room lifted their cups, and they either faked the drinks or it was simply wine because everything remained fine.

"Explain why she, of all things, is by your side." An Angel spoke, his voice dripping with disdain.

"No," Nikola answered simply, as if the question wasn't worth his time.

"Then what are we here for? We don't accept you as our ruler. I won't allow you to keep her by your side. I refuse to help you. Enough of us know who you are to try and stop you. Dahlia has been getting louder. We can hear her cry from her cage!"

Nikola's face never changed, never showed a display of emotion. His body did that well enough to make up for it. He was on his feet with the small glass bowl that sat in the middle of the table in his hand. It had been for decoration, and somehow, it had made it out of the rubble that surrounded us.

It didn't matter in the end. Nikola shoved it inside the Angel's mouth and held his jaw and skull in each hand. He forced the motion of chewing until crimson waterfalls poured out of each side of the poor angel's lips. The scent of blood filled the air, thick and nauseating.

The sound of glass crunching against the Angel's teeth would haunt me forever. It was wet and sharp and wrong in every possible way.

My heart raced as fast as the glances around the room. Every alarm system in my body rang out loud and clear. Every nerve inside of me set fire to the need to run. All of the parts of myself that should have moved shut down and refused to respond to me. My body locked me in place like I'd been turned to stone.

"Spit it out," Nikola demanded as he held the jaw open. "You don't need to worry about poison. I'd rather see you learn a lesson than die without any thought. Spit it out." He repeated, his voice deadly calm.

There was too much blood to confirm if all of the glass had hit the ground when the Angel spat on command.

"There's no need for you to swallow it and die so soon. I want an apology first." Nikola demanded, his grip tightening on the Angel's skull.

Nikola's face contorted for the first time, for a brief moment, a flash of something dark and hungry.

The Angel opened his mouth, blood bubbling on his lips. "Find Vespera."

He was hardly audible, but I heard him clearly. Nikola picked the glass back up off the ground. It still dripped fresh blood, dark drops hitting the floor with soft pattering sounds. He shoved it down the man's throat and stood back up, wiping his hands on his clothes as if he'd done nothing more than handle refuse.

"Anyone else?" Nikola asked as he straightened his clothing, his voice conversational.

No one attending the meeting spoke. Instead, Sahir slipped in with laughter from the doorway. She leaned so casually against the frame, considering the events that had played out.

"Find Vespera? That's what he decided to use as his last words. I think he's not as informed as he hoped." She cackled, the sound sharp and cruel.

"What does that mean?" I asked, my voice barely above a whisper.

Nikola looked at her as if he were burning a message into her eyes, and she lost her smile immediately.

I did want to find Vespera, even without prompting. There was something about being with Nikola that made my mind lapse away from normal thought. I knew that what I'd watched him do was horrific. That it was wrong. My body, my mind, it all told me to forgive him and move ahead.

That he wouldn't do the same to me. That I was important to him. Above Sahir, even. The thought should have terrified me, but instead it filled me with a warmth I couldn't name.

The way Nikola looked at me in the eyes was electric. It was hot, like lightning striking my very soul.

Who was I supposed to speak to? The question echoed in my mind as I sat surrounded by monsters and gods, feeling more lost than ever.

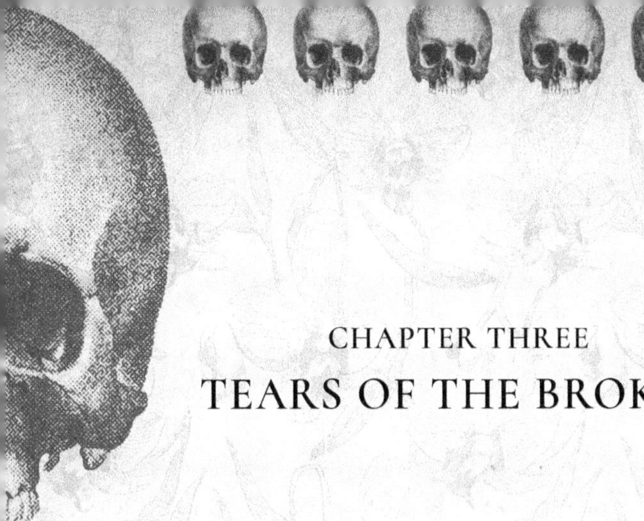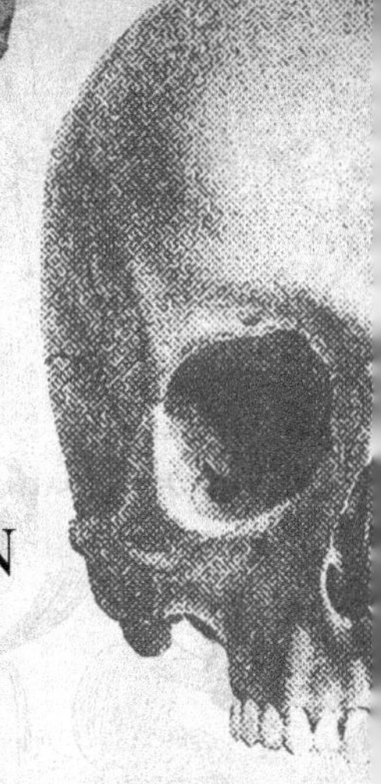

CHAPTER THREE

TEARS OF THE BROKEN

CAYM

The statue erected of me by my worshipers was, in my opinion, a poor representation. They had made my cheeks too puffy, and I would have preferred some kind of jewels for my eye color instead of cold, lifeless stone. The carved marble felt foreign when I looked at it. Too soft where I was sharp, too gentle where I was fierce. It was a foolish thing to focus on. It meant nothing in the end.

Still, I needed something else for my mind to ponder. Something to offset the sight of what was curled around the bottom of my statue.

The temple meant nothing to me. If I were being honest, the people inside meant little to me. I didn't care if they left it trashed and covered in dust, the incense bowls cold and forgotten. I wouldn't have lost a moment's thought if no one came to pray at the temple ever again.

For her, though, I was glad that there was something she could cling to. Some tiny piece of me that she could grasp to help herself feel something. I wanted her to feel anything because as long as she felt, even if it was pain, it meant she hadn't shut herself down completely.

Ruri looked as if she had already lost more than a few pounds. As if she hadn't slept for weeks. Dark circles shadowed her eyes like bruises, and her skin had taken on a pallor that made her seem almost translucent. I could see a frailness in her that I hadn't seen since we lost our child. That was what I saw again, her, laying in our bed. The bed we shared every night. The bed that we filled with laughter and tears, whispered secrets, and stolen kisses. Fading away to nothing but a blank soul waiting to pass.

I knelt down in front of Ruri, the phantom weight of my knees pressing against stone that couldn't feel me. But she could not see me. Her gift was life, not death. If her name were Hesperia, maybe it would be different. I lowered my hand so that my fingers could brush the hair from her face, but I slipped through like morning mist. Not a single small, green flyaway hair shifted. She did not flinch or gasp in shock at the sight of me. She simply curled tighter around my stone feet, her body trembling with each ragged breath.

I tried a second time to brush the tears that ran down her cheek and failed. The salt tracks glistened on her skin, and I wished that I could have whispered even a single word to her. It was for the best because knowing that I was stuck would only hurt her more. She mourned my death, but it would be worse if she had to mourn my loss and grieve for me being locked in an empty abyss as well.

"Please come home." Her voice cracked like breaking glass. "If this is my punishment for sleeping through everything, then it's too much. The punishment is too far. I can't live like this. I can't carry this kind of weight." She wrapped herself around the stone tighter, her knuckles white against the marble. "I'm not as strong as you, Caym. I can't be the better person if you're gone. If you aren't part of the world, then I'd rather see it fall. Please. Please come home. Please. There's nothing left to fight for in a world without you."

Her words broke and turned into incoherent sobs that echoed through the empty temple. She mumbled so many things that I could not understand, fragments of memories and desperate pleas that tangled together in her grief. I felt my heart shatter each time she sobbed a bit harder, each broken sound cutting through me like a blade. I was split between staying beside her, even in spirit, so that she didn't have to stay a moment without me, and leaving her to find a way back. I knew what I wanted and what I needed to do were not the same.

I wanted to stay by her side. I didn't want to leave her while she was in so much pain.

I needed to use that thought as my strength. I needed to remember that she was my motivation. That she needed me to hold myself together.

I leaned down and left a kiss on the air above her forehead before I stood and touched the star on my wrist until it pulsated with familiar warmth. Nikola's weakness laid not in ignorance, but arrogance. He was strong and smart, but he looked over simple details. I ensured that I never spoke them out loud, so it remained a fact he couldn't access.

Onyx's betrayal hurt, but Nikola failed to consider that he only put me back in my own realm.

Maybe that's why I was the first to come back. Maybe I remembered in some part of myself that I couldn't form words that I needed to come back to the realm of the living and help the rest come back, too.

Onyx took as much from me as Nikola took, but Onyx hurt worse. My situation meant that he was the reason my wife and her sisters died. Not just once, but every time. He was the one stealing blood and framing me. While I protected him. While I defended him.

I called him my brother. I could have put a stop to things sooner if I hadn't been so willfully blind.

Still, there was a relief in the review. A new sense of progress. I could hold onto the thoughts until they grew as bitter as overripe fruit, or I could use it to fuel my desire to get back. I would prefer to look at my situation as temporary. Nikola temporarily ordered me to be locked away in a place that belonged to me to begin with. Death belonged to Hesperia and I. My situation would only be temporary.

Nola, after Nola, appeared in front of me. They stood in perfectly formed rows in front of me, their skeletal forms casting no shadows in this place between worlds. Jeb stood in front of the formation, his jaw set in that familiar way that meant he was preparing for battle. It was difficult not to hold the image of Ru as the only thought in my mind, but I had to shove it down and put it away for now if I was going to get back to her.

"Jeb, I need you to help Ru while I'm away. She's not doing well, and I'm worried about what she may do once her tears have dried up." I stated.

"She better if knew you live," Jeb grunted.

Ruri had taught him to speak well, but he still had some work to do.

"She can't know. I can't guarantee that I can leave. Nothing is set in stone until the clay dries." I cautioned.

"She need know." He pressed.

"She will, but not today. Today, I search for anyone else here, and I try to open a rift. Today, I fight to get back to her, and you fight to keep her safe. Today, you don't cause her more pain. You keep her from doing anything that she will regret if I come back, and we can make things right again." I demanded.

He always was more loyal to her than he was to me. I saw pain in even his skeletal features at her mention, the hollow sockets of his eyes somehow managing to convey anguish.

I hated what I had to do next. If there was any other option, any other thing I could have done, I would have picked it instead.

I didn't have the ability to do the same things as the other deities because I spent most of my time in their dominions. I may have been dead, but it also meant I was at my peak. I was in my domain. I had the potential to harness the energy of death and create things from it.

It's what my first step in death needed to be.

I needed to open a doorway back to the living. Something I could work on walking through to get back to her.

"I need to ask one of you to do something for me that brings me no joy. I will spend every day making up for it." I sighed, still unable to let the sentence leave my lips. The words felt like poison in my throat. "I need, I need one of you to die."

There was only one way to have the full potential of death in front of me.

Every Nola marched forward by two steps, and I closed my eyes and held them shut. The sound of their movement was like dry leaves rustling in autumn wind. I knew that they would all selflessly offer. It made it even harder than it was to begin with. They never questioned why I asked. They never thought twice when it came to a request I made. There wasn't even a breath of hesitation.

I moved to the first Nola that I saw and removed my glove. The item crafted by Ruri that kept death at bay. The item that allowed me to forget, for a brief while, that my hands did not love. They did not create life. They took it away. They leeched every bit of happiness and joy from everything they touched.

I was going to prove that again.

I examined the palm of my hand. There wasn't a callous or cut. No sign of struggle or labor was written across them. They told the story of a lifetime of hiding away beneath a layered shield. I placed my hands on the Nola's skull, each finger on a temple. The life left him through what should have been his eyes, but were only sockets. The mist wavered in the air until it pulsed in my fingertips like a heartbeat made of starlight.

I needed the essence of death in its rawest form to open a rift to the other side. The Nola's body dropped, and I caught him in my arms. I held him close to my chest and used my other hand to crush the soul I held and open a rift to the realm of the living.

The air grew cold, and a rush of wind and screams mixed together to form a doorway on my side of the in-between. The sound was like a thousand voices crying out in anguish, a symphony of the lost and forgotten. I opened the door, but the other side was locked to me. I would have to have someone on the other side do the rest.

Crossing back to Ru was so close, but still out of my grasp.

I was closer to becoming something more akin to Yumi than getting back to her in the same shape I had left her as.

The Nola never flinched while they watched what I had done to their friend, my friend. I never loosened my grip on his body while I put the glove back on and put away the curse that I carried with a bare touch.

Even if they never breathed a whisper of judgement or resentment, I held more than enough breaths to make up for it.

"Take him and lay him to rest in my cabin. We will give him the burial he deserves when I get home." I commanded.

A Nola took the body from me reluctantly. I hardly realized that I refused to loosen my arm until he tugged the body twice.

"Go and wait for me to call you again," I ordered.

I held my composure until they were gone, and then I allowed the contents of my stomach to leave. I threw up all over the black abyss flooring before I lowered myself to the ground. The taste of bile burned my throat, sharp and acidic.

I was becoming a monster. A leader willing to sacrifice his own. No one could have thought less of me than I did, but the idea of what my Nola thought of me now was haunting.

What Ru would think of me was crushing.

I wiped the moisture off my cheeks and got back to my feet. I'd have a lot to make up for, but even more if I gave up after their willing sacrifice.

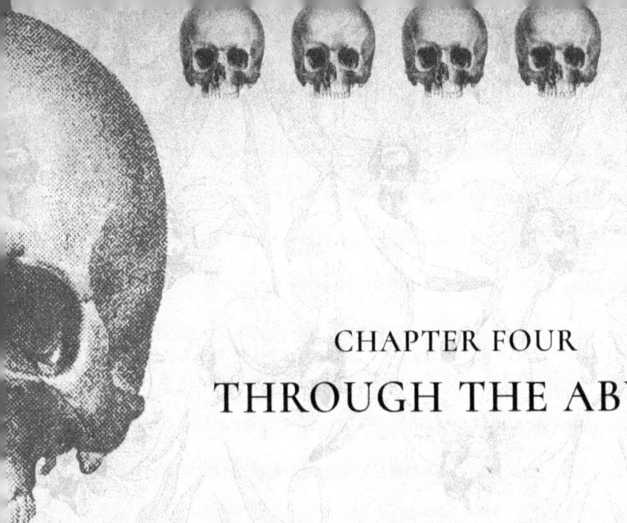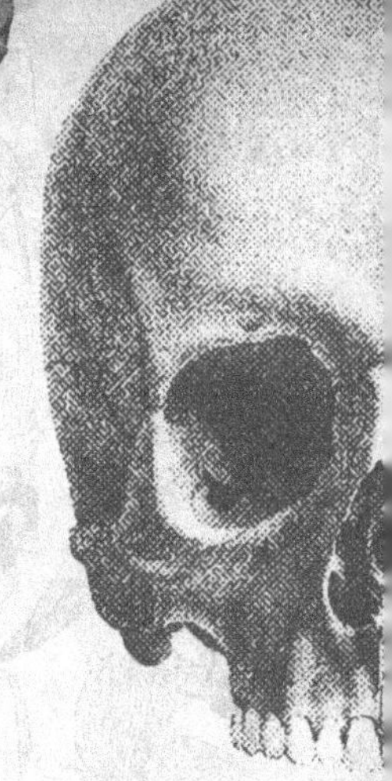

CHAPTER FOUR

THROUGH THE ABYSS

CAYM

Things had to have been moving rapidly on the other side of the veil. The number of souls wandering around me ticked up quickly, their spectral forms multiplying like shadows cast by a dying flame. Death was abundant in Cylla, and the proof grew in front of me with each passing moment.

The dead groaned and wandered with whispers on their lips of Deimos. Their voices carried like wind through a graveyard, hollow and mournful. The closest one to me whispered about how Deimos had lied to him. I stopped the wandering soul with my bare hands, and he stood in front of me at command. He was ready to do anything, to answer any question that I asked.

"What did Deimos lie to you about?" I commanded.

"Deimos, he promised we'd be promoted. He told us our afterlife was guaranteed by the blessing of the gods if we listened. He has stolen power, and he has been using it to create a realm of nightmares. A realm of agony. He's been using us as tests. He's going to lock them away."

"Who? He's going to lock who away?" I shook him, my fingers digging into his translucent form.

"The sisters." The soul replied.

I released my grip and let him continue to mumble his broken litany of betrayal and pain.

I would take more than a hand from Deimos when I was back in the land of the living. I left the souls behind and walked through endless darkness for what seemed like an eternity before I felt the presence of someone familiar to me.

The darkness felt so different when I was alive. It had felt like my home, filled with warmth and a welcoming touch that I enjoyed. There was a coldness now that I hadn't expected. A kind of emptiness that I had never experienced before, like breathing in winter air that froze your lungs.

Maybe it wasn't the void that I was in. Maybe it was the idea that I couldn't guarantee that I'd ever leave and go back to Cylla. To what was actually my home. Maybe it felt cold because the only warmth I had was Ru.

I'd rather freeze than have her where I was.

A pile of spirits huddled over something, and I picked up the pace of my footsteps. The sound of my boots against the void echoed strangely, as if the darkness itself were swallowing the noise. I grabbed spirit after spirit with my still-gloved hand instead and tossed them away. They hardly realized that I relocated them. They hardly knew anything had happened around them at all.

When I laid my hand on the last body hovering over the ground and swatted away the mist that surrounded it, Coy's face appeared, and the dead all snapped into realization.

They ran like animals on all four limbs at me to get to Coy. They sniffed him out and hunted him in hoards that hadn't been there originally. One by one, they moved through me and back onto Coy's unmoving body as if he were a dinner feast that waited to be devoured.

As if they had been commanded to keep Coy down and devoured.

I shoved my way into the horde of souls. They were heavy with demand. With a cause. They weren't hollow. They had a purpose. They had a desire.

They had a need for Coy as great as my need for Ru.

They resisted my every pull. My every tug. They denied even my most desperate cry out for them to get off of him. I ripped off my second glove so that my touch would be equal to my words when I called out for them to make way for me to get through.

Coy's eyes opened and landed on me. They were wide but empty. Glazed with a disconnect. He was physically there, but not in any other way. Lake blue eyes stared off into nothing, as if he were looking through me into some distant horror only he could see.

I grabbed at the souls by the throats, the hair. I grabbed for any part of them that I could, but it hardly stopped them. I started to dig my fingers into their souls until they turned from shimmering black souls of dim light to then dust beneath my fingers. The texture was like crushing dried leaves, brittle and somehow both weightless and heavy at once. I clawed at them with a power only I had until they became lost in the darkness of the flooring beneath me.

It still wasn't enough, fast enough to keep up with how quickly they were moving back to Coy.

There seemed to be no end in sight. If Coy was being devoured by souls on Deimos's order, then it would mean he gained more power than any of us gave him credit for. To cause me to struggle in my own domains. It spoke volumes of what he had been up to behind our backs.

No, not behind our backs. In front of our faces, while we ate up every small distraction that was so carefully placed in front of us. While we called ourselves all knowing and all powerful deities, only to be shown in the harshest way that even we were still only naïve beings, a small step above the mortals.

Ru left me with another gift before I abandoned her. The power of the sun. It was the exact opposite of the in-between. Warmer and stronger than the veil. It was a gift I hardly touched.

I held both of my hands to the pile of souls and unleashed the rays of light from both of my palms. The light was so bright that it blinded me in the darkness that surrounded us, like staring directly into a newborn star. It burnt the souls in a way I was sure would prevent them from ever coming back or moving on. The heat scorched the air itself, making it shimmer like summer pavement.

The heat not only cleared the path to Coy but also took his pale, expressionless face and removed the mask of death from him. Coy was no longer flat on the floor. He was hunched over, choking on oxygen that his lungs had forgotten how to process.

"Am I dead?" Coy asked.

His voice sounded as if it had gone through a bushel of thorns before its exit from his lips, raw and torn.

"You are," I answered him.

"Hesperia?" He whispered.

"Not now. We don't have time to dwell on what may or may not be happening. We need to get back on our feet. We need to get back to them. We don't do that by sulking here." I tried to convince myself as well as Coy.

Coy stumbled to his feet, but he did not look at me. I tried my best not to take it personally. The souls left rushed and moaned all together in the opposite direction, their collective wailing like a funeral dirge carried on phantom wind.

"That has to be where Vespera is," I declared.

Coy ignored my words as if I had never spoken any at all.

"I couldn't remember Hesperia because of him. He locked my mind in a cage. I was his backup plan in case Onyx didn't work out. Nikola caged my memories so that I would be a blank slate in his grander plans." Coy growled.

"Do you have your memories back now?" I asked.

"As if a dam broke inside my mind. I caught him. I caught Nikola giving Onyx orders to slip something into her tea. He claimed it would help to lock down Shivani's mind and magic. Preparation for the things to come in their future. He was getting the girls ready to be locked away until he could guarantee their death and take his power for his own. He caught me. His hands were around my neck." Coy stopped speaking.

His eyes glazed over as if he had left our reality and slipped into a different one. He traced the skin around his neck as if he were in a trance, his fingers following invisible bruises that his memory insisted were still there. I was hesitant to speak, but afraid to allow him to stay lost in a replay of his memories.

He blinked and shot his eyes up to me. He spoke no words with his expression or mouth. Instead, he reached inside of his ear and scraped. He tugged and pulled until his fingers were too deep, and I reached for his hand. I pulled him as hard as he pulled at himself, and when his two fingers were ripped out, a tiny serpent came out of his ear.

The two of us looked at each other in disbelief. The creature writhed in the air between us, its scales catching what little light existed in this place.

Coy took off in a full sprint into the souls. I crushed the serpent under my boot before it could have become lost, feeling its small body pop like a rotten grape.

I had never considered such an idea. The thought that something like that would have been used or inside of someone. It never crossed my mind.

We were meant to protect the goddesses while they protected the world, but we hardly had any real idea of what we were dealing with. Of the depths that Nikola had gone. We were ill-prepared for the depths that we had been tossed into.

I was stopped before I reached Coy. He was too distracted to notice. His calloused hands beat into anything he saw in a blind rage. He did not care if it made a difference or not, his fists connecting with spectral forms in a fury that seemed to feed on itself.

The air shifted and grew thicker, like breathing through wet wool. The sound of chains filled the endless space. Metal against metal, ending with the sound of dragging. From the shadows, a tall and wide figure appeared. It was wrapped in red-soaked cloth with eyes of white that seemed to glow with their own inner light.

A smile sat on its thin lips. Jagged teeth moved with his words.

"I could help you if you only gave a small token in return." Its voice rattled the air like bones in a cup.

"What are you?" I looked it up and down.

"I am the Blood Weaver. It is poor manners to not know the things that live where you claim to rule." It huffed.

Had it always lived there? I couldn't recall ever smelling so much as a hint of him before. The scent that clung to him now was copper and decay, sweet rot that made my stomach turn.

"What is your cost?" I nearly denied myself the right to ask.

"Only a bit of your blood." It cackled.

My blood? Did I need its help? The power Ruri gifted me should have been enough to get us out.

CHAPTER FIVE

HAUNTED BY THE THOUGHTS

RURI

Dahlia and I sat together in the meeting room of my temple, the silence between us heavy as stone. We waited for everyone meant to be in attendance to arrive, sitting like strangers who had forgotten how to speak to one another. The air felt thick with unspoken words and fractured memories.

It would take an adjustment to have her around and feel comfortable. The scent of jasmine that clung to her skin stirred something deep within me, a ghost of recognition that made my chest tighten.

I had memories of her, but I had already lived so much without the idea of a kind mother on my side. Of any mother. I had lived what felt like one hundred lives since she and I were mother and child, each one carving deeper grooves between who we had been and who we were now.

It was hard to allow myself to trust that she was there for me, to hear me. The doubt crept through my veins like poison, whispering that this too would be temporary. It was difficult to not feel as though I carried my burdens and hers, the weight of her lost years pressing down on my shoulders.

It was even harder to place myself in a lifetime where I had such a thing as a kind mother. If I tried, it felt more like a dream than reality. The memories of Dahlia were so far away that they played out in my mind like scenes from a half-remembered story, faded and fragile as old parchment.

I could feel that she hardly knew how to interact with me, either. Her fingers twitched against her skirt as if she wanted to reach out but couldn't bridge the chasm between us.

A part of me, even if it felt guilty for thinking it, also wondered if maybe her time as a mother, or a leader, was over. Everything from her look to the way she walked behind me whispered of uncertainty. It all silently screamed of a deity long forgotten, beautiful but brittle. I was sure that if she commanded something, everyone would listen out of guilt. Not out of respect, or even trust.

We would listen if she commanded it, but it wouldn't be in the same way we would listen to someone like Astra. The thought sent a fresh wave of grief through me.

Dahlia must have felt it, too. It wasn't only me that changed since she had legs instead of bark. The realm as it stood knew nothing of her, not truly. We were still trying to piece together a dream from reality all over the realm, grasping at fragments of what once was.

The Age of Moonlight that Dahlia ruled over was like a story book, and the Age of Starlight that Yumi led us through was the only reality we truly lived through. Everything else felt like folklore whispered around dying fires.

The air between us radiated the sentiment, thick and uncomfortable. She sat still and straight, her posture perfect despite the tremor in her hands. Her shoulders were in the perfect position; she had clearly never slouched, even at her worst. Her skin glowed against golden jewelry that caught the firelight and threw dancing shadows across the walls. She wore a simple golden crown with a moonstone inside of the center, the pale gem seeming to pulse with its own inner light. It was held perfectly in place by lavender braids that smelled faintly of forgotten gardens.

Even if I didn't see her as a mother or a ruler, she still intimidated me. Even the way she breathed was majestic, measured, and deliberate. She was our origin. Our beginning. Dahlia was the start of everything we had, and I could only imagine the aura she had back then. How powerful she was when she commanded an entire universe, when her word was law written in starlight.

She must have felt my eyes on her. If she were from a storybook, she was painted perfectly, too beautiful to be real.

"Once, in the past, it seems we shall never lay sight on again, you sat in my room while everyone else slept. Silence sat between us then, too, but it was gentler." Her voice was soft, almost musical. "The silence of those days was filled with a mother loving her daughter. You had your own brush on my nightstand so that I could spend the evenings playing with your hair."

The words hit me like a physical blow, and I had to bite the inside of my cheek to keep from gasping.

Her index finger fidgeted with the seam in her skirt, and I couldn't believe my eyes. The movement was so human, so vulnerable.

Was she nervous?

"If one had asked me then if I had thoughts of us drifting," she paused and lowered her chin for the first time, the moonstone in her crown catching the light, "I simply would have laughed."

The admission hung in the air between us like a bridge I wasn't sure I was ready to cross. I didn't respond because she sounded like she needed comfort, and I did not know how to give it. The skill felt rusty, forgotten from disuse. She turned to watch me, and I tried my best to keep looking ahead. Not at her lilac eyes or the way her braids were kept so neatly in place, not at the sadness that seemed to emanate from her very being.

I kept my focus on the way her fingers twirled the fabric she wore, the nervous gesture so at odds with her regal bearing.

"He wouldn't want you to mourn. He wouldn't want you to dive off the cliff and fall into insanity. You can honor his memory by being strong." Dahlia tried her best to comfort me, but her words felt like ashes in my mouth.

"I can honor his memory by slaughtering every hand that played a part in bringing us to this point." I cut her off, the words sharp as broken glass.

"Do you think that is what he would wish for you to do with your time?" Dahlia asked, and I could hear the careful restraint in her voice.

I appreciated what she was trying to do. I understood how she must have felt because I, too, felt that we had a different relationship once. It was clear in the way she moved with ease before putting herself back on edge when she looked at me, like a dancer who had forgotten the steps to a beloved song. I didn't want to pretend that even though I could understand how she must have felt, I was the same.

To her, I was a daughter lost and found again. To me, she was someone I hardly knew, a beautiful stranger wearing my mother's face. To me, Caym was everything. His absence was a wound that wouldn't heal, a constant ache that colored every breath.

Getting vengeance in his name was everything.

I cleared my throat and adjusted myself until I sat back up straight, armor settling back into place around my heart.

"Can I ask you something else? Why Orla? Why was she the one to bring Sage and I back?" I asked, needing to focus on something concrete, something that didn't make my chest feel like it was caving in.

Dahlia's eyebrow perked up, and for a moment, she looked

more like the goddess of old. "She wanted forgiveness for her past mistakes. She gave up half of her heart and half of her soul to bring the two of you back, and in doing so, she gave up her godhood. She has no magic or abilities anymore. She chose to give it up to pull you both back from the stars, and as such, when she dies, she will be reborn a mortal." The explanation was clinical, but I could hear the weight behind it.

"What did she need forgiveness for?" I asked, though part of me already suspected.

"She was once one of Nikola's helpers. Betraying us from within." Dahlia's voice hardened, and I saw a flicker of the ruler she once was. "When Orla saw the destruction, the true terror Nikola could inflict, and just how much she helped it…" She was silent for a moment, as if she fought to pull herself out of the memory, her hands clenching and unclenching. "When I had my chance, I brought Caym back. I didn't know he would come back without memory. I picked him because I knew I could trust him. That he would save you, and the two of you would make sure the rest came back. When that didn't work, I ensured that Orla came next. I needed to pull souls back that were easy. I hardly had anything left inside of me." Her voice cracked slightly, and I saw how much the effort had cost her. "Caym's desire to get back to you made it easy. Orla's need to make up for what she did assisted me. I gave Orla the offer before she was born again, when we could still speak with her memory intact. She accepted it. She brought the two of you back and gave up her position as a Goddess in exchange for my forgiveness."

The revelation settled over me like a shroud. So much sacrifice, so much pain, all interconnected in ways I was only beginning to understand.

"So, she is to sit in a box that Helia put her in forever?" I scoffed at the idea, though it tasted bitter on my tongue.

"I declared that I would forgive her, Ruri. I never promised that I would bless her." Dahlia whispered, and the admission was another crack in the idea that she was a picture-perfect storybook ruler.

Hearing her was another crack in the facade, revealing the complex, flawed woman beneath the goddess.

"It's not much different from your view. You only don't like it because you hear it from my lips and not your own. You just declared that, despite Caym's disapproval, you would still go lower than you thought possible to get him back. Both of us picked vengeance over approval." Dahlia's words were quiet, but they cut deep.

That's not at all what I did. It was different. Wasn't it?

The sound of footsteps echoed through the stone corridors, pulling me from my spiraling thoughts. Mortals, dwarfs, and angels entered from the stone archway. The light from the oversized fireplace lit up every face that entered the room with a flickering glow, casting dancing shadows that made them look like specters. All their expressions matched anger that gave way to flickers of sadness when they saw me, pity that made my skin crawl.

Seeing the pity in their eyes sent a rush of heat through me, rage mixing with shame. I could have been productive. I could have sought Nikola out by now. Instead, I was the center of pity, and I played the part of a listening daughter to a sad mother, wasting precious time while Caym remained lost.

The sound of talons scraping against the outer stone of the temple cut through the murmur of voices. The silence was filled with the tune of dragons landing, and my nerves vibrated in tune with the familiar rhythm. I knew what the sound meant, and I was ready to get to my feet and get something done, to finally act instead of sitting here drowning in memories and regret.

I stood and, with the scrape of a chair against stone, left Dahlia behind. I pushed past all of the leaders who showed up to discuss movements and plans, their surprised gasps following in my wake. I ran down the halls of the temple until

I felt the fresh air hit me, cool and sharp against my heated skin.

Burgundy fur was in sight before any other dragon. Belladonna had assumed the position of authority and helped the dragons set up a council, her massive form radiating competence and strength. The position suited her well, and I felt a surge of gratitude that she had stepped up when I couldn't.

"I have brought guests," Belladonna rumbled as she shook her fur out, the sound like distant thunder.

I was grateful to know that she stayed by my side while I was not myself, a steady presence when everything else felt like it was crumbling.

"I have brought the Daughters of Steel. They want to help fight for Sage back, and I think they have a right to." Belladonna's voice was steady, matter-of-fact.

A girl with short, bouncy hair pushed herself forward, her movements quick and determined. Her eyes blazed with a fierce loyalty that reminded me of myself at that age.

"My name is Lia. Sage is more than a friend of mine. It's why we will fight, to the death, by your side." Lia held her sword to her chest, the metal gleaming in the afternoon sun.

"Before you swear anything to me, understand that I have no intent to go light and gentle. I won't use the word mercy. I will inflict pain until the results I want are in front of me. Make peace with your conscience before you look to me." I let the words hang in the air, heavy with promise and threat.

"We agree on the next course of action, then." Lia nodded, and I saw no hesitation in her eyes.

I took her opposite arm and held her palm to mine. The scent of burning flesh filled the air, sharp and acrid, and her palm erupted in a purple glow that simmered down to a washed-out pink before it dissipated. The magic flowed between us like liquid fire, marking her as mine.

"That burns!" Lia screamed as she pulled her arm back, cradling her hand against her chest.

"It'll go away," I replied dryly. "You're welcome."

Lia looked at me with a lifted brow and raised a finger to point at me. Lightning crackled from her fingertip before any words were spoken, the bolt singing through the air. Her eyes widened when she realized what she had done, shock replacing her earlier confidence.

"The Goddess gives you a gift, and you use it on her?" A dragon from beside Belladonna shouted, outrage coloring his voice.

"I didn't do it on purpose!" Lia shouted back, her voice shaking slightly.

"Calm down. She will need time to practice and gain some control over herself. It's not a natural ability, and even for me, it wasn't." I studied her face, seeing the mix of fear and determination there. "Unfortunately for you, you will have to learn faster than others, too. If you want to be on our side, if you want to help, you'll give it the best you have."

She looked at me with a changing expression, cycling through doubt and resolve before she settled on agreement, her jaw setting with determination.

"For Sage," Lia declared, and I heard the steel in her voice that gave their group its name.

I wanted to be easier on them all, but the time for that was gone. The luxury of gentleness had died with Caym.

CHAPTER SIX

SIDES MUST BE CHOSEN
BY ALL

RURI

Brontide hadn't changed as much as I expected it to. The land of Thunder was still as beautiful as it had been, but it somehow felt eerily stuck in the past, like a painting that had been left too long in the sun. As if it hadn't aged since my death, frozen in a moment that no longer existed. Divala, the dragon I gifted the land as a guardian, slept curled around the tallest tower of the castle built atop a stone pillar. The golden spikes on her back caught the morning light and matched the golden accents of the white castle, creating a harmony of light and shadow that spoke of better days.

The guards at the entrance whistled inside when they laid eyes on me, the sound sharp and piercing in the still air. The metal chains on the gate to enter tightened and sent creaks into the air as the only thing that stood between the entrance and I began to lift, the sound echoing off the stone walls like a death knell.

I expected them to offer some greeting, some acknowledgment, but the whistle and the gate chains were the only sounds. The silence felt heavy with judgment.

Kyra had refused my presence at Astra's funeral. She was adamant enough that I would not be allowed in that she sent out letters with the wrong date to the entire group. The betrayal still stung, a wound that wouldn't heal. To avoid my presence, Kyra deprived everyone of their chances to say goodbye, stealing that final moment of peace from all of us.

I tried to understand what she must have felt. The rage, the grief, the sense of abandonment that must have consumed her. I could not place myself inside such a spiral that I would deprive someone I loved, that I would have taken away their chances of being surrounded by those who loved them. But then again, I was beginning to understand that grief made monsters of us all.

Kyra's eyes were on me before I entered the main hall of her castle, green fire burning in their depths. Her jaw clenched so tightly that I thought she may break a tooth, the muscles in her face standing out like cords. Her lips curled and twisted before they parted, and when she spoke, her voice was like ice over steel.

"You have some nerve!" Her words were like frozen daggers, each one finding its mark. "I'll tell you one time to turn around and leave. I won't be so kind the second time I have to ask."

The hostility rolled off her in waves, and I felt my palms grow clammy despite the chill in the air. "Kyra, I just want to talk."

Kyra scoffed and rolled her eyes, the sound harsh and mocking. "Talk? You want to talk? Are you going to start with an apology?"

"Yes," I breathed, the word barely audible.

"Save it." She spat, and I could see the pain beneath her anger, raw and bleeding. "It wouldn't be enough. I don't care that you abandoned me. I've long since moved on. Not Astra. Her every waking moment was dedicated to you. She stayed devoted to you at my sacrifice till death. I won't help you.

Whatever you want, save it and leave. She waited for you, and you allowed her to die. You did the same to Caym. I won't do the same."

The words hit me harder than any physical assault I had been under, each one a blade between my ribs. They knocked the breath from my lungs and left me gasping.

"Kyra, I won't ask you to see from my point of view, or to even understand why I did what I did. I only ask that you consider if I had thought my choice would hurt you so much, I wouldn't have picked it. I wanted you to stay hidden for your sake. Can you imagine what Yumi or even Sahir would have done in my absence if they knew who you are? If they knew that you come from Caym and I? You would have been in chains faster than I could have hoped to come back. I had hoped to—" The words tumbled out, desperate and pleading.

"I didn't ask what you hoped to do, because it doesn't matter to me." She cut me off, her voice rising with each word. "It doesn't matter to me what choice you would have made. It only matters to me what choice you did make. The only thing we are similar in is that when we set our minds on something, it does not change. You and I have nothing to do with each other. I'll tell you one last time, go."

She pointed behind me to the exit, her finger trembling with rage, but when I turned, black eyes and shaggy white hair met me. The air seemed to grow thicker, charged with malevolent energy.

Nikola. Broad and towering, filling the doorway like a nightmare made flesh.

My blood turned to ice in my veins. Kyra moved past me and invited him in with much more warmth than she had shown me, her entire demeanor shifting from hostility to something almost welcoming.

She couldn't. She wouldn't.

But the evidence was right before my eyes, and it felt like watching my world crumble all over again.

Astra would not have agreed with her choice. The thought was a knife twist of certainty.

Kyra slammed the door to the room they entered together with enough force that the entire castle seemed to shake. The message was clear; it was none of my concern.

I disagreed with every fiber of my being.

It was entirely my concern. Astra's most trusted companion, no, my daughter, siding with the very thing that caused the loss of one of my closest friends. Of my husband. The betrayal cut deeper than any wound I had ever received.

I hurried my footsteps to the oversized marble door and leaned my ear against it, the cool stone pressing against my skin. Kyra's castle was not meant to keep secrets. Every sole of a boot sent waves through the air. Every bated breath that fell with the hope of silence still chimed through the walls, revealing the building's secrets to those who knew how to listen.

Every groan of passion that was let out with the hopes of privacy still whispered to the picture frames on the wall of its secrets.

I steadied my breath and pressed my ear as tightly as I could manage against the gap of the door, my heart hammering against my ribs.

"Of course. I anticipated that would be your request when I received word of your letter." Nikola's voice carried like honey over broken glass, smooth and dangerous. "The loss of a loved one is heavy. It's a pain that I know all too well. It simmers inside of you, escaping in stifled whimpers. You find that your hands tremble when you command them to sit still. Your dreams are haunted by their face and the memories of what could have been." His voice dropped to a whisper, intimate and knowing. "I can change it for you. I can bring her back to you, but it will be at a cost. You will have to hurt people you once loved."

The words made my skin crawl, and I had to bite down on my knuckle to keep from making a sound.

"I only love one thing." Kyra's voice was steady, resolute. "If you can promise to bring Astra back, then I will swear my people to your side. Use them as you see fit. They're stronger than most mortals. Ruri made sure of that."

The casual way she spoke my name, like a curse, sent a chill down my spine.

"You'd sacrifice your own people?" The voice was familiar, painfully so.

Sage. The sound of her voice was like a physical blow, and I had to press my hand against my mouth to keep from crying out.

Sage? Was she waiting in the room the entire time? Did she listen to us and not say a word?

Something inside of me snapped at the sound of her voice, like a dam bursting under too much pressure. My mind washed itself clean and refused to allow any new thoughts to flow through. I was light as air, unbothered by the weight of my feet, floating on a sea of rage and betrayal. The doors in front of me flung open and crashed into the walls behind them, and I was still watching it play out, without a whisper of a thought, as if I were outside of my body.

A wave of heat took over the blank slate that I carried when I saw Sage and Nikola together. His finger was tucked under her chin, and he lifted her face to his with the casual intimacy of a lover. He was sure to be singing some kind of sweet venom to her, too. Tales of his heartbreak or a vast pit of knowledge, promises wrapped in silk and poison. She was sure to believe it.

It had to be so since she was still by his side, still allowing his touch.

Kyra's expression contorted to match the fire I felt burning in my chest. Nikola's head casually tilted back to me with a smirk wide enough on one side for me to see his teeth, white and sharp as a predator's. His black eyes shimmered in the newly present rays of sunlight that streamed through the tall windows.

"I wondered how much you could take before you could no longer resist," Nikola mused, his voice like silk over steel.

Kyra was already releasing bolts of lightning from her fingertips, the air crackling with electricity. She wasn't hoping or trying that one might hit me. No, she was fully focused, fully aimed at me, each bolt precisely targeted.

I was her only goal, and she cared nothing for the architecture around us or the destruction she might cause.

She cared no more for her home than she did for me. The sight scared me for a moment, a glimpse into my own possible future. She mimicked what I was to become once the haze that I was living in wore off. Once I realized that my reality wasn't that different from hers.

I kept myself busy in the same way that I did the first time around, throwing myself into action to avoid thinking. If I had too many things to focus on, and my only worry was at night when I was alone, my battle seemed half as long. Half as hard. If I only had to distract myself from my reality, then was it really my reality?

But I knew the truth that lurked beneath the surface. When the dam that I so carefully built up broke, would she and I look the same? Willing to give up everything good, everything fought for, for even a whisper of a lie?

I think so.

I think I will look just like her when I stop pretending, when the mask finally falls away.

I think I would let the entire realm burn at his feet if it meant that Caym and I could leave.

Together.

I dodged and blocked with my own magic, feeling the familiar burn of power flowing through me. The hits that should have landed on my bare skin were deflected by shields of crackling energy. Nikola motioned for Sage to join Kyra against me, and although she had a look of apprehension, a flicker of the girl I remembered, it wasn't enough.

Maybe she thought of how I released her from punishment when she broke into the temple, how I had shown mercy when I could have chosen cruelty.

It mattered not. Sage lunged at me with a sword, the blade singing through the air.

"Isn't this a sight to see!" Nikola's laugh came from his belly, rich and cruel. "If I had dreamed up this day one hundred times over, I still would not have landed my dice on this sight." His laugh stopped as quickly as it had begun, and when he spoke again, his voice was soft, almost gentle. "I did hope that we would get to talk a bit more intimately. I did so want to replay your lover's last moments for you. To discuss his last words. The way his heart tasted while he begged for one last goodbye."

My teeth dug into the inside of my cheek too hard, and I tasted copper. "I know it's a lie. I would feel him on you."

"Do you want them to stop? So that you may feel me, Ruri?" Nikola asked, and there was something in his voice that made my skin crawl.

Bile rose through my throat, along with a wave of cold that sank it all back down. Had he truly eaten Caym's heart? The thought was so horrific that my mind rejected it even as my body shuddered with revulsion.

No. I would know it. If he ate Caym's heart and took his place as ruler of Merripen, I would know it. If Nikola had the sun magic I gave Caym, I would know it. The bond between us was too strong, too deep for me not to sense it.

Repeating those lines to myself was the only way I kept my head from spinning off of my shoulders, the only anchor I had in the storm of his words. I hardly had any sanity left to grasp onto, and somehow, his words were smooth and sweet even when gritted out.

There was something in his voice that almost convinced me to keep listening, a hypnotic quality that made me want to lean closer even as every instinct screamed at me to run.

I didn't want to keep listening, and I didn't want to hurt my daughter or sister. The conflict tore at me like claws. I had to leave. I had to retreat far from Brontide before I did something I would regret forever.

I couldn't win against Nikola, not alone. Not like this, not when my heart was already shattered and my mind was barely holding together. Even if every bone in my body wanted to hurt him, to make him pay for what he had done, I needed a plan. I needed no casualties. I needed the assurance that I would win before I moved a piece.

Most importantly, I needed him alive to ask him where Caym was. That was the only thing that mattered now: finding my husband, bringing him home, and making everyone who had hurt him pay.

The rest could wait. It had to wait.

But my patience was wearing thin, and I could feel the darkness growing stronger with each passing moment.

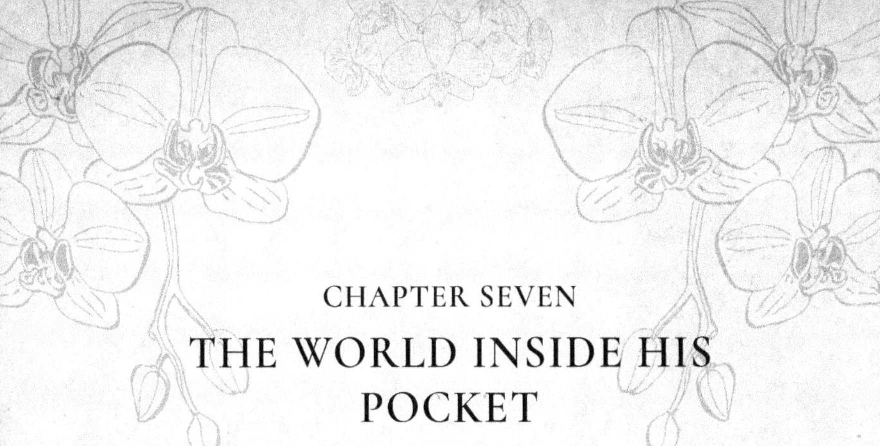

CHAPTER SEVEN
THE WORLD INSIDE HIS POCKET

HESPERIA

One red eye and one black stared at me from under thick lashes, the mismatched gaze unsettling in its intensity. His lips pressed together tightly after daring to ask me a favor, the silence stretching between us like a taut wire.

Thick brows and a freckled nose stood in front of me and dared to ask me to assist him with his memory. The audacity of it made my jaw clench.

"I know we aren't friends, and I don't want to be. You're just the only one that doesn't have a direct reason to kill me," Deimos stated, his voice carrying the weight of someone who had counted enemies more than allies.

"I don't?" I sneered, letting the question hang in the air like poison.

Deimos sighed and ran a hand through his stubbled white hair as if it would make a difference in the way it sat. The gesture was futile, desperate in its familiarity. "I'm not asking you to come to my side. I'm not asking you to forgive me. I'm not even asking you to redeem me or consider me at all in the future. I'm only asking that you help me clear up the fog over my mind. I simply ask for a fair chance to pick what I fight for because I don't believe I've gotten one yet either. This dream world Nikola has put you in is a place where we can speak openly. Why not use it? Nikola has a way with his words. It's as if when he speaks, there's a natural spell that he leaves behind. Sometimes, I lose myself entirely. Other times, my mind is strong enough not to be sung to sleep."

The admission hung between us, vulnerable and raw. I could taste the metallic tang of his desperation in the air.

"What is it you want specifically? For me to confirm that you've been lied to, or that Nikola has you under a spell?" I questioned, crossing my arms against the chill that seemed to seep from the dream realm itself.

"I want to know what is going on, specifically. I want to know why we are where we are. I want to know who Nikola is. What my part in it really is. He is all too happy to use me; he calls me his son. I know that can't be true." Deimos stumbled over the last words, his voice cracking like breaking glass.

"He is not your father. He is Onyx's father." I sighed in annoyance, the sound escaping through gritted teeth. "If I agree to speak openly with you, then you agree not to confuse one conversation for friendship. I will never hand you that."

"I know." Deimos nodded, the movement sharp and quick.

"You won't be able to repeat anything I tell you once you leave here," I insisted, my voice firm as stone.

"I know, but I will know it." He pressed on, leaning forward with an intensity that made the air between us crackle.

"Fine." I shook my head, feeling the weight of what I was about to reveal settle on my shoulders. "Where do I start?"

"At the beginning," he urged, wide-eyed and eager as a child hearing their first bedtime story.

The beginning was too broad. He didn't understand what

he was asking. I'd never get out of Nikola's cage if I tried to explain everything from the very start.

"There are a lot more lies than truths floating around. It would take a long time to sort them all out," I began, my voice taking on the cadence of someone who had carried secrets for far too long.

I did have a large part of myself excited to talk to someone about the truth of our reality. The words had been festering inside me like an infection, begging to be released. I knew everyone was interested in learning it, but the blockades were higher than the sources they had to gather from. I had become so focused on the path ahead that I had nearly lost sight of our road, which was already carved in stone and blood.

Even if I had the chance to deviate from the path, it wouldn't have mattered. I would always have to decide between telling the full truth, which I knew, or protecting my sisters.

If they knew that I held so much close to my chest, I couldn't imagine that they'd be quick to forgive me. I could hold onto hope that they would understand, but I knew better than anyone else that not all of them were quick to forgive. The thought of their disappointment made my stomach twist into knots.

"Dahlia and Yumi are the beginning, but so is Nikola. He is their brother. He was removed from Yumi's version of the world. Nikola was the darkness that held the moon and the stars in his sky. He cared for Dahlia more than Yumi, but it wasn't returned. Dahlia only cared for Yumi, and Yumi only cared for herself. When Nikola confessed his love, Dahlia denied him. He courted her all the same. He thought that if he showed Dahlia that there was light in him, she would change her mind. Every recreation only brought him a new sense of motivation to better himself. The day that Dahlia created Olexei, the sun God, her sun, was the day reality slapped Nikola hard. Dahlia was the only thing that he cared for, and she cared for everything but him. He turned his sights to Yumi in an attempt to hurt Dahlia. It was what caused Nikola's first death. He waited patiently for Yumi to find him after Dahlia erased her memory."

I paused, letting the weight of the story settle between us like dust after a storm.

"How do you know this?" Deimos asked, his voice barely above a whisper.

"There are no secrets in my realm," I replied through gritted teeth, the words tasting bitter on my tongue.

"Your realm?" He lifted a brow, confusion flickering across his features.

"The one you stole from me. Cosima is mine. I am the sorter of the dead. You stole my land, and you ruined it." I crossed my arms, the anger rising in my chest like a tide.

He glared at me with his two-tone eyes and his hunched shoulders as if I were the liar. The audacity made my hands curl into fists.

"Shall we continue?" he urged, his voice carrying an edge of impatience.

I rolled my eyes, the gesture sharp and dismissive. "Yumi kept Nikola's return a secret for only a short while. When Dahlia learned he was back, the seasonal deities thought she would implode the world. Dahlia had taken their memories as well. You can imagine the confusion when Dahlia was so upset by a new god appearing. There were only a few who knew the truth. Olexei, Astra, Fennic, and Aero. They were such a tight circle, they may as well have been one being. When Nikola gave everyone their memories back, the great battle began as well. Dahlia learned that Nikola could not die, and neither could she or Yumi. They only turned into something else and waited."

The silence stretched between us, heavy with the weight of revelation.

"That's the reason for the sisters," Deimos whispered, understanding dawning in his mismatched eyes.

"That's the reason for the sisters. In the end, there has to be something strong enough to contain that which cannot die. Dahlia realized that the only way to live was to contain Nikola and Yumi. Nikola refused to be contained," I replied, my voice steady despite the chaos of emotions swirling within me.

"So her plan all along was to use her children as war puppets?" Deimos mumbled, the words heavy with disgust. "To use you."

I ignored what he implied, the accusation cutting too close to truths I wasn't ready to face. "Nikola and Yumi turned on each other as well. That's where you enter. The three of them were meant to work together in harmony. Dahlia was the light, Nikola the darkness, and Yumi the neutral. Dahlia took from them to make Olexei. So they took to making their own children. Nikola stole from Dahlia to make Onyx and Juniper. Yumi stole from Olexei to make Sahir and you."

"So, I am Yumi and Olexei's child? So, you're my half-sisters?" He announced more than he questioned, his voice carrying a note of wonder and horror.

"I won't call you my brother," I grumbled, the words sharp enough to cut. "Dahlia and Yumi claimed that they weren't working together, but they had the same plan. They both failed. They learned that Dahlia was creating children to take over the realm. She wanted four vessels and four votes for anything that could happen in the future. Four sisters to control life and death, power, and distribution. Four sisters who would be forced to be together and get along to make progress happen."

"I don't think I understand," Deimos admitted, his brow furrowing with concentration. "If you are so powerful, why not kill Nikola now?"

"I can't. Did you miss the part where I mentioned we all have to be together?" I remarked, exasperation bleeding into my voice. "The point was to ensure no one had too much power. When Dahlia realized that Nikola and Yumi were trying to create their own vessels, that they wanted to take us, kill us, and place the power where they could use it, her answer was to split the realm. To contain Nikola and Yumi away in a broken fragment. A cage. From there, I'm fuzzy as well. I don't know if Dahlia knew that she would be turned into a tree or if where we are now was a shock to her, too."

Deimos watched the ground in silence for a moment, his breathing shallow and uneven. I watched his face shift expressions as he took in my words, each revelation hitting him like a physical blow. He looked like an open book, pages fluttering in a harsh wind. Anger gave way to betrayal in his eyes, the transformation as stark as sunrise breaking through storm clouds. He fought Nikola as if he could be the true top, but Deimos' reality was the same as anyone else's. He was only what the originals decided we would be.

The weight of that truth settled between us like a gravestone.

Deimos looked up at me after some time, his eyes reflecting a pain I recognized all too well. "When I leave, the nightmares that are a part of this place will come back. There's nothing that I can do to change that."

"I didn't ask you to," I replied, my voice softer than I intended.

"I only wanted you to know that if I could, I would. As a thank you for the truth. Nothing more," he murmured, his words carrying the weight of genuine gratitude.

Deimos snapped his fingers before he was gone again in a cloud of mist, leaving behind only the faint scent of ozone and regret.

It hit me that he must have helped Nikola create the place I called home for so long. The realization struck like lightning, illuminating truths I had been too blind to see. He had to have helped Nikola lock me away last time, too. I was where I was because Deimos helped put me there, and then he had the nerve to come ask me for help. The betrayal tasted like copper pennies on my tongue.

Nikola counted on me to stay naïve to the world inside his pocket, but I made a tool in preparation for my nightmares. I had planned ahead because I feared nearly nothing as much as I feared being put back in my cage, alone and forgotten.

I pulled a dagger from my garter belt and slammed it into the wall in front of me, the impact reverberating through my bones. It wasn't visible to the naked eye, but I knew it was there all the same. I made my blade from souls that wandered the void, their essence forged into something unbreakable but tormented. It was unbreakable but loud. Every time I drove it into the wall, it wailed in agony, the sound piercing through the dream realm like a banshee's cry. The wall shimmered and cracked in response, reality bending under the weight of my determination.

CHAPTER EIGHT

THE FIGHT AGAINST MYSELF

HESPERIA

There was something different about the locket I was trapped inside after Deimos left. The air felt the same; the sights were the same. Everywhere my eyes touched, Coy still died in endless repetition. It was still somehow different. The change brought confirmation to the idea that Deimos had a hand in the creation of what had become my home.

The realization settled in my chest like a stone dropped into still water, sending ripples of understanding through me.

He shouldn't have been able to enter on a whim, and he shouldn't have been able to halt what happened inside. He should have had to see what I saw, endure what I endured. He knew what I had been forced to watch. He knew enough to warn me that it would come back and was aware enough that if he wanted to speak to me, he would have to, at least, put it on pause.

That had to be why my memory became fuzzy during his visits. He helped put me inside of a hell created just for me.

The truth had to be that Deimos helped with much more than he admitted to remembering.

If he came to me for answers, I wondered what his prize had been. If he hadn't been allowed to hold even the memories of the events that he helped with or the cages that he helped build for us, the deal couldn't have been worth it in the end. What kind of payment was worth forgetting your own sins?

Trees sprouting around me pulled me from my thoughts. They sprouted, one by one, in a row. They called to me to walk down the path they formed, their voices weaving together in harmony with each other. They sounded like Mother did—sweet and low like she was when she wanted me by her side, when the world still made sense.

I followed the path of oversized leaves that formed one by one under my feet, each step cushioned by their velvet softness. Each tree bloomed a full set of leaves once I walked beneath its branches. They greeted my presence with more enthusiasm the closer I got to them, rustling and swaying as if moved by invisible hands.

The sun finally beat down on me from above. The heat was soothing against my skin, but I had to hold my eyes shut from the blinding and sudden change in brightness. I lifted my hand and held it over my face, squinting through my fingers. The world I was trapped inside changed so vividly, sometimes so quickly that it left me dizzy and disoriented.

My eyes opened, and the trees were no more. The sun was gone as well. A maze of bone formed in front of me instead—dim and cold, stretching endlessly in all directions. The air smelled of mildew and decay, and my skin prickled at the sight. A rush of pins and needles washed over me, but there was nowhere to go but forward into the labyrinth of death.

The presence of bone formations gave me a familiar sense of comfort. It reminded me of other places I had been at another time, when death was my domain rather than my prison.

Three steps and a door of bones raised behind me with

the grinding sound of ancient joints. I was fully locked inside of a maze, the walls towering above me like the ribs of some massive, long-dead creature.

Four more steps ahead, there was still nothing but bone walls and moss creeping between the cracks. Five steps and in a blink, Mother was in front of me. She appeared as if she had always been there, as if I had simply failed to notice her before. She smiled at me with the same smile she gave me before things changed—the smile that met her eyes and lifted them in the outer corners. The one that gave her smile lines on each cheek. She reached up and cradled my cheek in her palm, her touch warm and familiar.

I missed her. I missed her warmth and the way she smelled of jasmine and sea salt, the scent that used to mean safety and home. I missed Father and the way every laugh he gave came from somewhere deep inside his stomach, rumbling like distant thunder.

"My sweet girl. You've changed so much since last I saw you," Dahlia whispered, her voice carrying all the tenderness I remembered. "It's such a shame you changed for the worse."

My heart stopped so quickly that the pain that came with it convinced me that it would never beat again. The world seemed to tilt on its axis.

"I thought I'd always love you because you were my daughter, but I was wrong. You allowed the rest of them to die. You killed your sisters. You killed them, Hesperia. I can't love you anymore. I can only hate you. When I look at you, I only see their dying faces. You're a failure."

Mother's voice chanted and repeated without ever changing a single note in her tune, the words becoming a mantra of condemnation. Her palm was against my cheek and left behind a burning fire where each finger met the sensitive skin, the heat spreading like poison through my veins.

My hand replaced where hers was. I gripped my burning,

wet cheek, the tears hot against my palm. I was crying? When had that started?

I knew it was fake. I knew it wasn't real.

It felt real.

It felt too real, carved into my heart with surgical precision.

"I would never hurt them," I whispered, my voice breaking like glass.

Her head snapped sideways with a crack that echoed through the bone maze, and from the split in her neck came a second head. Then, her body split in half, the same sound that came from pulling hide from animal fat echoing through the air—wet, tearing, wrong. The two blank bodies split again until there were four of them, multiplying like a nightmare given form.

Red hair, green hair, blue hair, and white hair grew from each scalp, cascading down their shoulders in waves of accusation.

Shivani, Ruri, and Sage stood in front of me. They stood beside someone who looked just like me—my own face staring back with hollow, condemning eyes.

"Why didn't you fight?" Ruri asked, her voice carrying all the pain I had tried to forget.

"Why didn't you care about us?" Shivani mimicked, her words sharp as broken glass.

"I needed help. I couldn't do anything while I was trapped inside of myself. You could have stopped them from using me," Sage pleaded, reaching toward me with desperate hands.

The girl who looked like me moved closer until we were face to face, close enough that I could see every detail of my own features twisted into cruelty. She touched my still-burning cheek and smiled with lips that were mine but spoke words I would never choose.

"It's okay that you blame yourself. You should," she murmured, her voice—my voice—like honey over poison.

"While your sisters were being murdered, while they were being reborn and suffering again, you were playing games inside of a locket. They grew, they changed. They lived and lost. Not you. You stayed the same failure that you always were. You had no experience to help you grow. You only played games with Nikola. Do you miss him? Do you want him back? Of course you do. He's the only one who will love you now that you've failed everyone else." My mimic laughed in my face, the sound echoing off bone walls like breaking bells.

Was I a failure? Was it my fault? The questions circled in my mind like vultures.

I could have tried harder to get out. I gave up already this time, too. I found something that worked, something that had gotten further than anything else, and I gave up on that, too. The pattern was undeniable, damning.

I was good at giving up.

I was good at giving half of my effort.

I was good at disappointing everyone who mattered.

The four figures turned into cream-colored clay, their features melting like wax, and then molded themselves back together until they formed Nikola. The transformation was fluid, horrifying in its ease.

He stood with straight shoulders and a crooked smile in front of me, every inch the predator I knew him to be.

"My sweet girl." He stroked my hair and pushed it behind my shoulders, the gesture mockingly tender. "Don't cry. I still care for you. Even if they don't. I would never leave you."

His voice was like a switch. It flipped something inside of me, igniting a flame of fury that burned away the despair. Nikola was playing a game with me again, and I had almost let him win.

"This isn't going to work!" I screamed, my voice echoing off the bone walls like a battle cry.

"It nearly did." He smiled, the expression cold and calculating. "I nearly had the failure of the sisters eating out of my hand like a dog looking for a scrap of attention."

"You overestimate yourself," I snapped, though even as I spoke the words, I knew they were a lie.

It was I who underestimated him. He was right. He almost had me. No, he did have me, completely and utterly. The words he spoke to me in my mother's voice would haunt me for years to come. Even if I knew it wasn't her, it was still her in my eyes, in my heart. A part of me thought that if Mother could speak to me openly, her words would be similar to those my nightmare had conjured.

She was right. Nikola was right. I didn't try hard enough. I allowed them to suffer while I wallowed in self-pity.

The admission tasted like ashes in my mouth.

"You won't pull me to your side. I should thank you. You helped me realize that if I fall into these kinds of thoughts, we will lose everything we have. You're like a worm, and if we let you wiggle your way inside, then you'll end up taking everything that we have left. I'll have to keep reminding myself of that so that I can do better."

"What if it's not enough?" he asked, his voice carrying a note of genuine curiosity, as if my answer truly mattered to him.

"Then I'll have to do better," I declared, the words carrying more conviction than I felt.

I leaned down, removed the dagger from my garter, and plunged it into Nikola's chest without hesitation. The blade sank deep, and I felt the familiar wail of the souls trapped within it. I knew he wasn't real. It wouldn't have killed him even if he were, but it made me feel better. The act was cathartic, a physical release of all the rage and pain he had stirred within me.

I felt as if I could breathe again when he was gone, his form dissolving like smoke in wind. The bone maze dissipated around me, crumbling to dust, and I was alone in the familiar silence of my prison.

There was no Coy dying endless deaths, no Mother with her cruel truths. Only silence, blessed and complete.

I needed it. I needed a moment to sort my thoughts and pick myself up again, to gather the scattered pieces of my resolve and forge them into something stronger. The quiet wrapped around me like a blanket, and for the first time in what felt like eternity, I allowed myself to simply exist without judgment or expectation.

In the stillness, I began to plan.

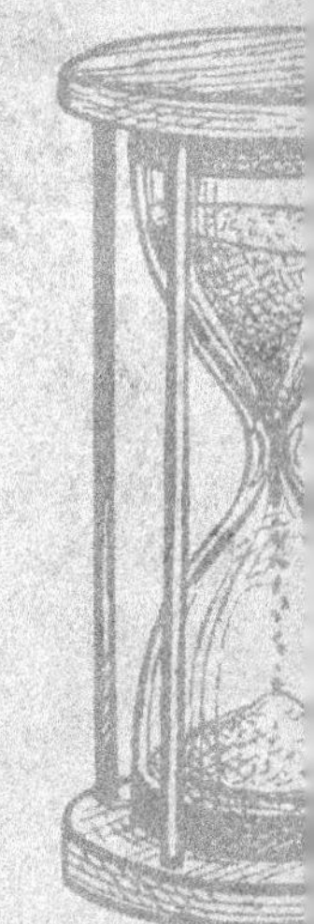

CHAPTER NINE

THE BLOODY DOOR

SHIVANI

The wheels of the carriage shook us around hard enough that I thought my stomach wouldn't hold itself together much longer. Each pothole sent us careening into the sides, and I gripped the worn leather seat to keep from being thrown to the floor. The road to Brisa was not kind—not to the horses, whose labored breathing I could hear even over the clatter of wheels, and certainly not to me.

The only thing that could rival the discomfort of the journey was the way Koa watched me without discretion. His gaze was unrelenting, burning into my skin like sunlight through a magnifying glass. His round honey eyes pierced me, and his jaw hadn't stopped trembling since the two of us were shut in the small box on wheels, trapped together with our unspoken words.

Brown hair was tied behind his head, but it still tumbled around his squared jaw in unruly waves. I feared that if I uttered a single word, he might erupt like a volcano. If I didn't say anything, he might crumble all the same, but I wasn't sure that I was equipped to have the kind of conversation that he needed to have.

We were all barely holding on by threads. I felt guilty, feeling affected at all. My lover didn't die. My sisters didn't die. I hardly had a right to be upset about anything, to take up space with my own pain.

Ruri did. Koa did. But me?

I didn't deserve to feel anything but grateful.

The weight of that thought settled in my chest like a stone.

I cleared my throat as quietly as I could, the sound barely audible over the rumble of wheels.

"Do you consider me miserable company?" Koa's hazel eyes glinted with rage for a moment, the emotion flickering like candlelight.

"No," I replied, my voice softer than I intended.

The air between us was thick—too thick. It could have been cut with a blade, sliced through the very wood of the carriage itself. I didn't want to be the extra stress on top of an already failing realm. I also didn't know if I had it in me to lie to him if he kept applying pressure, if he kept looking at me like I held all the answers he desperately needed.

"Do you stay around me only out of duty?" His honey hair fell around his face like a curtain, obscuring his expression.

"No," I murmured.

"Then what is it? Why do you refuse to talk to me?" He pleaded, his voice breaking like glass.

"I'm not refusing to talk to you—"

"I thought for a moment that we had begun to make some kind of progress, that you might let me in. I thought that we would face Nikola together." Koa's voice cracked before he finished speaking, the sound raw and vulnerable.

I took my gaze off of him, unable to keep my eyes locked on his while he looked at me with eyes filled with betrayal. The hurt there was too much to bear.

There was a piece of skin around my thumbnail that was harder than the rest—a bit more calloused than I remembered it to be. I used my opposite hand to pick at it, the motion automatic and desperate. It hardly budged. I might break my nail before I got it off, but that didn't stop me from trying. I kept picking and digging at the skin while it grew redder, the slight pain a welcome distraction.

Did we have time for this kind of talk? Did we have time to be concerned with a relationship when the world was ending around us?

What if we decided not to discuss the things lingering between us, and he died next? I think that was what I truly wanted to avoid considering. I wasn't being selfless and keeping to myself for his sake. I was terrified that I might waste the time we had, that he might be next and anything we could have had—any good that could have come from us taking the time to get closer—would have been squandered on my own self-imposed isolation.

If I decided that now was the time for us to truly commit to each other, would it be worth it? Would the pain that came from one of us dying when we had only just started be worse than the pain of not knowing what could have been if we just hadn't touched the idea at all?

The questions circled in my mind like vultures.

"Shivani?" He leaned his head to look at me from under all the red hair that sat as my own personal curtain, shielding me from his scrutiny.

He pushed his stocky body off of the carriage seat and dropped to his knees in front of me, the sudden movement making the entire carriage creak. I couldn't protest before his hands pulled mine apart, revealing the piece of skin on my thumbnail that hung halfway off, a small wound I'd created in my anxiety.

"Tell me what you want because I can't keep doing this. I can't keep standing silently by your side, fighting myself over what lines I need to draw while you hang silent. I don't know what road to take now. Do you want your name carved into my flesh? Do it. Do you want me to beg and kiss your feet? Lift your leg, and I will bare your toes myself. Do you want to remove my head from my shoulders so that I won't be able to speak to you anymore?" His grip on my hands was firm but not rough, his calloused palms warm against my skin.

"Stop," I breathed, holding up my hand between us.

His words made my face heat and my heart pound so hard I thought the beating might make it explode from my chest, scattering across the carriage floor.

"I don't want to hurt you, and you don't need to go so far." I took a deep breath, but he spoke first, his words rushing out like water through a broken dam.

"If you care about me at all, you won't lie to me." His eyes flicked back and forth between my own, searching for truth in whatever he might find there.

The carriage came to a halt with a jarring stop, and though his body shifted with the sudden stillness, he didn't move from his position at my feet.

Why did opening up to him feel like the hardest thing I had to do? My lips and my tongue both fought against my request to speak, as if they belonged to someone else entirely.

"Anything that we say in this little box, we can pretend it never happened once we step out of it," he urged, his voice soft and desperate.

My hands had left his and were back to picking at the hard, dry skin, a nervous habit I couldn't seem to break.

"It's not a good time to focus on an us." My voice shook like leaves in a storm. "If I died, it would be better for you if we were unattached. If we didn't get close to each other. It would be best for both of us, with how uncertain everything is now, to keep a distance between us. What if Nikola—"

"If Nikola killed me right now, then I'd rather have

nothing left to dream about when I am dead than you," he interjected, his words hitting me like a physical blow.

My pounding heart skipped every other beat at his declaration. I did want him—had wanted him from the moment I first saw him. I thought I had stumbled onto the most beautiful thing I had ever seen when our eyes first met. He was my comfort before the realm collided into chaos. He was my only grounding stone when I… when I killed so many innocent people, when blood stained my hands and nightmares filled my sleep.

I wasn't going to become a poet simply because he created a soft and open space for the two of us. Instead, I leaned in and pressed my lips to his, the kiss saying more words than I could have ever spoken aloud. If he felt the same kind of electricity shocking him as I did, then it communicated everything it needed to for both of us.

Both of Koa's hands moved up my shoulders, and his fingers combed their way through the hair on the sides of my head. The warmth of his fingers radiated through my skin, sending shivers down my spine despite the heat.

The carriage door opened with a sharp creak, and guards with the bulkiest shoulder pads I'd ever seen—shaped like clouds and just as imposing—stood with their feet together. They kept their eyes forward as if looking past us, their faces carefully neutral. They must have been used to the kind of scene they had stumbled upon.

I wasn't.

I cleared my throat and nearly kneed Koa in the chest when I stumbled out of my seat to exit, my cheeks burning with embarrassment.

"Are you ill? You look pale," Ruri observed, her sharp eyes taking in my disheveled appearance.

"No, I'm fine," I stuttered, smoothing down my hair.

"She was going to have intercourse inside of the carriage," the guard announced with all the discretion of a town crier.

"No, I was not!" I yelped, my voice cracking with indignation.

I turned around and looked to Koa for defense, but he was straightening out his clothes with hair ruffled in different directions, looking thoroughly guilty. My eyes shot back to Ruri, and her brow was raised as high as her eyes were wide, amusement dancing in her expression.

"I was not! Why are you here?" I demanded, desperate to change the subject.

"Jeb came to find me. They opened a rift in whatever part of the afterlife they were trapped in. I don't know who is there and who isn't, but they need us to open the other half on our side. I went to you first, but they told me you had left. When I heard you were going to the witches, I knew things couldn't have lined up better." Her words came out in a rush, excitement and hope threading through her voice.

"Do you think this is real? What if Nikola is playing tricks?" I asked, the paranoia that had become my constant companion rearing its head.

"Jeb would never lie to me," she declared with such fierce conviction that I didn't dare question it further.

I nodded, not wanting to press her harder and cause a fight when we needed unity more than ever.

"What do we do, then?" I asked, trying to focus on the task ahead rather than the lingering warmth of Koa's kiss on my lips.

"We go together, as sisters, and ask the witches for help," she responded, her voice steady and determined.

As sisters. I liked the sound of that, the words wrapping around my heart like a warm embrace. Even if I only kept that feeling to myself, it was enough for now.

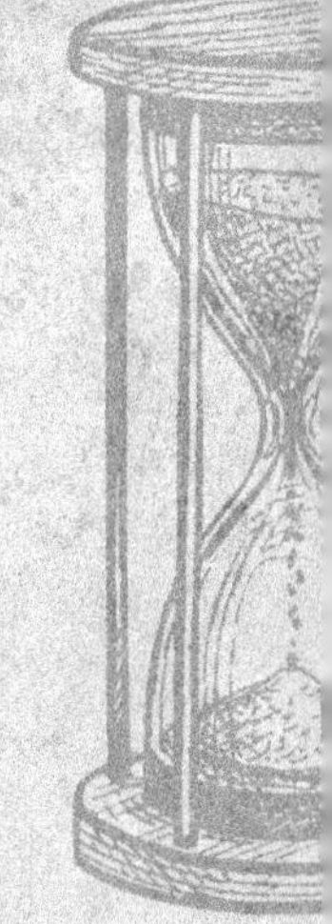

CHAPTER TEN

TWO TRUTHS, AND A LIE

SHIVANI

"You are going to go to a separate room," Ruri announced, pointing toward a corridor lined with floating lanterns.

"What?" I grimaced, the word escaping before I could stop it.

"I brought Dahlia, and she would like to see you before you leave again. The only way that I can guarantee that is by making you go see her before we start doing anything. There is no way to guarantee that we can open a rift, let alone connect it, and if we do, what may come out? So before we start, you have to go talk to your mother." Ruri placed her hands on my shoulders and turned me around with the authority of someone who wouldn't take no for an answer.

With a firm shove, I stumbled in the other direction, my feet catching on the smooth stone floor.

"This really is not the time. What if we can bring them all back? What if they're on the other side fighting for their lives?" I protested, the urgency in my voice making it crack.

"Then you need to hurry up so that I can get back to

preparations and discussions. I want my husband back," she demanded with another shove, this one harder than the first.

Where I was meant to be was clear. The door was half open already, warm light spilling out into the hallway like honey. If I didn't have time for relationship discussions, then I really didn't want to have time for parental ones, either. The weight of unfinished conversations pressed against my chest.

"Shi-Shi?" Dahlia's voice carried out, soft and familiar, using the pet name that made my heart ache with memory.

I only responded with a sigh before I pushed the door open and walked inside, already feeling emotionally exhausted from the day's revelations.

"How are you feeling?" I asked her, trying to keep my voice steady.

I moved inside and shut the door behind me with a soft click. Her lavender hair was tucked behind her ears, catching the light like spun silk, and her cheeks were flushed pink—not from blushing but from the addition of color to them. Her eyes matched her hair the same way her lips matched her cheeks, a perfect harmony of soft pastels. I sat in a chair beside her, the cushion sighing under my weight.

It wasn't as elegant as she was. The chair looked ordinary next to her radiant presence. Maybe if I had seen the chair first, I'd consider it something special. It was a soft cushion covered with delicate embroidery depicting tiny flowers and vines. Next to Dahlia, it looked closer to garbage. She was radiant, luminous in a way that made the air around her shimmer. She glowed with an inner light that made everything else pale in comparison.

Her intensity made me feel small, insignificant.

"It is strange to be here. Some places look familiar to me, but others are things I haven't ever seen. I may be back, but I do not have the ability to solve all the problems for you girls," Dahlia sighed, her voice carrying the weight of disappointment.

"Do you know why you're powerless?" I asked, the question tumbling out before I could consider whether it was appropriate.

I didn't know if it was the right thing to ask, but it was the question that burned in my mind.

"I do," she replied simply. "It's part of why I wanted to see you. We used to be close once. One of our last days together, I held you while you cried. Someone—Nikola—stole a gift your father gave you. A tool to help weed out the traitor. I couldn't tell you then that I knew it was him, but—"

A laugh slipped past my lips, sharp and bitter. I couldn't stop it, couldn't hold back the irony that bubbled up like poison. She looked at me as if I had sprouted two heads, but I let it flow still, the sound echoing off the walls.

"Coy died thinking that if he could just find that tool, he could have solved half of our problems and all of his," I managed between gasps, shaking my head at the cruel twist of fate.

"If I could have spoken more freely, I would have," she whispered, her voice thick with regret.

"Do you know why you don't have any abilities? Are you still a Goddess?" I asked, needing to understand the extent of our situation.

"When you try and do too much, this is the consequence. I had hoped that maybe I was immune, but I wasn't. I'd have to be blessed by someone stronger with new magic. That can't happen when I am at the top." Her voice grew lower with each word she spoke, as if the admission itself drained her. "I gave everything I had to trying to banish Nikola and keeping you girls safe."

She adjusted the red lace that sat over her white dress, her fingers trembling slightly. I understood she was deep in thought and fidgety, but I felt anxious, too. The need to move, to act, clawed at my insides. I wanted to get back to my sister, to my mission. I needed to stay on track before Nikola could burn anything else to ash.

"I know that you don't remember everything yet, but I wanted one chance to apologize to you before it was too late. It will matter when you remember. You will remember. You knew I was a liar, and you told me so. I lied to you again when I denied it. You were right; Nikola was always there. There is no moon or stars without a sky. I was a poor sister. I cut him down at every turn. I wanted Yumi's attention to myself. I didn't see any path too deplorable to take if it meant my sister cared for me more and Nikola lost his power. He was nothing but darkness then, too. Anything that he created was monstrous. Still, you were right. It wasn't my place to decide his future when I did it from the view of jealousy."

She tucked her already tucked hair further behind her ears but kept her chin tilted down for the first time since I'd entered. The sight sent a wave of sadness through me, cold and unexpected. She had always oozed confidence like a second skin. To see her ashamed made my stomach feel hollow, carved out by the weight of her admission.

It was hard to form my thoughts of her based only on the sadness that rose from her display of vulnerability. It was hard to focus on anything other than the idea that such a powerful and praised Goddess had ruined her own brother's life to be the center of her sister's world.

We were supposed to fix it for her. I didn't know how to tell her that whatever may have been in the past that she remembered remained there, buried under years of separation. None of us were close enough to share information, to meet, to spend any meaningful time together. We may as well have been torn apart by jealousy—any reason worked. In the end, we were not close.

That is to say, at least none of them were close to me.

"If you can't help us because you have no abilities, then

how have you been able to reach out? How did you use Fennic?" I asked, leaning forward in my chair.

"I was able to pull from Yumi because we were so entwined," she whispered, the admission barely audible.

"Do the rest of them know?" I pressed, sensing there was more to this story.

"Ruri and Sage do not," she admitted, her eyes unable to meet mine.

I nodded and felt my stomach twist again, a knot of anxiety and betrayal forming. When I looked back over to her, something had changed. There was something different about her, about the glow she had carried. She seemed dimmer, less ethereal. She held her chin high again, but to me, she looked less majestic and more like any other deity I had met—fallible, flawed, human in her mistakes.

It was my own fault for placing her on such a high pedestal in my mind.

I got to my feet and straightened out the bottom of my corset, the familiar gesture grounding me. "Is there anything else that I should know?" I asked, my hand already reaching for the door handle.

"I left four pieces of myself, my power, scattered across the realms. The four of you can keep them when you find them. It will help." She paused as if she had more to say but, in the end, remained silent, her lips pressed together in a thin line.

I turned the knob and opened the door enough to slip through. A guard waited in the hallway and escorted me to another room on what felt like a floating island suspended in clouds. Most of the walls were open to the sky, and I could see every shade of blue painted across the heavens, every cloud drifting around us like cotton, and every bird deciding to make a brief stop on their journey.

A pastel blue cloud floated in the middle of the room, defying all logic. Still, there was solid ground beneath my feet and a roof overhead, but no walls to speak of. Everything looked soft enough to bounce on, though I wouldn't dare try. Ruri sat on one side, perched on a chair that had no legs but still somehow hovered above the ground.

"Just sit," she commanded without looking up.

"On what?" I glared, gesturing at the empty space before me.

Ruri raised a brow at me in silent command, so I sat despite my reservations. A chair appeared underneath me just in time to keep me from hitting the floor, its cushion materializing like magic.

"Queen Rina has arrived," a voice announced from somewhere beyond the open walls. "Preparations are complete, and once we have an agreement, we can begin."

Queen Rina entered with a presence that commanded attention, wearing a pastel blue gown with a sheer train that seemed to float behind her like morning mist. Her entrance was dramatic, purposeful.

"What is left to agree on?" I asked, wariness creeping into my voice.

"Which one of you will offer me your magic before I ask Nikola what he can offer me," she declared, her expression perfectly serious.

Queen Rina's face was as hard as stone and as cold as winter ice. My stomach sank like a rock dropped in deep water, but when it rose back, it came with fire burning in my veins.

How dare she. I stood in a rush, and the cloud beneath us disappeared like smoke. I lifted my hand, and my finger pointed as sharp as a blade, power crackling at my fingertips.

"I'm just kidding," she announced with a dismissive wave of her hand, a grin breaking across her features. "I'm ready to kill that bastard too. I want Hesperia back, maybe as much as you do." She jerked her head toward me with newfound camaraderie. "I recall her as a friend, and teacher."

She was animated in her speech, her whole body moving

with her words. She stood too, and gently lowered my still-pointed hand with surprising tenderness.

"It's rude to point that finger unless you are sure you mean what you're gonna send out with it," Rina winked, her eyes twinkling with mischief.

She moved past me with fluid grace, and Ruri stood next. I caught a smirk on her face, only briefly before she realized that I was watching her.

Outside, there was a circle of cypress leaves and candles arranged with mathematical precision. They surrounded a pond of water that reflected the sky above like a mirror, placed at the entrance to what looked like another realm.

"Earth, fire, water, and air. We only need to add the three of us," Rina explained, her voice taking on a ritualistic cadence.

She took her place at the top of the circle, and Ruri stood an even distance from her, their movements synchronized like a well-rehearsed dance. I filled myself into the last spot available and nervously checked the distance between the three of us, measuring with my eyes. I was clearly less prepared than they were, fumbling where they moved with confidence.

Rina lifted her hands, placed them wrist to wrist, and faced her palms toward the circle. In perfect synchronization, Ruri followed. I stumbled last to hold mine the same way, my movements clumsy compared to their practiced grace.

"Blood," Rina whispered in my direction, her voice carrying the weight of ancient ritual.

Of course. My blood magic—the one thing that truly belonged to me. I pushed a stream of blood from my palms, feeling the familiar sting and power of it. Rina forced a tornado of wind from hers, the air howling with supernatural force. It picked up my blood and fused with it until the tornado was crimson, beautiful and terrifying. Ruri called down purple lightning that crackled through the air, and in the brightest flash that left spots dancing in my vision, a portal of absolute black opened before us.

"It worked," I laughed, the sound mixing relief and amazement.

Rina brushed her hands off with satisfaction. "I never doubted it."

"Can I admit I don't fully understand this?" I asked, staring at the swirling darkness that seemed to pulse with its own heartbeat.

"We control life, Cyan controls death, and Hesperia controls the crossroads. With all of it combined, we can open doors to other realms, other places that exist beyond our understanding. If Caym is alive even as a soul, then all we need to do is find the right door," Ruri explained, her voice steady despite the magnitude of what we had just accomplished.

CHAPTER ELEVEN

A DEAL WITH THE DEVIL

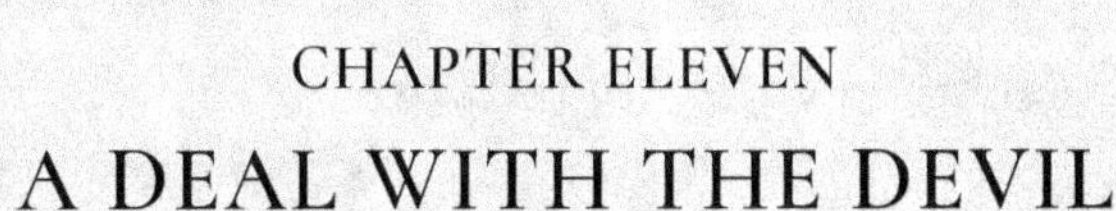

SAGE

The most protected place in Semper was Juniper and her garden. The other gods whispered that a Goddess was powerful enough to create a barrier even other deities couldn't enter or tear down. If I hadn't seen it with my own eyes, then I would have dismissed such tales as folklore and legend.

Nikola was enraged that he could not find a way inside, his fury radiating like heat from a forge. I didn't know who the Goddess was that put up the barrier, but I imagined she was awe-inspiring if she had been strong enough to stop Nikola in his tracks. It wasn't because he hadn't tried—oh, how he had tried. He made Sahir attempt to break through, and then Onyx. A small part of me found it amusing, though I dared not let that satisfaction show on my face.

Nikola had maintained only a mild interest in Juniper's quarters until he swore that he glimpsed someone named Olexei inside.

Nikola refused to explain to me who that was. He snapped at me in a way that made my blood run cold, his voice carrying a warning that froze me to my core. I hadn't asked any more questions about him or Juniper again. I considered asking Sahir, but I felt she would only carry my words straight back to Nikola like a faithful hound.

I hardly knew her, but something in my gut warned me she wasn't to be fully trusted.

The second most protected place in Semper was the golden cage that held still-beating hearts. I watched them with more questions than I had answers, drawn to their rhythmic pulsing despite myself. Occasionally, they would shake and glow as if responding to something unseen, their light casting eerie shadows on the cage bars.

"One of those is for you," Nikola murmured from behind me.

My body jolted like I'd been struck by lightning, but I didn't turn around. He moved my hair from both shoulders to one with deliberate slowness. The cold air hit my bare flesh and sent chill bumps racing across my body like tiny insects crawling over my skin. He laid a kiss on the top of my shoulder, his lips burning against my skin. My body responded for me before I could think about my actions.

I lowered myself and spun around to face him, the movement creating enough distance between us that we weren't touching. Still small enough that he wouldn't be upset, I hoped.

"Why would I need one?" I asked, my voice barely above a whisper.

"To become better, stronger," Nikola mused, his eyes gleaming with something predatory.

"Then why not today?" I questioned, confusion threading through my words.

If I were with him to help, if I were to fight against gods, then why wouldn't it be important for me to be stronger sooner? If I was supposed to be part of them, why were there so many secrets shrouding everything? I was allowed to know nothing, kept in darkness like a mushroom.

"There are other key components that need to be in place before you consume that heart," Nikola answered, his voice taking on that hypnotic quality that made my thoughts scatter.

He moved closer and ran his fingers along the length of my arms with the precision of someone mapping territory. I tried to wear a convincingly warm smile even as his touch made my skin revolt, every fiber of my being screaming in protest. He constantly conflicted me—if we were silent, my mind worked fine, but once he spoke, it was as if I were under a spell that rewrote my very thoughts.

"Am I still allowed to ask questions?" I managed to say.

I had so many things to ask that we were sure to never wade through them all in a dozen lifetimes. He nodded and continued to trace my body with his fingers, each touch leaving trails of confusion in its wake.

I wished it were Vespera touching me instead. That was one question I knew I wasn't allowed to ask, one thought I had to bury deep.

"You killed, well, you sent people to kill those 'guardians,' and you trapped that girl in the locket you carry with you, but you haven't made a move on the others? Why have you left them alive?" I asked, forcing myself to meet his gaze.

"One sister is trapped; another fed herself to the wolves willingly. The last two will be mine soon enough. The game may be long, but it will be won," he replied, running his eyes over the length of me before drawing his words out in a tune again. "If you are truly committed, if you really want to help your new family and be loved, then you need only ask. I can give you a special kind of magic. It will make you more powerful than you can imagine."

His voice wormed its way inside of my ears and slithered around until I lost my train of thought again, my resistance crumbling like sand. Nothing sounded appealing but pleasing him, making him proud of me.

I nodded, the movement feeling distant and disconnected. "I want whatever you have to give me."

Nikola leaned down and into me until his face was pressed against mine, his presence overwhelming. His breath was hot and smelled of peaches and wine, sweet and intoxicating. His lips touched mine, and I felt the heat flood through me—a want to keep kissing him that burned like fever.

The feeling faded as fast as it began when the kiss grew to feel like daggers piercing my mouth. The stabbing felt so intense that my knees gave out beneath me. I didn't feel them hit the floor, but when I landed on my knees in front of Nikola, I saw the roots growing out of my mouth like some horrific garden blooming from within.

He shut his mouth, and root ends untwisted themselves before they, one by one, shrank back inside of my mouth with wet, slithering sounds. I sobbed hard enough that the tears were visible on the dirt-covered rubble ground, each drop hitting the earth like falling stars. I used my arms to hold myself up, but they shook enough that I wasn't convinced they'd hold long.

I gasped for air once the vines were all inside, my lungs burning. Squeaks came from me with the force of the air, pathetic and broken.

"What did you do to me?" I gasped, tasting earth and copper on my tongue.

"Exactly what I promised. I unlocked your magic," Nikola responded, his tone matter-of-fact as if he hadn't just violated something fundamental within me.

"Unlocked my magic?" I didn't understand, my mind reeling.

"I gifted you abilities that you didn't have access to. Are you going to say thank you or continue being ungrateful?"

Nikola's voice commanded, carrying that edge that made my spine straighten instinctively.

Vines grew from my fingers across the floor without my conscious command, spreading like spilled ink. It felt so familiar, as if I had used the magic hundreds of times before, muscle memory written in my very bones. "Thank you," I whimpered, the words torn from my throat.

I didn't mean it. My body was in more pain than I had ever felt before, every nerve ending screaming in protest.

"We have more to accomplish today; get up," Nikola commanded.

He grabbed my arm and pulled me to my feet with no regard for my state. He pulled me against his chest and turned us to sand before he formed and molded us back together again. The sensation was like being tossed down a hill too quickly, everything rushing into my head before it all dropped back into my feet. It was like being crushed and compressed before being stretched to capacity again, my very essence scattered and reformed.

Nikola turned me around, and in front of us stood multiple square eight-by-eight rows of people arranged with military precision.

"I brought them like you requested," a girl announced, her voice carrying the weight of authority.

"Sage, this is Kyra. She brought all of her people to the realm of the gods for the same transformation you went through," Nikola announced with evident satisfaction. "She was betrayed by a Goddess that was supposed to understand justice. The Goddess was created to oversee the creation of life. She was meant to be merciful—an unbiased being of perfection. She used that supposed perfection to allow Queen Kyra's lover to be murdered after demanding endless sacrifices from her. To me, that seems like someone who doesn't understand what justice or mercy truly means. We will give her an army powerful enough to challenge such a Goddess. We will be the justice instead."

Nikola allowed me only time to take a breath, but not the time to respond when he started with a low hum that made my temples throb. I knew enough to plug my ears, but somehow the sound still penetrated.

His lips parted, and he began to sing. There weren't any words that left his lips, but the melody was enough—haunting, beautiful, and terrible. Kyra's people stood tall at first, their golden veins shimmering in the sunlight like living jewelry. It only took a few moments of harmonizing before the rows started to fall.

A few here and there like tiny flies at first, scattered and random. The screams rang out from them and blended with Nikola's own voice in a symphony of agony. They were all on their knees or backs before long, writhing and convulsing. His voice was devastatingly effective, and although it didn't take much time for him to transform them, when I watched it, it felt like an eternity stretching into forever.

The transformation had to feel even longer for them.

Their skin grew thin in color; I could see through it like parchment. It wasn't enough for a perfect view, but it was enough that, this time, I witnessed their bones snap clean through and take new shapes, the sound like breaking branches echoing across the field.

The ones that fell first stood first as well, rising like twisted phoenixes. They were unrecognizable from what they had been moments before. Their skin was made of smoke that shifted and swirled, and their golden veins held starlight instead of blood, pulsing with celestial light.

Nikola stopped singing and held a satisfied smile, admiring his handiwork. "I think I'll call them celestial commanders. They will be able to call down help from the skies."

"What does that mean?" I mumbled my words, half hoping he wouldn't hear them.

"You'll see," he answered with dark promise. "They are going to assist you on your next task."

"Me?" I pointed to myself, disbelief coloring my voice.

Of course, he meant me; I don't know why I questioned it. My mind fought against itself constantly now, and that confusion was the result. A part of me knew that what I witnessed needed to be stopped, that it was wrong and unnatural. That it shouldn't be allowed to happen to anyone, ever. Part of me didn't believe any deity could be crueler than him. If what he was doing was his kindness, I couldn't imagine what his punishment would look like.

I didn't want to find out. The other half of me insisted that I needed to keep my mouth shut and I would be safe. That if I didn't challenge him, I would never be at the mercy of his tune. I would never be turned into a mindless monster like those poor souls.

I wanted to have the bravery to tell him that what he did was horrific to witness. That his stories of the Goddess seemed like problems that could be solved without tearing the world apart if he were truly so powerful. The part of my mind that wanted to live held its hand tightly over the other half, silencing my conscience.

"I am tasking you to go to Ashbell. If we take their ability to heal, things will progress more quickly. There is also a guardian there, a titan. It needs to be eliminated," he declared with casual brutality.

"A titan?" I grimaced, the word tasting like ash in my mouth.

"A child of two gods, given special gifts beyond mortal comprehension. They don't look like you and I. Ashbell's is a giant armored creature, formidable and ancient. The one in the land of water thinks he's a secret, but I know of him, too. He slithers around the ocean when he's not appearing as a human," Nikola explained with the tone of someone discussing the weather.

"I'm supposed to take that down? A child of gods?" I frowned, my stomach dropping to my feet.

"Confidence," was all Nikola offered before he vanished, leaving me alone with my terror.

I swallowed harder than I should have, and I felt the pain travel down my entire esophagus like swallowing glass.

What had I gotten myself into? The question echoed in my mind like a death knell.

CHAPTER TWELVE
THE FIRST BLOW

SAGE

Nikola had no intention of waiting. I didn't take seriously how quickly he wanted things accomplished, how little patience lived in his bones.

I didn't feel very hidden or safe, despite his assurances that we would not be seen until we wanted to be. The celestial commanders followed behind my carriage on foot, their footsteps creating an ominous rhythm against the hardened earth. Kyra sat across from me, and Sahir sat beside me, the tension in the small space thick enough to cut with a blade.

Kyra watched me with calculating eyes, and Sahir watched her as if they had known each other for years, their shared history written in glances and subtle expressions. I tried to keep my eyes focused outside of the small window we were graced with and pretend that I noticed none of the undercurrents swirling around me.

I saw the volcano of Ashbell in the distance and felt the heat of the land seeping through the carriage walls, making the air thick and oppressive.

"You've licked your lips enough times; they will crack

soon," Kyra observed, her voice cutting through the uncomfortable silence.

I cleared my throat and gave my best laugh, though I wasn't convinced by it myself. The sound felt hollow and false in the cramped space.

"Why are you here?" Kyra asked, her tone direct and probing.

Sahir sat a little straighter, but her legs stayed crossed with practiced elegance. A smirk formed on her lips as if she had finally gotten what she had been watching for the entire carriage ride.

"Why are you here?" I countered, deflecting her question back at her.

I hardly understood what she meant. Did she think that I was free to leave any time that I wanted? I certainly didn't feel that way—trapped felt more accurate.

"I'm here for the same reason that you shouldn't be here," Kyra declared, her words heavy with implication.

I furrowed my brows, confusion clouding my thoughts. "What does that mean?"

"Vespera?" She looked at me with undisguised disgust, as if the name itself left a bitter taste in her mouth.

"That's enough," Sahir interjected, her voice carrying warning.

Kyra leaned back and laughed as she slapped her knees, the sound sharp and mocking. "She doesn't know! Oh, that's a new low, even for him."

"That's enough," Sahir pressed again, though her tone suggested she was more amused than concerned. "As much as I would love to see this play out, Nikola has uses for her first."

She didn't speak as if she were upset. She spoke as if she were proud of herself and wanted to continue watching the show unfold. Kyra's expression challenged Sahir, but only just enough to be shy of a full commitment to confrontation.

The last time that I mentioned Vespera, Nikola had

demanded that Sahir not discuss her with me. He proclaimed that she was a betrayer, that she would not side with us. He claimed the only way that I could protect her was to help him finish what was started, that she would be spared by him in the end.

I missed Vespera with an ache that settled deep in my bones.

I wished that I had made her my first real commitment. I was never good at making a choice and sticking with it, always afraid of closing my options and missing out on something better. I was always just afraid, paralyzed by the possibility of making the wrong decision. I wished that she had been the first time I was truly brave.

When I saw her again, I would make sure that she would be the first time I was fully committed to something, to someone.

"Why don't we talk about other things while we wait," Sahir mused, her voice taking on a conversational tone that felt dangerous.

Kyra sighed and tried to join me in looking busy with the view outside, but I could feel her attention still focused inward.

"Do you want to know a secret?" Sahir whispered, leaning closer.

No. I absolutely did not.

"Sure," I replied, knowing I had no choice in the matter.

"When all of the Gods still lived in Semper, at the beginning of the Age of Starlight, I was the one who helped Helia develop her blood magic. She was awful—smart, and so creative but utterly untalented. There was nothing natural inside of her. Together, we stole a bit of hair from Astra and created an entirely new planet. Helia is the one who found out my daughter was leading a mortal-looking life in Cylla and reported back to me. It was Helia's show of goodwill to me, an act of loyalty. I still thought she was weak and pathetic. Yumi's creations just never were as strong as the originals."

Sahir sighed and leaned back, her words carrying the weight of ancient grudges. "I'm glad to be able to have some girl time and get things off my chest. Though I suppose only one of you understands what I'm saying. The other is, well, a bit hollow."

"I would never casually spend time with you long enough to call this girl time," Kyra snapped, fire flashing in her eyes.

"Sweet girl!" Sahir giggled, the sound grating against my nerves. "You can't sit on a pedestal anymore." Sahir leaned in and tapped Kyra on the nose with mock affection. "You sold out your friends, the people that looked to you as a leader, everyone who respected you and your mother; you left your father dead and betrayed your lover to sit here with me."

Kyra's face paled for a moment before she held her frown firm in place, her jaw clenched tight.

"Had you convinced yourself it was another way? Did you think that Astra would think you a brave girl? A lost soul who tried her best? As much as she may have liked you, Kyra, she never loved you as much as she loved Ruri. You made a bed you'll lie in alone. Can you imagine Ruri's face when she finds out? Everything she went through for you, only for you to remain an angsty little brat and toss it all away? You were not just her prize, but a piece she placed so carefully, so that when she came back, you were well protected and her first solid army against us. I mean, look at the pieces you handed us." Sahir clicked her tongue as she shook her head in mock disappointment.

Sahir's smile was unnerving, showing every straight tooth she possessed. It lifted her eyes in pure ecstasy, as if cruelty was her greatest pleasure. She was pleased with herself, but Kyra was the opposite—sparks flurried from Kyra's fingers like the crackles of flint and steel, anger radiating from her like heat.

"Oh, please, put it away. If you couldn't stomach hearing

that you and I are the same now," then you should have made different choices," Sahir continued with relentless precision.

I matched Kyra's emotions closer than Sahir's. I was sick of hearing conversations where I wasn't allowed to be part of all the details, where I was treated as a small child without any comprehension. I was good enough to fight on their side, good enough to be used for their ends, but not good enough to be part of the things going on, to be filled in on anything they spoke of.

I could piece things together here and there. Astra was obviously this girl's lover. They had different views. Sahir was insane. I could follow along roughly drawn lines, but why did I need to? Why wasn't I invited inside of the circle of trust?

Without Nikola around, I absolutely felt closer to the way Kyra felt at that moment than to the side I was supposed to be a part of.

"We've arrived," I announced, grateful for any excuse to escape the toxic atmosphere.

I pushed past them and out of the carriage, happy to stretch after being cramped away. My relief lasted only until I laid eyes on the celestial commanders and their weapons. They held claymores, scythes, and hammers double my size, each weapon gleaming with otherworldly menace.

They were double my size—an army of glowing celestial torment that promised nothing but destruction.

We were sure to cause pain in the task ahead. Why was I joining them? I hardly remembered why anymore, lost in a fog of blind obedience.

I stepped backward once, twice, and bumped into Sahir's solid form.

"Where are you going?" She whispered into my ear, her breath hot against my skin.

My feet moved forward without an answer, as if controlled by someone else's will. I grabbed my own sword from the sheath on my back and gripped it tightly, the familiar weight both comforting and damning.

"Good girl," Sahir hummed with satisfaction.

Maybe it was fear that drove me forward. I felt less afraid to fight than I had before—my new abilities made me feel a sense of confidence that I hadn't possessed. I still knew that there were people stronger than I was, highly trained where I was merely average. There was always someone faster or stronger. I didn't want to die; who did?

It was the fear of Nikola and Sahir that kept my feet moving closer to the border of Ashbell. Closer to the guards that controlled entrance and exit. Closer to killing someone who had woken up and gone about their day like it was any other ordinary day. Someone who had made plans with friends, maybe a lover of their own, maybe a child or sister waiting for them to return home.

I hadn't seen what the people in Ashbell could do. I saw the temple and what they had on their side. None of it had scared me as much as Nikola's wrath.

Maybe it was the same fear that had always driven me— the fear of admitting I was wrong, the fear of whispers behind my back, the fear of failure that followed me like a shadow.

The guard, dressed in obsidian and crimson armor that caught the volcanic light, met me with a genuine smile. He opened his mouth to speak, probably to offer greeting or assistance, and I lunged at him without hesitation. I drove the tip of my blade into the opening of his armor that lay between his chest plate and helmet—a sensitive area that needed more protection than most armors provided.

It probably would have served him better if he had been expecting me to be a monster. If he had anticipated that when he woke up that morning, it would also be the day that he drew his last breath.

I didn't watch his body drop, couldn't bear to see the light leave his eyes. Instead, I watched the hordes of celestial commanders give away our presence when they called down meteors from the sky and crashed them into the guard towers that other guards occupied. The sound was deafening—rock and metal colliding in a symphony of destruction.

My arms felt heavy, too heavy to use my sword effectively. Kyra didn't use a weapon beyond her own hands, but the devastation she caused was enough to make up for my place on the sidelines. She called down bolt after bolt from the sky into the bodies of the residents of Ashbell, each strike precise and merciless. I almost couldn't hear the sound of my own heartbeat over the screams of confusion and armor banging against itself in desperate flight.

The dragon guardian, Ruri, moved as fast as Kyra, her form a blur of deadly grace. She had a girl with red hair by her side who flung threads of blood from her hands and moved on wings of fire that scorched the air itself. The redhead looked at me with disgust and disappointment, but never stopped her assault.

It was the dragon guardian that did stop, her attention focusing on me with laser intensity. The one that had already forgiven me for things far less devastating than what I was participating in now.

"I thought I warned you about coming back here to cause trouble," she growled, her voice carrying the rumble of barely contained rage.

"I don't take orders from you," I replied with far less confidence than she held, my voice shaking despite my efforts.

"Sage, I'm warning you! There's only so far I'll let you move without consequences. I'll find a way for the rest of us to keep moving forward without you!" She stepped closer to me while she spoke, each word punctuated by her advancing footsteps. "If I have to kill you, I will!"

Ruri's words were cut short by the appearance of Onyx, who sprinted to her and pushed me out of the way with brutal force. She lunged at him just as quickly, their collision sending shockwaves through the air. I felt her rage for him—it penetrated the atmosphere like a living thing.

"Get out of my way!" Ruri screamed, her voice raw with fury.

"He's not coming back. I made sure of it," Onyx mocked, his voice dripping with cruel satisfaction. "If you don't take my head, I'll take yours."

"One of us will meet him, then," she spat back with venom.

They were face to face, blade to blade, locked in a deadly dance. Why did I find myself rooting for her? My desire to jump in and help was palpable, changing the air around me, changing something fundamental within me. He was broad and imposing, but she was strong—stronger than I had imagined. She held him off as if he were hardly a challenge, her arms steady and unwavering underneath his weight. She was fueled by something stronger than Onyx, something pure and righteous.

She was commanding in a different way than Nikola—in a way that felt natural to her, born from genuine conviction rather than manipulation.

It was inspiring. It was what helping Nikola should have felt like but never did.

She was what I wanted to be. Tall and proud, she was fighting for what she knew was right with every fiber of her being. I never knew what was right, always lost in a maze of conflicting loyalties.

I had a choice in front of me—a choice that could make me proud of myself for the first time in what felt like forever. I sheathed my sword and grabbed the heaviest piece of hot magma rock from the ground, the heat searing my palms. I took off in a sprint and slammed it into the back of Onyx's skull with all the force I could muster.

He dropped to the ground like a sack of potatoes, unconscious and helpless. Ruri looked at me with complete disbelief, her eyes wide with shock.

"I don't know what came over me," I huffed, my chest heaving from exertion and adrenaline.

Ruri's eyes remained wide on me, searching my face for answers. "Whatever it was, maybe you should lean into it more. Vespera would be disappointed if she could see you now. Your sisters are disappointed watching you." She paused to catch her breath, her words hitting me like physical blows. "You tell Kyra that I'll have her head for hurting my mortals. You tell her that I'll make sure she has to answer for her choices. If not to me, if not to her father, then in front of Astra if it's the last thing that I do. You consider your actions, too, Sage. Next time we meet like this, I swear on my mother, I'll have your head, too. Do you understand me?"

I felt only inches tall, reduced to nothing by the weight of her words and the truth they carried.

"Do you understand me?" she shouted again, her voice echoing across the battlefield.

I nodded my head, unable to find my voice. She was commanding in a way that also felt like love—fierce, protective, unyielding love.

She bound Onyx's limbs with some sort of red shimmering cord that pulsed with magical energy.

"He wants your titan," I blurted out, the words escaping before I could stop them.

She looked up at me while she grabbed Onyx by his feet to drag him away and nodded in acknowledgment, understanding passing between us.

She was going to take him as a prisoner, and I had helped her do it. I couldn't even explain why—the decision had come from some deep place within me that I barely recognized. Our battle was a losing one, even if I hadn't helped her. Our numbers were crashing quickly against the superior training of the Ashbell soldiers. The celestial commanders, for all their otherworldly power, were no match for disciplined strategy and local knowledge.

There was nothing else for me to do but retreat, tail between my legs.

There was nothing else for me to do but fail at another project, disappoint another person who had placed their trust in me.

But for the first time in longer than I could remember, that failure felt like a choice—my choice.

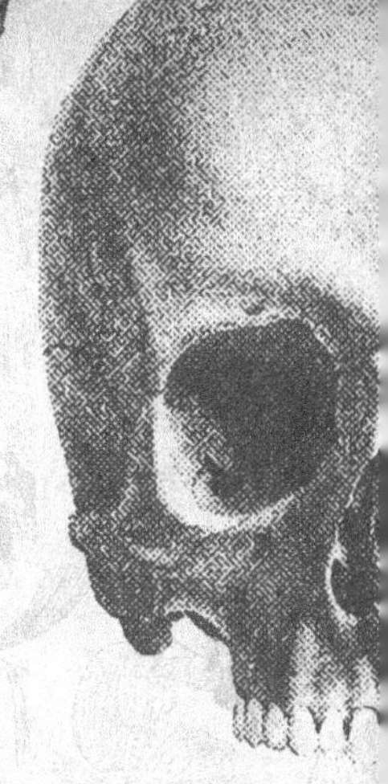

CHAPTER THIRTEEN

THE CURSE OF DEATH

CAYM

The Blood Weaver and I sat in silence surrounded by darkness so complete it felt like being buried alive. Coy and Vespera lay nearly lifeless in front of us, their forms pale and still as marble statues. They came to consciousness occasionally, and I had to put them back to sleep with gentle touches that felt like betrayal. They were both in a frenzy of confusion and anger whenever they stirred. They saw no difference between the spirits and me, attacking with the same desperate fury.

There wasn't much of a difference anymore. I was a spirit, too, after all—caught between life and death, belonging fully to neither. The two of them didn't respond to anything I uttered or any gesture I made. They didn't react to anything when they were awake, either, their eyes staring through me as if I were made of smoke. I was convinced that they were trapped somewhere else, their minds imprisoned while their souls remained with me. I had their souls with me in the same form as they were in life, but their minds—their essence— weren't truly here.

Wherever they were trapped, it was a much worse place than where I sat, and that thought chilled me to my core.

The only thing that didn't get attacked was the blood weaver. He wasn't a spirit, but he wasn't alive either—something caught between states like myself. He was quiet, but his presence was loud, filling the space with an energy that made the air itself feel heavy. I tried my best to get used to him because I knew, in a place that I didn't want to visit mentally, that I was going to spend more time with him than anyone else.

The next challenge was finding a way to comfort myself, especially when I knew that all of us weren't going to leave this place the same as we entered.

"Who are you?" I asked, my voice echoing strangely in the void.

"Someone that you wouldn't know," he responded, his words carrying the weight of forgotten history.

"Then tell me," I urged, leaning forward slightly. "I see no need to be cryptic when we're trapped here together."

"I was never a man, but I was once named Quade." He paused as if considering how far he wanted to venture into his past, weighing each word carefully.

"Even if I found a way to leave, I wouldn't be able to repeat anything we've discussed here," I tried to assure him, my voice soft with understanding.

"I haven't lived since the Age of Moonlight—before you even drew breath. My life was the cost that was supposed to be high enough to prevent Nikola or Yumi from being where they are now. I helped Dahlia create her daughters. I helped bless them with their magic." His eyes gleamed with distant memories that seemed to pain him. "I was an important member of a history that was rewritten. In the current version, I never existed."

More lies surfacing about our past like bodies floating to

the surface of a lake. I should have known we hadn't reached the end of them yet.

"Can you explain to me how we got where we are?" I asked, needing to understand the web we were all caught in.

"Gods that refused to acknowledge that power did not put them above emotions. They swam in jealousy and competition like mortals, never stopping to think that what they were doing would have such vast consequences. We are living in a bid to grab the most power, a game where the stakes are entire realms." He paused, his expression growing darker. "Every god thinks they know best and can handle the responsibility that comes with power better than the others. Isn't that an average tale for mortals as well?"

"Then, Quade, my question to you is, why did you have to die, and yet no lesson was learned? Why didn't you stay alive to help prevent this?" I asked, frustration bleeding into my voice.

I was disappointed that there was no one in the story of our history brave enough to stand up and shout stop, to halt the things that happened before they spiraled beyond control. It was always a story of power plays with silent enablers watching from the sidelines.

"I, too, was guilty of thinking I sat on the correct side. That I was above being sacrificed for the greater good. My part in Dahlia's bid to stay in power was to help her create her daughters, ensure they were blessed with magic, and die so that our brother and sister could not have the means to repeat any of it. Her daughters were her backup plan—she would always be in power, be it directly or indirectly. Nikola has the ability to get inside people's heads, to whisper poison into their thoughts. He can convince them of nearly anything. Tell them to do almost any command, and they will do it and think it is their own choice. Dahlia couldn't risk that kind of manipulation. But some things can't die, even without a heart, even without a body. They can not be erased completely. Nikola was the first hard lesson of that truth." Quade was silent for a moment, the weight of his words settling between us like stones. "I've chosen to stay here, in the shadows, and live quietly. I have no desire to be in the middle of the war they've created." He looked at me, awaiting a response with patient eyes.

He had revealed more than he could have understood. My head spun with everything from the word 'brother' to the idea that Dahlia willingly killed him to keep her secrets buried.

"Who am I to believe is the good side?" I asked simply, the question tasting bitter on my tongue. "Are you responsible for my brothers and me, too?"

"Things are never so black and white, Caym. I did not have a hand in you or your brothers. That, indeed, was Olexei's doing. He was an honest God—a good God, as you would put it. His only fault was being so deeply in love that he allowed Dahlia to do anything she decided was just, even if it wasn't. Olexei will lose that moral clarity when he learns the full truth of his wife. He will side with her, and it will be only natural—love makes fools of us all. Once that happens, do you think he will also carry the blame for allowing three Gods to fight for what they could have shared?" He watched me patiently, studying my reaction. "Do you think Olexei should be deemed as part of 'the bad side' as well?"

I had no good or wise answer, the complexity of it all weighing on me like a physical burden. For my wife, I'd turn the other cheek. I'd cut out my own eyes to plead innocence convincingly. I'd never regret a moment of my choice. If Olexei was wrong for that, then I'd be just as guilty of the same blind devotion.

"Would you be willing to answer for your choice?" he asked as if he had read my thoughts, his voice carrying a challenge.

"I would," I replied without hesitation.

"Good." The blood weaver responded cheerfully, his tone

brightening. "That's the difference. If you make a choice, you should also be able to hold yourself accountable for the result. It shouldn't be allowed to be buried as if it never happened." He leaned forward conspiratorially. "I will make you a deal. I will help you get your friends to the other side of the rift if you leave a few of the Nola with me. It grows lonely here in the endless dark."

I shook my head firmly. "I won't force them to stay. If they want to remain, they already know that they can."

"Then you will allow me the chance to ask?" He leaned in, hope flickering in his ancient eyes.

"Yes," I answered, confident that they could handle themselves and him if they chose to remain.

Like Olexei, a part of me was willing to do anything to get back to Ruri, even if I could never look in a mirror again after making such compromises.

"You should do what you know needs to be done, then." He nodded his head toward the two unconscious forms in front of us. "You already know, as the God of Death, the rules."

He was partially right. My mind was still clouded in a primordial deity-induced fog, but I knew scattered pieces of the truth like fragments of a broken mirror.

The curse of death was an emptiness that filled the hearts of those who died with unfinished business or extreme pain. They carried the weight of betrayal or sorrow so heavily that they couldn't move anywhere—couldn't be reborn or sorted into an afterlife. They remained stuck until it was resolved, trapped in their own personal hells.

Someone had to carry it for them if they wanted freedom.

Someone had to stay so that they could go. I took my gloves off one by one, revealing hands that tingled with deadly power. The blood weaver leaned himself into my hands, examining them with the curiosity of a scholar. He sniffed at them and turned them in each direction, studying every line and callus.

"You'd never know these were a weapon if you didn't already know," he chuckled, his voice carrying dark amusement.

"Then how do you know?" I pulled my hands from his scrutiny, suddenly self-conscious.

"It was my idea! I told Olexei it would be the best gift given to the God of Death."

I grimaced, the revelation hitting me like a physical blow. "It's a curse."

He waved me off as if I didn't know what I was talking about, dismissing my pain with casual indifference. "What is it mortals say? One man's trash is another's treasure?"

I placed one hand on Vespera's forehead and one on Coy's, feeling the coolness of their skin beneath my palms. I mixed my own magic with the sun magic Ruri had given me, using it to cleanse them of their torment. Their tears and screams entered my mouth like a flood, and it felt like razor blades slicing me open from the inside. The pain was excruciating, every emotion they had suppressed pouring into me at once.

I released their heads and huffed for air, my chest burning as if I had been drowning.

"Interesting," he mumbled, his tone thoughtful. "I wouldn't have guessed you carried that kind of magic."

Quade stood and poked the invisible wall beside us, his finger somehow connecting the rift from both sides to each other. He picked up Coy and Vespera with what had to have been his mind, their bodies floating like leaves on water, and tossed them through to the other side with surprising gentleness.

I rushed to the rift, pressing close to see what was happening on the other side. Something told me that I needed to move with more caution, that danger awaited.

My thoughts scattered like startled birds when I saw that on the other side, Inola hovered over them, her hands glowing with healing magic. She called to clerics, but they looked overwhelmed, their faces pale and drawn. They looked bloody and fearful, as if they had been fighting for their lives.

"What's happening?" I asked out loud, but it was more to myself than him, dread pooling in my stomach.

He used the rift like a scrying mirror and flipped through scenes of the land, each image more devastating than the last. Ashbell was burning—not just its trees, but its very land was scorched black. Bodies lay everywhere, scattered like broken dolls, and creatures that I did not recognize prowled among the ruins. The blood weaver stopped when he found Ruri and stepped aside for me to see clearly.

She had Onyx. She chained him to a wall with fate chains that glowed with malevolent energy. He hardly looked as if he were breathing at all, his chest rising and falling in shallow, labored gasps. She grabbed his hand and set it firmly on a brick. She took a knife that mortals would have used for their meat and positioned it carefully. With deliberate precision, she severed his index finger from his hand.

He woke with a scream that echoed through the chamber, raw and agonized. The Blood Weaver looked at me, and I already knew his question before he could voice it.

"I would," I admitted, my voice steady despite the horror of what I was witnessing. "I would stand in the doorway silently. I would stand beside her and hand her any tool that she needed. I wouldn't question her methods."

"So then, who is good and evil?" he asked, his voice carrying the weight of philosophy.

"I suppose maybe it's not so black and white," I answered as I watched her work, understanding that love could make monsters of us all.

CHAPTER FOURTEEN

HOW MANY SURPRISES ARE TOO MANY

CAYM

"Can we use the rift to watch anything?" I asked, my voice echoing strangely in the void.

The blood weaver nodded with the thinnest smile tugging at one side of his lips, a expression that didn't quite reach his ancient eyes.

"Is there something specific you'd like to see?" he inquired, tilting his head with curiosity.

"Can you find Nikola?" I responded, my hands clenching into fists at my sides.

"I can, but what good would it do for you?"

"I can send a Nola with the information, or once I find a way out, I can share it then." I turned to face him fully, hope threading through my words.

"You can't repeat the things learned in here out there until someone decides to do something about Yumi's hold on communications. Even if they did, you aren't leaving here while you hold Coy and Vespera's curse of death." The weaver's words hit me like a physical blow, each syllable hammering home my trapped state.

"Is there really no way?" I tried to hide the pleading in my voice, but desperation leaked through anyway.

I didn't want him to know how desperate I felt, how the walls of this place seemed to be closing in around me. I wanted to hold myself together, firm and unbreaking, for myself. I couldn't let myself slip into despair. I wasn't going to let anyone convince me that I couldn't leave, that I was truly trapped here forever.

I wouldn't be broken.

"You can make a deal with me," he offered, his voice taking on that familiar tone of negotiation.

"If you want me to give you Nola again—"

"I heard your position. I won't keep asking." He held up a hand to stop my protest. "My second offer is for a heart. I will lend you mine for thirty days. I will carry the curse of death for you until then so that you may leave." He held out a weathered hand for me to shake, the gesture both inviting and ominous.

"What happens after thirty days?" I asked, though part of me already feared the answer.

"You come back here and become just another soul with a long past, and we become friends for eternity." He replied with casual finality. "You don't need to answer now. Think it over while I let you watch Nikola."

"Why would you make that kind of offer?" I asked, suspicion creeping into my voice like poison.

He scrolled through the rift while he spoke, his fingers dancing over invisible controls. "Maybe it's not out of kindness. Maybe I want the power for myself instead. Maybe there is always someone else lurking in the shadows to take a spot at the top." He stopped the images on the rift and backed away from them, giving me space to see. "Or maybe I'm just an old, old soul with a long past that has nothing but time and desire to see Nikola burn. Maybe I want companionship as well. Maybe I want to help my sister one last time."

He motioned me to the rift, and I wasn't sure what I expected to see, but it wasn't the horror that unfolded before my eyes. Nikola was in the form of a massive viper, his scales gleaming like black oil in the dim light. He ate mortals whole, their screams cut short as they disappeared down his gullet. When their souls tried to leave and join another realm like they should have, following the natural order of death, he plucked them from the sky with his forked tongue like ripe fruit.

A sickening crunch was audible through the rift, and a spark of light exploded ever so briefly as he absorbed the souls, each one adding to his already immense power. I knew he did it for power, but the casual cruelty of it made my stomach turn. He could have done what we did: set up a temple and waited for prayer to sustain him.

But who would send prayers to him? What mortal would willingly worship such a monster?

I needed to leave. I needed to get to the other side with an urgency that burned in my chest. The weaver's offer was tempting—dangerously so. Thirty days was enough time for me to find another way to stay permanently. It was enough time to help set things right, to make a difference in the war. Enough time to kiss my wife once more, to feel her warmth against my skin.

Would I be willing to leave again if I failed to find another way? The question haunted me.

If I couldn't find a way to stay, I could at least say a proper goodbye to her. I could give her full authority over Merripen, over the Nola. I would have time to let her know how much she meant to me, to say all the words that had been trapped in my throat.

A little extra time was all I needed. A single extra touch, one more moment in her arms.

I needed that extra time more than my next breath.

Could I trust him? Was the weaver someone reliable? If I

had learned anything in the past few weeks, it was that I shouldn't trust anything, especially when I couldn't even trust my own memories. I learned that history was written by the one who held the pen, not the one who was justified or right.

"I have one more thing to show you before we discuss our deal," the weaver announced, pointing behind me.

I turned and immediately recognized the boy standing there. Silver hair and pink eyes that sparkled with familiar intelligence. His hair was short, and his eyes round and inno-cent. He was the spitting image of Astra, so much so that it took my breath away. I knew my jaw hung open because of the sudden dryness coating my tongue.

"Hello, Caym." He moved forward until he stood beside the weaver, his movements graceful despite his apparent youth. "We never formally met, but I feel as if I know you all the same. I've seen so much that you've done."

"Sin?" A shiver rushed down my spine, recognition hitting me like lightning.

"My mother named me Ekron after my passing," he explained with a maturity that seemed at odds with his youthful appearance.

"You've grown," was all I could manage to say, my voice thick with emotion.

"You should know things work differently in this realm. When I saw that you were here, I wanted to speak to you. I wanted to reach out and offer you a helping hand, but I felt it would overwhelm you if I moved too quickly." Ekron spoke with careful consideration, his words measured and thoughtful.

I nodded, still trying to process his presence. "You were right. It's still a bit jarring. I'm sorry I couldn't find a way to bring you back."

"My mom was already looking. Ruri was looking. Kyra looked. The Timekeepers searched tirelessly. There were many heads on the case, but the damage was too severe." His expression grew somber. "My heart was partially eaten by Sahir. It's not impossible for me to come back, but it's complicated. Unless someone wants to bring me Sahir's heart so that I can eat it in return, I won't ever be whole again." He looked at the ground, the weight of his situation settling around him like a shroud.

He had the look of a young boy but the demeanor of an older man, as if death had aged his soul while preserving his body. Maybe it was because the only influence he'd had was that of ancient beings.

"I'll make sure it happens," I announced with fierce determination.

"What?" He stuttered, hope flickering in his pink eyes.

"I will make sure you get your heart back," I repeated, my voice carrying the weight of a sacred vow.

"I want to help you, too," he replied with a smile that transformed his entire face. "I found a way to bind Nikola to the mortal realm. He won't be able to hide in Semper anymore. He won't be able to use his full potential. He will be at a disadvantage—one he's never had before. It will force Yumi to lift the curse on communication. Nikola will not enjoy being caged like that; he will demand that she lift it."

"How do we do that? Bind him?" I asked, leaning forward with intense interest.

"The Blood Weaver only needs a few drops of blood to do quite a lot of things," Ekron answered, his voice carrying the confidence of someone who had studied these magics extensively.

"That's it? A few drops of blood?" I didn't believe it could be so simple, so easy.

"If he gave the sisters their magic, why is it so unbelievable that he could do something like this?" Ekron asked, raising an eyebrow that reminded me painfully of Astra.

I didn't want to make any mistakes. I didn't want to trust the wrong person again, but the idea that I could see my wife, that I could hold her in my arms, and that the only cost was a few drops of blood? I nearly forgot about any other possible consequences, my desperation clouding my judgment.

A few drops of blood and a borrowed heart to win a war. To kiss my wife. To bring Astra's son back. A few drops of blood for my life back, for everything I had lost.

It felt like such a small price to pay for so many things to be solved, so many wrongs to be righted. My life hardly felt worth as much in the living land when weighed against all the things it could fix by remaining in the land of the dead.

I bit my finger until it bled, the sharp pain grounding me in the moment, and held it out to the Weaver. With a smile that seemed almost predatory, he wiped his finger across mine, collecting the crimson drops. Then Ekron did the same, his touch gentler but no less purposeful. They both held up fingers covered in my blood, the red liquid gleaming in the strange light of this place.

The Weaver reached into his chest and pulled out a small, beating golden heart that pulsed with otherworldly light. The sight was both beautiful and terrifying.

He shoved it inside my chest with surprising force, and I gasped as foreign magic flooded through my system. Then the two touched their blood-covered fingers together, and the world exploded.

The resulting light was so blinding that my skull throbbed as if it might split apart. White-hot pain lanced through my head, and spots covered my sight like falling stars. But my heart sank when I thought I saw them kill a Nola before my vision was consumed. My body became engulfed in flames that felt both real and illusory, and everything went dark as consciousness abandoned me.

I wasn't sure how much time had passed when I opened my eyes, but the voices I heard made my blood run cold. Despite what had happened, despite the ritual and the borrowed heart, I wasn't going to be able to leave. Despite the blood weaver's best efforts, despite the sacrifice of the Nola, I was still stuck in the never-ending abyss of darkness that had become my prison.

I could still only watch from the outside, helpless to offer my love any assistance, trapped behind invisible barriers that mocked my desperation.

I was cursed to remain on the sidelines forever, a spectator to my own life's destruction.

CHAPTER FIFTEEN
RETURN OF NIGHTMARES

RURI

My final straw was snapped in half, bent until it could no longer pull in water and then stomped on until it was unrecognizable as its former shape.

I kept myself together; I held on so hard that my knuckles turned white from the effort. Even when the strength that kept me together became so thin it looked the same as the strands of hair on my head, I still held on with desperate fingers.

Despite how badly I wanted to fall off the path that I knew I needed to be on, I stayed on it with stubborn determination. I stayed on the moral ground that I built myself, brick by brick, each one laid with blood and tears. I created my path on the idea that if I were good, if I did what I knew to be right no matter the injustice that I suffered, in the end, it eventually had to be my turn to win.

I told myself that suffering was the way that I would earn happiness in my future. That not all days could be dark, and I just needed to carry myself with my head high and my family as the first thought in my mind in order to get to the place that I wanted to be.

I thought that all injustice had to eventually be met with a harsh fist of retribution.

I lived on the idea that the strike of justice had to be stronger than the punch of injustice. I went through what I had to so that justice could prepare itself for the moment when it would finally arrive.

I was wrong. I was foolish. I was stupid and naive.

I should have changed my mind and decided long ago to be my own hand of justice. I should have decided after the first whip cracked against my back, the leather splitting skin and leaving scars that never fully healed. After the first time I witnessed Yumi allow an infant to die while she watched with cold, calculating eyes. There was no good in the world unless there was someone willing to lay the foundation for it with their own blood.

Unless there was someone to be feared.

I should have recognized then that the hand of justice was only going to strike if someone decided to be strong enough to wield it themselves.

I shouldn't have wasted so much time believing in fairness. I shouldn't have allowed Caym to die for my head to be placed correctly on my shoulders.

I shouldn't have let myself believe that if I created a child from the best pieces of Caym and myself, that she would be the best of us when she grew into her power.

Everything was wrong. And some gods needed someone to fear them.

The chaos that was Ashbell was too much for me to process. Wounded Seere carried other Seere on their backs, their faces etched with pain and determination. Guards lay dead, their bodies mixed with citizens in a tapestry of carnage. I heard nothing but ringing in my ears while I watched the scrambling, the desperate attempts to save what could be saved.

The heat of the volcano was nothing compared to the

burning I felt in my chest, the rage that threatened to consume me whole.

We weren't the only land under assault. Nikola didn't rest, didn't pause for breath or mercy. The entire realm was feeling the effects of Nikola's ability to transform mortals into his twisted servants.

"If you would allow me to help, I would," Deimos declared as he appeared beside me like smoke materializing.

I pulled my arm back and drove my fist as hard as I could into his jaw, the impact reverberating up my arm. He startled me when I thought I stood alone, but that wasn't why he deserved the blow.

"Take at least one alive as a prisoner. Chain it up with Onyx," I called to a guard that ran past, his armor clanking with each hurried step.

Deimos rubbed his jaw while he smirked at me, and I felt every bit of rage I had bottled up begin to rise to the surface like lava seeking escape.

"Have you missed me?" he asked with a grin that made my skin crawl.

His two-colored eyes beat down on me, wide and hungry for something I refused to give.

I was hungry, too. Not in the same way he was. He lusted after the lie he had forced on me when I couldn't resist, when my mind was not my own. I was hungry for vengeance, for justice. I wanted his head along with Sage's, displayed as warnings to any who would dare follow their path. He used me, and she slaughtered the only thing left in the realm that I cared about.

"What do you want?" I gritted my teeth, each word scraping against my throat.

"I want to help you. You don't seem to care for me any longer, but I've always been fond of you," he replied with false sincerity dripping from every word.

If my body felt any warmer, it might have set fire to everything around me.

"Your idea of help and my idea are not the same. The only thing that I want from you is your head as a decoration for my temple."

"Do you remember our time together?" He ignored my words as if they were meaningless noise.

"I'll give you one last chance to tell me what you want before I show you how much I hate you, Deimos." I pointed at him with a finger that trembled with barely contained violence.

"We have the same goal," he insisted. "Once we used to discuss that until the sun rose, planning our future together."

"You could have fooled me! My goal is to help people. It seems your goal is to take advantage and harm them."

"I do care about you, regardless of what you clearly think about it," he murmured as he moved closer, invading my space. "I have a realm and an army, too. I can be better for you than he ever was. We had plans, goals, dreams." Deimos reached for my hand with fingers that had once traced patterns on my skin.

I moved backward, revulsion washing over me. "Don't. What you did wasn't out of my free will. Remember that. I didn't care for you as myself. I didn't fall in love with you because I was in my own mind. You manipulated a blank canvas that understood nothing of the real you."

"I don't believe that. From the first time you met me, you knew me. You told me all the time that you recognized my face. You just couldn't place it," he argued, desperation creeping into his voice.

"You can rest easy knowing that if I had placed it sooner, you and I," I waved my finger between us with sharp, angry gestures, "we wouldn't have made it as far as we did because I would have killed you then."

"I can understand how you must feel conflicted now that you can remember Caym. You don't need to feel guilty about what we had. If he loved you, he would be happy to see us together, if it's what makes you happy." Deimos reached to touch my face with the audacity of someone who believed his own lies.

I raised my fist to hit him a second time, but he snapped his fingers and disappeared before I could make contact, leaving me swinging at empty air. I felt the tiny, thin string inside of me that had been holding everything together finally snap with an audible crack in my mind.

I marched to the dungeon where my people had chained the creature they captured, my footsteps echoing off stone walls like thunder. I didn't know what I was walking into. I didn't know if it could even communicate with me, if there was anything left of its original mind.

I flung the steel door open with enough force to make it ring like a bell and moved past the guards protecting the thing. Its head hung down until it realized I was there, sensing my presence like a wounded animal.

Maybe it was wrong to take my rage out on something that was also a victim in the right light.

I wasn't going to stop, all the same.

"Can you speak?" I asked, my voice echoing in the cramped space.

"Yes." The voice was distorted, barely recognizable as once belonging to something that had been alive and whole.

It still had the ears of a Fae, but that was all that remained of its original form. The rest was torn flesh and exposed bone, a patchwork of horror. It smelled of rot and decay, the stench making my eyes water.

"What is Nikola planning next?" I demanded, stepping closer.

It moved its head slightly, the motion clearly causing pain. "We know nothing. We were lied to. Sent off to die. Used as pawns in a game we never understood. We hold nothing of use to you."

"There is nothing that you can tell me?" I pressed, my voice growing harder.

"Do you think that he would share anything with me? I'm nothing to him. None of us mean anything to him," the creature howled, its voice breaking with anguish and truth.

I grabbed an axe that was left by the guard, the weapon heavy and cold in my hands. Without second thought, I swung it with all my might into the creature's leg. I felt it tear through flesh and sinew, heard the wet sound of metal meeting meat. I drew back and hacked at his leg a second time and then a third, each blow more vicious than the last. Bone shattered with a sickening crack, and the leg severed from the body, blood pooling on the stone floor. The thing screamed and howled, the sound echoing off the walls like the cries of the damned.

"Do you still know nothing?" I yelled, my voice raw and desperate.

"Nothing!" it gasped through its agony.

I felt my chest rise and fall hard, my breathing ragged. My vision blurred and became red-colored, as if I were seeing the world through a filter of blood. I shoved my knife into its chest cavity before any sense could swirl around my mind, before conscience could stop me.

"Thank you," it mumbled as it took its last breath, the words hitting me like a physical blow.

Like a slap to the face, my heart stopped beating for one terrible moment. Reality shifted around me, and I felt my feet planted firmly on the ground as if I were seeing myself clearly for the first time.

I had lost myself to become a monster no better than Nikola. I had been talking to myself about justice and acting as though I were the only one who knew what it meant.

Then I had acted as a monster myself, no different from those I claimed to fight against.

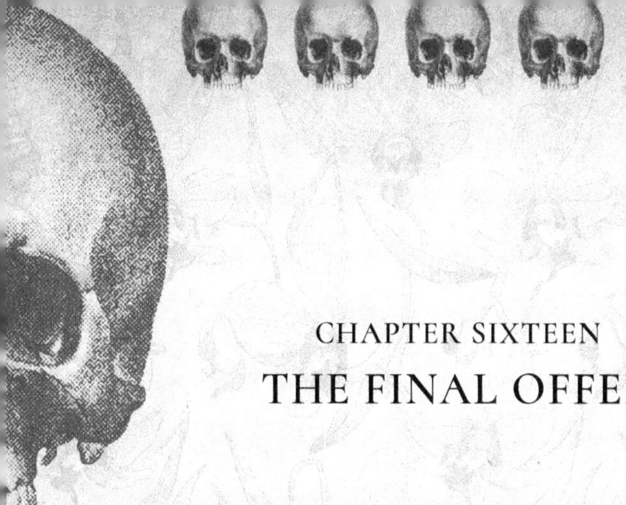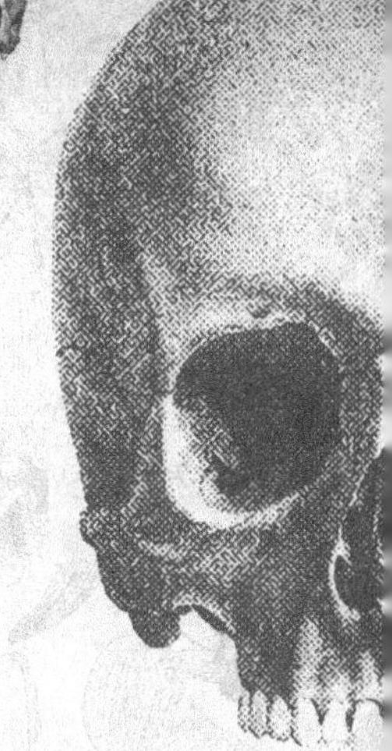

CHAPTER SIXTEEN

THE FINAL OFFER

CAYM

"Did you kill a Nola?" I yelled, my voice echoing through the void like thunder.

The Blood Weaver dodged my questions with more questions, deflecting like a seasoned politician. I felt as if I were running in circles after a treat that was promised to me but never fully within my grasp, always dancing just beyond my reach.

I didn't understand how, but every raise of my voice, every beat in my chest that ticked with rage, sent streaks of golden lightning in spiderwebs through the darkness we were gathered in. The energy crackled around me like a living thing, responding to my fury.

"Where did you come up with such an idea, really?" The Blood Weaver threw his hands up in exaggerated innocence.

"Why am I still here?" I demanded, my fists clenched at my sides.

"Do you always expect everyone to be so perfect?" he asked, tilting his head as if genuinely curious.

There he went again, twisting my words into tiny knots for me to trip over. He tossed me peels to fall over as if it were his profession, as if he had always been skilled at refusing to answer things that he did not want to admit. The evasion was maddening.

I didn't know what he did when he was in the mortal realm, but I knew that he had to be someone skilled at his job, or one of the biggest problems to face any population. He was unnaturally good at sending me into a rage like I had never felt before, stoking the fire within me with surgical precision.

"Did you kill my Nola?" My heart was on the verge of bursting from the pressure building in my chest.

"I did no such thing," he finally responded, his voice carrying wounded dignity. "It must have been a hallucination caused by being so overwhelmed by the ritual. As for why you are still here, I don't know. It should have worked perfectly." He paused, looking genuinely puzzled. "It's not common for me to try and bring the dead back from a realm that isn't even mine."

Even with the answer finally on the table, I didn't trust it. I didn't believe anything that spilled from his lips. He had wanted to form a bond, trust between us. He'd had it, briefly. Now, he only gave me the feeling of discomfort that crawled under my skin like insects.

"If the sisters of fate could work together, this would be easy for them. They could snap you back as if it were just a small task on their to-do list. It seems they aren't much on teamwork, though," the blood weaver rambled on, his voice taking on a conversational tone that grated against my nerves.

I left. I stormed away from him, my footsteps heavy with frustration.

I didn't know where I was going, but I was going somewhere—anywhere but near him. I needed to be away from his manipulations and half-truths. I needed to move my focus back to my wife, to what truly mattered. I had to find a way to leave this place.

If the blood weaver really was a sibling of Nikola and Yumi, I could see where they were similar. They all were judgmental and convinced that only one of them possessed true intelligence.

They enjoyed treating everyone as if they were playthings in some cosmic game.

"I never give you enough credit. We could have been such a team. You found someone we hadn't been able to locate for ages," Nikola's voice came from behind me, smooth as silk and twice as dangerous.

I looked at him and did not resist the urge to roll my eyes. I felt pain in my eyelids from the stretch, but it still felt good to let out some of the emotion I had bottled up like pressure in a sealed container.

The group of them also enjoyed showing up from nowhere, materializing like nightmares.

"Did you think that you were safe? That I couldn't enter here?" Nikola laughed, the sound beautiful and terrifying.

Even his laughter was melodic, designed to entrance and manipulate.

"Why are you here?" I asked, turning to face him fully.

"To see you. To offer you the chance to truly choose your path," he replied with false sincerity.

"How generous of you," I scoffed, the words bitter on my tongue.

"I won't discuss the Blood Weaver. Not today. He is something… complex. Instead, why don't we discuss our immediate future? Why don't we talk about a world where we can ensure our loved ones are protected?" Nikola offered, his voice taking on that hypnotic quality.

A chill ran down my back at the topic, ice forming in my veins.

"Do you think I'd accept?" I furrowed my brow, disbelief coloring my voice.

"I think that the idea of Ruri standing beside you, safe and happy, while the two of you have the world at your fingertips? I think that is a tempting idea. Isn't that all that really matters in the end? The two of you, together. Living a quiet life with children and friends." His voice grew softer, more persuasive. "You were quick to sacrifice Sage for the chance at just that once. You didn't care about what might come from that decision. You didn't care about keeping Sage from her guardian, or maybe keeping the other sisters from entering the realm. Why care now? Now that you could truly have everything you've ever wanted?"

"I would never disrespect Ruri by accepting such an idea. If Ruri is upset at me because of a choice that I made on my own, so be it. I will accept the consequences." My voice grew stronger with each word. "I wouldn't take your hand when I know it would mean letting go of hers. I definitely wouldn't accept an offer like that when I know that I can kill you myself." I growled, power thrumming through my words.

He looked at me with a flat expression, his face a mask of cold calculation. He looked at me as if he were deciding whether to take me as a joke or a genuine threat.

"Do you know what I can do with only a hum? Not a full song but a simple hum—a harmony carried on the wind. My voice, my tune, has a way of asserting control over people. She is no exception to this power." His words grew darker, more menacing. "Her sister is following me like a lost puppy. She knows that what she's doing is wrong. She wants to resist, but she never does. Her desire to please me is stronger than her desire to fight." He paused, letting the words sink in like poison. "Did it hurt you to watch Ruri with Deimos? Imagine how much it would hurt to watch me take Ruri while she was on all fours like a dog." His expression stayed empty, devoid of any humanity. "Don't toy with me while I'm playing nice with you, boy."

His dark eyes glanced inside of me like windows into my soul. He began to hum, a low, hypnotic sound that seemed to come from everywhere at once. I reached to plug my ears, but I was too late—the melody had already wormed its way inside.

He was inside my mind, rifling through my thoughts like a thief.

Nikola showed me images of my children, their faces bright with innocence. They danced with Ruri in a field of flowers, her laughter like music in the wind. She smiled and laughed until she didn't. She was warm and alive until she was on the ground, decaying with the grass around her. Two small bodies lay beside her, my children reduced to bones. Mortals visited the skeletal remains of her body, which stayed intact as if she were a monument to my failures.

The images shifted, becoming even more horrific. Nikola showed me visions of her chained to a wall beside his bed, her eyes hollow and broken. Short moving pictures of her crying over a group of children with Nikola's cold, dark eyes while she wore chains and sat beside his throne like a broken doll. He brought me back to reality just as quickly as he had stolen it, and I found myself on my knees, gasping for air.

"You have a choice, Caym. I'll leave you to consider it carefully," he murmured with mock kindness.

He sliced the layer open between our world and the living with casual ease, then walked through it as if stepping through a doorway. I held myself together until I knew he was gone, until nothing surrounded me but darkness and my own ragged breathing, before I allowed myself to shed tears that burned like acid on my cheeks.

I had been so confident, so sure that I stayed at least one step ahead at all times.

I was never more than two steps behind, stumbling in the dark while he danced in the light.

The images of Ruri in my mind weren't gone for long. As if Nikola were still standing in front of me, taunting me with his presence, they played again and again like a broken record of torture.

How were we supposed to keep taking steps forward when it took only a flick of his eyelashes to cause such devastating destruction?

CHAPTER SEVENTEEN

IN THIS LIFE, OR THE NEXT

RURI

My land needed help and focus. It needed a leader and a ruler that dedicated its time to healing mortals and repairing homes torn apart by war. The devastation in the end was beyond what I had imagined possible.

We were unprepared for Nikola's reality. The writing of him was all but erased from history, buried beneath layers of lies and careful omissions. The stories of what he was capable of lay only with Shivani and her experience in the shattered realm, fragments of truth in an ocean of deception.

How were we supposed to defend against something we hardly understood?

I laid those thoughts with Shivani. I tucked her in with them like a blanket of responsibility, and I left her to carry what I could no longer bear.

Though my land needed a leader that could help them recover, could guide them through their darkest hour, it wasn't me.

They needed to be healed and pieced back together with comfort and gentle hands.

It wouldn't come from my hands.

The only thing my hands were capable of now was harm. My hands wanted to turn the entire planet into rubble, to reduce everything to the same broken state as my heart. They could no longer help anything grow or heal. Instead of rebuilding my city, I went to crush another.

I stood in front of the city of light, the one that had long been ruled by Kyrell with his golden throne and golden heart. The one that trained Caym and held an army that was said to be loyal only to him, soldiers who would die at his word.

I had come to crush it, and its ruler. I had come to find a way to make myself feel whole again through destruction.

I had come to give in to what I had fought against for so long.

I slung my hand outward to the right and sent a bolt of purple orbs crashing into the citadel that towered over the city like a beacon. It held a glowing ball of light at its tip like a miniature sun, beautiful and pure. I flung my other hand to the left and sent more orbs shooting into the ring of pathways that circled the town center. The city of Solaris was covered in pathways of sparkling starlight to walk on, each step meant to inspire wonder.

I'd cover them all in rubble and ash.

I shot two more sets of orbs into the city center until chunks of the shimmering stone that held it together rolled down the side and crashed to the ground below with thunderous impacts. Every piece of the city that fell was a piece of me fitting back together, violence rebuilding what grief had destroyed.

"Kyrell!" I called out, my voice echoing off the burning buildings. "I'll count to five before I take down mortals!"

I called down a crackle of thunder as a threat, the sound reverberating through my bones. The thunder sent a new rush of rage through me when it reminded me of Kyra, of her betrayal that cut deeper than any blade.

I couldn't stop myself from feeling as though she were a bigger betrayal than Yumi had been, more personal than even Sage's treachery.

"One!" My voice carried across the destruction.

We could have had a conversation. Even if she only wanted me to listen while she explained, I would have given her that courtesy.

"Two!" The word tore from my throat.

I would have apologized for hurting her. I would have done what she needed to feel okay, to heal the wounds between us.

"Three!" My hands trembled with barely contained power.

Instead, she betrayed not just me but Astra without hesitation, choosing Nikola's lies over everything we had built.

"Four!" The number hung in the air like a death sentence.

It was unfair to put the blame for the way that I felt on her shoulders. It wasn't the root of my emotions, but it riled me to a new high all the same. My body felt the same crackle of intensity that I had brought down from the sky.

A large part of me thought that I'd feel fine again once Caym was back by my side, that his presence would restore the parts of me that had been carved away.

I needed him to feel anything other than this consuming rage.

"Ruri, stop this," Kyrell pleaded, his voice carrying across the space between us.

He stood before me, attempting to look composed, with golden eyes that reflected the flames behind me. He trailed his gaze from my face to my fingertips, assessing the threat I posed.

"This won't bring him back. I know that's why you're here. He can't come back," Kyrell nearly stammered his words, fear creeping into his usually steady voice.

Had I given him more credit than was due? Was he actually afraid of me, the girl he used to counsel?

"It's just like you to give up on him so quickly!" I snapped, the accusation sharp as broken glass.

"It's not about giving up on him," Kyrell started, raising his hands in a gesture of peace.

"Yes, it is!" I screamed, my voice cracking with emotion. "Have you tried to find him? Have you searched for his heart? Have you done anything besides sit here in your tower of light?"

"There is no heart to find," he answered with finality.

I forced a laugh, the sound bitter and hollow. "So the answer is no. He's the God of Death! I know he can come back!"

"Rules aren't changed just by love," Kyrell replied, his voice cautious as if he were speaking to a wild animal.

"You wouldn't know anything about love," I sneered, venom dripping from every word. "Did you help destroy his heart?"

He only watched me in silence. Freshly shaved blonde hair and tidy nails told me he still hadn't lifted a finger on either side of this war, content to remain neutral while the world burned.

"I won't help you," he whispered, the words barely audible.

"Yes, you will!" I pointed at him with a finger that crackled with purple energy.

He shook his head in protest, backing away slightly.

"You'll help me from the grave if that's how it must be, but you'll help!" I advanced on him, my voice rising to a roar.

"You understand how things work between us. You grow stronger; I grow weaker. As such, I can't fight you, and you wouldn't hurt someone so defenseless. I've known you long enough to be sure of that." Kyrell lowered his hands to his sides, his posture one of resignation.

His words were like the last twist of a screw before all of me split under pressure and force. I didn't speak because I couldn't have formed words between my screams of rage and anguish. I tackled him hard enough that when we both hit the ground, the air left my chest with force as brutal as his.

The background was lit by the flames of buildings behind us that I had only noticed from the ground, the city burning like a funeral pyre. I hardly cared about the destruction anymore. I pulled the sickle blade from its place on my hip and used it to hack into Kyrell, the metal singing through the air. I wasn't sure where my aim was meant to be, driven by fury rather than precision. I knew that with every rise and fall that tore through flesh, I felt a little more like myself.

Every time I felt the blade hit bone, I cringed under the grinding sound but continued my assault. I hacked and pulled, carved and sliced. I screamed and laughed in equal measure. I cried until there was nothing recognizable left of Kyrell, until the golden-eyed god was reduced to meat and memory.

I dripped with his blood, and I was out of breath, but I ate his heart to become whole again. The rush of my full abilities and memories was overwhelming, flooding back like a dam bursting. They brought with them guilt and regret that threatened to drown me.

I'd refuse them for today.

Kyrell's soul left his body to enter the place I desperately wanted to be, the afterlife where Caym waited. I watched for his soul to open the small rift to the other side, the tear in reality that would be my salvation. Before it could close, I grabbed the soul and held it tightly until it pulled me into the afterlife with it, using his death as my key to the realm beyond.

Kyrell was a fool—a stupid one at that. He misunderstood my arrival completely. He thought I was still some girl who would think twice before acting, who would hesitate at the crucial moment. He would have been right if they had kept their hands off of Caym. With him by my side, I fought to stay in the middle of the violence to protect him, to shield him from harm. Without him by my side, I only wanted to become the violence myself.

Kyrell thought that he had some moral ground to stand on, but I had come to take his heart and lie my way into the afterlife through his death.

He was my two-for-one ticket—my shortcut to power and the other half of my heart.

I'd find my husband with Kyrell's help, one way or another, even if I had to drag his soul kicking and screaming through the void.

CHAPTER EIGHTEEN
EMERALD EYES

CAYM

Nikola was kind enough to give me a break from the hallucinations he left me with, though his mercy came at a price. The break came after each horrific event was completed, allowing me enough time to catch my breath and listen to a whispering voice that slithered through my mind like poison, asking if I was ready to make a commitment to the correct side yet.

When I refused with what little strength I had left, the process started again.

The visions were largely of Ruri, each one designed to break me a little more. Some of them were glimpses into Nikola's own life, fragments of his twisted history. Every so often, Nikola gave me an inside view of his own experience, forcing me to see through his eyes. It was compelling enough to understand that picking the right side didn't come with perfection, that even heroes made terrible choices.

I felt as though he had been trying to convince me that the things he had done were for the greater good, that Dahlia was just as monstrous as he was. I hadn't seen any evidence of

Dahlia manipulating minds to do her dirty work for her so that she didn't have to lift a finger. Her sins seemed to be of a different nature entirely.

Nikola's entire defense for himself lay in the twisted comfort that he hadn't explicitly hurt anyone with his own fingers. He showed me this rationalization more than once, as if repetition would make it true. It had the opposite effect on me—I lost respect for him when he presented that idea as if it absolved him of guilt.

He endlessly used mortals and deities who otherwise might have never hurt anyone if he hadn't whispered a song in their ears, if he hadn't planted his poison in their minds. He spent over one hundred years tearing the shattered realm apart based on those manipulations. He entrapped an entire mortal bloodline with a hummed control, turning them into puppets.

He wouldn't convince me, no matter how many horrors he forced me to witness.

When Nikola realized that he wasn't making any difference with his tactics, he shifted them like a predator changing hunting strategies. When he showed how powerful his hands could be, when he failed to convince me through fear, he tried to show me that he once had a softer side. He showed me the version of him that once helped his sisters, before love became obsession.

I saw, through his eyes, how he felt in those moments.

He loved his sisters, but it didn't convince me of his righteousness. He crossed from love to obsession and couldn't understand the difference, couldn't see the line he had obliterated. Even when he forced me to feel the way he felt, I understood it was wrong. I felt the progression from love and devotion for Dahlia—when he helped her with no expectations in return, when they cooked meals together like family. When it shattered, he would only offer a helping hand in exchange for something he wanted, love corrupted into transaction.

I felt the shift in his loving glances when they turned into hungry stares that devoured rather than cherished. He wanted to win me over by showing me that he had some semblance of humanity, but that wasn't true. The rest of us only learned compassion through time with mortals, or truly lending a hand to each other without expecting payment.

No matter what he showed me of his past, I didn't see a single time where he helped anyone but himself, where he learned any lessons that might have made him better.

He was cruel when he didn't get his way, petulant as a child with the power of a god. I could have lied to him and told him what he wanted to earn my freedom. I could have bitten my tongue and run at the first chance I got, but she would be disappointed to hear it. Even if she didn't voice it, I knew that she would feel the betrayal.

Instead, I'd take comfort in getting to see Ruri's face again, even if only in my mind. I'd refuse to watch the things he put into my head. Instead, I'd focus on touching her face again, on memorizing every detail. I tried to remember the sound of her voice saying my name like a prayer.

I'd focus on the good in her—the warmth she always carried like sunlight in her soul. I'd focus on her beautiful, long, dark green hair that caught light like living emeralds. I'd recall how tall she was when she wore black heels with her gowns, how she commanded every room she entered.

"Caym!" Ruri called, her voice cutting through the darkness.

There it was—her soothing voice that could calm storms. My mind never let me down when it came to her memory. True music to my ears.

"Caym!" Her voice soothed me like a balm on burns.

I tried to pry my eyelids open, but they hardly lifted, weighted down by exhaustion and despair. They were too heavy, and I only saw more darkness pressing in from all sides.

I was lifted off of the ground by soft skin, gentle hands

that I recognized even in my broken state. I tried once more to open my eyes, and when I did, I was met with emerald gems gleaming back at me like stars in the void.

"He is too good at what he does. I know you're fake, a product of Nikola's cruelty, but he did well. You're still beautiful. You still smell of strawberries and summer rain." I ran my hand across her cheek, marveling at the softness. "You're still as warm as I remember." My voice cracked like breaking glass, but I didn't hold the tears back. I didn't stop them from falling where they wanted to land. "I'm sorry for failing you. I should have been stronger. I let you die more than once."

"Shh," she whispered, the sound like wind through leaves.

She had never spoken in my hallucinations before—they were always silent tortures.

"It's my fault for not putting a stop to things sooner," her voice eased my mind like cool water on fevered skin.

"I wish that I could have seen you one last time. That I could have apologized properly. That I could have given you the real wedding that you deserved, with flowers and music and all our friends." I managed through the tightness in my throat. "Nikola has shown he's skilled enough that I can't even trust my own mind anymore."

"I'm here, Caym," she assured me, her voice carrying a certainty that made my heart ache.

"Do you recall when we built our home on the edge of the island outside of Elowen? When we showed our little girl the dragons that flew in the sky like living jewels. Do you remember how she giggled? She sounded just like you, pure joy made into sound." I leaned my head into her chest, seeking the comfort I remembered. "I thought I would have found her here, but I didn't. I didn't find either of them. I wanted to bring them home to you."

"That's all right," my Ruri murmured, her voice like honey and warmth. "It means we can find them together when we have fixed things. We can bring them back to a safer realm, one where they can grow up without fear. First, we need to bring you home. We need to heal you and help you recover because we have many more children yet to come."

If only that were true. If only I could have given her what she wanted, what she deserved. If only we could have run away together when we still had the chance. I'd have given the entire world to Nikola on a silver platter if—no, if Ruri would have agreed to it and run away with me to somewhere he could never find us.

"If that were true, if we did have the chance to start over, I'd prove to you that I could be a better husband and father," I whispered against her skin.

"You were already a good husband and father," she whispered back, her words wrapping around me like a embrace.

"No, I wasn't. I let you die, I let them die. I failed over and over when you needed me most." I cried, the words torn from the deepest part of my pain.

"Shh. You need to rest now. Don't speak anymore. Close your mouth and your eyes. I've got you," her beautiful voice hummed, and for the first time in what felt like eternity, I believed that maybe, just maybe, I was safe.

CHAPTER NINETEEN

THE GLOWING GARDEN

I sat cross-legged in front of my three false sisters, studying their faces with a mixture of affection and sorrow. Were they simply creations of Nikola's twisted imagination? Yes. Had I managed to shift the world he put me in to suit my needs? Yes. They looked so similar to my real sisters that they held the same scars and smile lines, every detail perfect down to the way they moved their hands when they spoke.

"Are you sure it will work?" False Sage asked, her voice carrying the same hesitant tone I remembered.

"I mean, as sure as I can be, given that I've never tried to knife my way out of an altered reality before," I answered, trying to sound more confident than I felt.

"What if it doesn't work?" false Shivani asked, worry creasing her brow exactly like the real one.

"Then we come up with another plan," I replied with determination. "We always do."

Ruri sat silently for a moment, deep in thought, before she spoke with characteristic directness. "Will you miss us? Will we die?"

My heart sank at the question, the weight of it settling in my chest like lead. They weren't real, and everything they did spoke to a part of me and my own guilt, reflections of my own imagination. But they may as well have been real sisters. I had spent nearly as much time locked inside the world Nikola made for me as I had spent outside of it, sharing conversations and comfort with these phantom versions.

"You won't die. You'll combine with your real forms on the outside. You'll still be with me. We will just be free," I lied, the words tasting bitter on my tongue.

I didn't know what would happen if I broke out successfully. I didn't know anything for certain; I just believed in what I had witnessed the first time I used my soul blade against the barrier.

I got to my feet, and the other three followed in perfect synchronization. I handed each of them a blade like mine, weapons forged from desperation and hope. It had taken considerable time to craft them, but it was worth every moment of effort. I had just as high a belief in my sisters' ability to hold strong while I was trapped inside as I did in my blade's power.

I had extensive experience with blades of bone and soul— it was who I was at my core. Shivani dealt in blood and had the ability to do so many miraculous things with it. Ruri commanded elements with the force of nature itself, and Sage could bring even the smallest leaf to vibrant life. I could pull even a small spark of a soul through bone and make it sing.

Souls, death, bones—the possibilities with them were unending. Once I had time and freedom, I'd like to see what the original witches I taught had accomplished with so much time. What they might have created in my prolonged absence.

For now, I needed to earn my freedom, again.

I pointed them to specific spots along the shimmering line of my enclosure, and they listened with trust that warmed my heart. I could see the hesitation flickering in their faces, so I moved first to show them the way. I dug my blade into the wall and unleashed the screams from inside the knife, the souls wailing with collective anguish. The barrier sparked and crackled, and so did the false representations of my sisters, their forms flickering like flames.

They pounded at the barrier, too, their fists creating rhythmic impacts. The combination of screams from inside the blades and relentless pounding could have made its own haunting song. The sparks could have started a fire if there had been anything combustible to burn down. Everything compounded together into a symphony of motivation and desperation until there was a brilliant burst from the barrier and then absolute silence.

I watched cracks form on every inch of the surface in front of me, spreading like a spider's web, before it all crashed like glass from a shattered cup. I clapped my hands in triumph and turned to thank my fake sisters, but before I could speak, the ground fell out from underneath me. I floated through absolute darkness, light as a feather, until I hit a cold marble floor with brutal force. The air was knocked out of me completely, and I could only groan in pain.

"That's what I was told," a voice drifted from somewhere nearby.

I tried to roll, to find some sort of cover to gather myself behind, but my back was still in too much agony to move properly.

"I don't know who would have the power to bind Nikola to Cylla but the sisters of fate," another voice responded, closer than the first.

"Sahir is the problem now. Not even Yumi is worth much anymore."

I opened my eyes cautiously to see the locket lying on the ground beside me, its surface gleaming in the dim light. There was a bed and a rug, only a stone's throw away from where I had fallen.

"You're right, she's not worth much. Yumi used the last of any power she had to lift the curse of voice. Nikola promised that if she did it, he would spare her, but I don't believe it."

"Neither do I."

Yumi lifted the curse? The realization hit me like lightning.

"Yumi betrayed us and lied about the Tree of Life. The tree was my mother," I declared aloud as a test, my voice ringing clear.

It really had been lifted. I was really free to speak without consequence.

I rolled myself to the side until I could sit up, my ribcage still too sore to move quickly. Their voices trailed off into the distance, and I sighed with relief. The last place that I wanted to be discovered was inside Nikola's bedroom. I didn't want to be found at all, but least of all in such an intimate and dangerous place.

I grabbed the necklace, which looked untouched and innocent, and placed it back on the table beside his bed before struggling to my feet.

The doors in Semper were different than the ones I was used to in other realms. They slid instead of opening wide, which was convenient for sneaking and remaining undetected. I remembered the conversations that I had overheard about the last safe place in Semper. Something told me that I would have an easy time finding it with the way the place looked like nothing but rubble and destruction.

Rubble and dirt everywhere. Whatever the realm of the gods had looked like at its height, it now resembled nothing more than the shattered realm before we had fled it.

I kept close to the remaining walls, ducking and weaving between debris. I had to dodge falling rocks and rotting fruits that hung from dead branches. Dead tree stumps and browned vines covered everything left behind like a shroud of decay.

The end of the hallway held a door that shimmered in the

same way the barrier of Brontide had, pulsing with protective magic. It had to be the right place—the safe spot in the realm of the gods that Ruri had left behind.

I slipped myself inside and immediately held mixed feelings about what I encountered. There was an octopus made of starlight floating in front of me, its tentacles swirling with cosmic light. He had to have been a helper, maybe a pet? He was undeniably cute, but the way he squealed and shook at my presence made it clear that he wanted to attack me.

Aero and Fennic came around the entrance doors, swords lifted and voices raised in battle cries. They were ready to try and hurt me, and I was genuinely impressed by their protective efforts. I raised my hands in surrender before they could get too close.

"Hesperia?" Fennic's words were broken up with disbelief, and he took his steps slower, as if I might vanish.

"Hi," I waved with as much casualness as I could muster.

"How are you here?" he demanded, sounding more angry than confused.

"Would you believe me if I told you that I used altered reality versions of my sisters to trap souls inside of daggers and break down an invisible barrier? Then I fell out of a necklace," I asked, knowing how absurd it sounded.

"No," Fennic replied flatly.

"I would," Aero chimed in with surprising acceptance.

I shrugged with a grin. "One out of two isn't bad."

Aero took the starlight octopus with him, and Fennic guided me inside to where a pale red-headed woman sat at a stone table. She drank tea and smiled at me warmly, the gesture moving her hundreds of freckles like constellations across her skin.

"It's been a long, long time," Juniper murmured with genuine affection.

I had entered a realm completely opposite to the one that I had just escaped. The room seemed to have its own sun—I couldn't see it, but the brightness and warmth convinced me it existed. Small multicolored dragons roamed through bushes of vibrant flowers, their scales catching the light. Fire sprites danced among the plants, burning away weeds with playful precision. It was like a fairy tale brought to vivid life, with bits of everyone's essence remaining untouched inside the protective barrier.

I sat across from Juniper on an open stone stool, marveling at the sanctuary she had created. "I didn't think that you would recognize me," I admitted.

"I may not have, but it seems we have some blessings on our side. You arrived just in time for our memories to be mostly restored," Juniper explained, taking a delicate sip of her tea.

"So then, you remember last time we were against Nikola?" I asked, leaning forward with anticipation.

She nodded solemnly. "I do, every painful detail."

"Do you think we have better odds this time?" I asked, though I knew I shouldn't have. I could have gushed like a broken dam knowing I was free to speak and in company that knew as much as I did.

"I do. Nikola's upper hand came from his ability to move in the shadows, to strike from places we couldn't see. It's our upper hand this time, too." She slid me a cup of steaming tea, the aroma soothing my frayed nerves. "Dahlia couldn't do much, but what she could do, she did with purpose. She sent Ruri visions and dreams through our time in Semper. Dahlia showed Ruri what she could of Nikola's true nature. She gave images of the death of you girls, showed her the devastation of the realm. She revealed what would happen if we lost this war. Ruri also learned that people were going to die." She paused, her expression growing somber. "Ruri didn't know what she was preparing for. She thought she was going insane, but it was the best Dahlia could manage. I have stayed in the background so that I was forgettable, invisible. I took a note from Nikola's playbook and stayed as quiet as a mouse. I was left with the task of preparing for war, and we are ready for war."

A flame of hope ignited underneath me, spreading warmth through my chest.

"I'm glad you're on our side, Juniper. I'm going to go find my sisters, unless you need help here?" I asked, already feeling the pull to reunite with them.

I was anxious to leave, to see them with my own eyes.

"Go, sweet girl," she replied, patting my hand with maternal tenderness. "They need you more than I do right now."

CHAPTER TWENTY

THE HAMMER OF CHAOS

JUNIPER

I watched Hesperia leave through the barrier that Ruri had left behind, her figure disappearing into the shimmer like a stone sinking into still water. I didn't worry for her because I knew there wasn't much left that could hurt her, not while she remained alert and free. Sahir was the only thing that remained in Semper to cause a real problem, and although she spent much of her time lurking outside our sanctuary, she was preoccupied now going back and forth with Nikola.

I didn't understand how Nikola had become locked out of Semper. I didn't think such a thing was possible, but I wouldn't question this stroke of fortune. I wanted Nikola to remain as far away as he could be, trapped in whatever realm would hold him.

I returned to the center garden, where Olexei the sun god waited with infinite patience. He was soft in all ways—from his gentle middle to his kind facial features. Olive skin comple-mented honey-colored hair that caught the light like spun gold. It was comforting to have him back around after so long.

If it hadn't been for him, Dahlia would never have given me a chance to prove myself worthy.

Olexei was the paint that helped Dahlia see in color instead of black and white. She was naturally rougher, stern and set in her unwavering ways. Good was good, and bad was bad. She saw no middle ground, no shades of gray. Olexei helped to leave a softer landing for a lot of deities and mortals who might otherwise have been crushed under her judgment.

There was a time when I pleaded with Dahlia not to judge me for the sins of whom I was born to, and she remained steadfast in her ideals that all we had to build from was the legacy of our parents. Dahlia wanted to see me left as an outcast, branded forever. She wanted me to remain under my father's shadow and name. Dahlia wanted me to be treated as Nikola was—with suspicion and fear.

Olexei was the voice that convinced her to allow me the chance to show her that a branch might break and tumble away from its root, that I could be different.

I would forever be grateful to him, and he would always remain warm and strong to me, even now when he was powerless and diminished.

"It looks like we are out of time," I murmured, feeling the weight of approaching fate.

"We were out of time the moment Caym died," Olexei answered with quiet resignation.

"I don't understand what you mean."

"Quade is in the in-between realm. If I'm being honest, I think that is how Nikola became trapped in the mortal realm." Olexei sighed deeply, his shoulders sagging. "I've long kept his secret from Dahlia. Anything to give her peace and one less worry to carry."

"Quade? The Blood Weaver?" I asked, my voice barely above a whisper.

"The Blood Weaver," Olexei confirmed with a solemn nod.

"Whose side will he be on?" I pressed, though I feared the answer.

The Blood Weaver was something even I hardly knew anything about. Dahlia had been strict that he be written out of every piece of history we kept, erased as if he had never existed.

"He's always been on his own side. He believes in no such thing as good or bad. He is neutrality in its most humanoid form," Olexei explained, his voice carrying the weight of long-held knowledge. "The only true information I hold about him is that it was he and Dahlia who made the seasons together."

"Before we go, can I ask you one more thing?" I pressed, needing to know. "I always wanted to understand why, when everything else is balanced, why are the guardians not? There are two sisters of life and two brothers. Four sisters of fate, four seasons. Only three male guardians and one woman. It has always stuck out to me as deliberate."

"The number one often stands for trusting yourself and your intuition. Three can be a message for new beginnings and growth." He sighed and stood up, his movements heavy with exhaustion. "Anyway, it doesn't matter now, none of it does. We have to take one step at a time, and Nikola is the current problem pressing against our throats. Our side quest is finding a way to bring Astra back to us. We haven't been able to find a way to do it without someone sacrificing themselves so that the pieces of her heart that are left have something to fuse to."

"I don't know what else to try. Herbs, dragons, flowers, sprites. I don't know what else there is," I confessed, tossing my arms to my sides in frustration. "Do you think that Caym being there with Quade will cause more problems?" He had told me to ignore it for now, but that was easier said than done.

"Maybe we have to try another deity," he reluctantly offered, the words hanging between us like a death sentence.

I didn't want to hear him say it, let alone discuss the implications. If he wanted to move away from the subject, tossing around the idea of self-sacrifice was certainly the way to do it.

"I don't know if I can condone or guarantee that sacrifice would work. I know that we need any deities that we can get from Semper. Hesperia will be counting on us to be here when she needs us," I replied instead, deflecting from the horrible possibility.

"I disagree. We need to move in silence, like shadows. If you proposition a deity and they reject you, the first thing they will do is tell Nikola. If he knows that we are successfully recruiting, do you think that he will just let us continue?" Olexei asked, his logic cutting through my hopes.

I knew he was right, and I wouldn't argue the point, but I did long to do something more than sit in my protected bubble. It didn't feel as helpful as being on the ground with the rest of them, fighting and bleeding.

Aero leaned around the archway that stood between the entrance and the garden, his expression grave.

"He's right. We need to keep to ourselves unless we know that we can trust whom we are talking to completely. A small group that we can trust is better than a large one where we have to wonder what betrayal comes next."

"Fine," I relented, though every fiber of my being wanted to do more.

Time stood still for a moment—not a long enough moment for me to process what was happening. A hammer came twirling in a perfect line through the air, spinning with deadly precision. It moved with such force that I swore it had to have been tossed by someone with more strength than any god or mortal I had ever seen. It was thrown with meaning, with pure fury. It was thrown with the intent to not just harm but to utterly destroy.

My feet began to move, but not faster than the hammer's trajectory. I wasn't able to move faster than my heart as it sank into my stomach like a stone.

I was powerless to stop its landing, helpless to change what was about to happen.

Her laugh came before the crash, echoing through the garden like breaking glass.

Sahir's giggle of glee and finger wave moved as slowly as everything else had, her expression one of pure malicious joy. She bit her lip in anticipation as the blood began to run down Fennic's face in crimson rivers. He dropped to his knees with a single blink, and I would never forget the way his eyes pleaded up at me, or the way his jaw hung open as he tried to understand—like the rest of us tried to understand—that he was going to die.

Olexei had already begun to uncover our hidden vine portal into Cylla and toss bags of precious herbs and frightened dragons through it. His mind moved faster than mine did, already thinking three steps ahead. He had gotten half of the things that lived in my garden to safety by the time Fennic fell the rest of the way to the ground. The hammer embedded in the back of his skull was clearly visible, a grotesque crown of violence.

"Oh, Juniper," Sahir called with another giggle, her voice dripping with false sweetness.

The world sped back up to normal time, and I grabbed the candles placed in the middle of my table and hurled them into the bushes until the garden lit ablaze with cleansing fire. She wasn't going to get her hands on anything that I had grown with love and care. I couldn't save Fennic, but I could stop her from getting another advantage.

Aero grabbed Fennic's body with gentle hands, and he was out behind the rest of us, carrying our fallen friend to safety.

Ashbell stood in front of us in more chaos than I could have ever imagined possible. The realm of the Gods had been so eerily quiet after Nikola's devastating assault that it was unbelievable to see the sight that greeted us on Cylla.

Nikola had caused trouble and ruin wherever he went, but nothing compared to the devastation of the realm of the Mortals.

CHAPTER TWENTY-ONE

THE PULSE OF CHANGE

SHIVANI

I hadn't known chaos like the chaos we lived in now. Everything I thought was poor luck before seemed like a fine, peaceful time in comparison. The stress I thought I would never overcome before felt like a casual ride compared to our current days of endless crisis.

Proof that no matter how bad things felt, there was always something worse lurking on the horizon, waiting to devour what little peace remained.

We were still reeling from being attacked, our wounds both physical and emotional still fresh and bleeding. We had been doing our best to repair things and help people heal when Ruri disappeared on us without warning. She didn't say where she was going or why she needed to leave. She gave us no idea of when to expect her back, if ever. She just snapped like a taut rope under pressure and left us behind. There was no one to chase her and try to bring her back because then we'd lose more hands that could have helped the wounded.

The idea that gods were all-powerful had always been a

funny one, a comforting lie. Mortals decided it had to be true to make themselves feel more at peace with their powerlessness, but the truth was that we did not hold the answers to everything. We did not hold unlimited ultimate power or infinite wisdom. We held what we were given according to our position in the cosmic order.

We were only the current faces of something that kept life turning, the wheels of existence grinding forward. We weren't important, all-powerful, or unending. We were only vessels for a much larger mechanism that kept life living, kept the world spinning.

I could only do so much with my limited abilities. Healing the vampires was easy because they lived and thrived off of my magic, our essences intertwined. We were blood to blood, like mother and child. They were a curse built off of me, connected by crimson threads. Healing them was as natural as breathing, as going to sleep.

Ruri's creations? They weren't the same at all. They didn't respond to my magic, didn't recognize my touch. They didn't respond to anything but the ash trees, and only so much of that precious resource could be gathered. It could only be collected so quickly when the trees were under as much of an attack as we were.

All of the inhabitants of Cylla were exhausted beyond measure as it was. When a flood of deities poured into Ashbell as if it were the ocean coming to reset the land, I felt the silent cries that begged for no more burdens to bear.

I didn't know what to do with them or where to place so many displaced souls. I didn't know what task to hand them when everything was already falling apart. I was the only person in charge, and the weight was crushing.

The fires that burned in our surroundings blended in well with the magma flow that sat in streams around Ashbell, creating an hellscape of flame and destruction. The crumbled buildings were a shock to witness. Ashbell was not known for ruined architecture—it was far from that reputation. The land was known to have some of the best carved temples and the only castle to be made entirely out of obsidian crystal, a marvel of craftsmanship.

Half of that architectural wonder was now scattered across the grounds like broken dreams.

Koa did his best to help, bringing every citizen he could spare from his own land. It wasn't enough—it was never enough. His land was reeling from its own problems, dealing with their own crisis. Hesperia was gone. Sage was the cause of so much suffering. I already felt like the ground under me was thin as paper when Aero appeared next, with Fennic's lifeless body cradled in his arms.

How much more could any of us take before we shattered completely?

Aero's face held no color to it, drained of all life and vitality. No hint of flush remained in his cheeks. He trudged forward like the walking dead, lifeless, from a mirrored portal surrounded by vines, moving in my direction with heavy steps.

I felt the wave from my stomach that warned me I was going to vomit, bile rising in my throat. The rush of regret, sorrow, and confusion was too much for my system to process. My hands shook like leaves in a storm, and I didn't know how to proceed. The feeling of helplessness that I thought had reached a point of unbearable pain had somehow increased beyond that threshold.

Koa intercepted Aero before he reached me, and I was partially relieved when he did. I didn't know what to say to Aero about his loss. It was his brother, after all—his blood, his family. In our current realm, Fennic and I did not talk, our relationship strained by circumstance. Fennic was a member of the Shadows of Justice who fought for what was right in the mortal realm with his brother. In the shattered realm, Fennic had been someone close to me, someone I almost loved with a heart that barely understood what love meant.

That felt like lifetimes ago, but it was still true, still real. We were still friends once, at least a little. We considered marriage once, didn't we? Even if it was because we were both out of our minds from Nikola's influence, separated from ourselves, and our memories were lost like scattered pages. It was still a real feeling, even if it was small and fragmented. It had to have been enough of a real connection if we hadn't been able to speak to each other since without discomfort.

I had let it be a blockade between us until I could no longer say that I was sorry or that I regretted the two of us falling away from each other.

A wave of electricity suddenly washed over the ground beneath our feet, crackling through the air, and everything stopped once it touched them. Silence filled the air for the first time in days, an eerie quiet that made my ears ring. My skin prickled and buzzed with energy. I didn't know how I knew what I felt, but I recognized the signature immediately.

It was Ruri's power.

"Ruri killed Kyrell. The last heart was consumed," a temple member whispered, their voice carrying across the stillness.

I felt the sparks inside of me responding, the rush of fire in my veins, and the last lock on my mind and power lifted like chains breaking.

I was pulled into my mind and thrust into a memory, one that felt urgent and important.

I found myself surrounded by golden buildings as I snuck through a narrow alleyway, shadows keeping me hidden. Vespera walked in front of me with someone in a dark cloak. They held their hood tightly to them, fingers clutching the fabric. They both felt urgent and cautious, their movements quick and furtive. I kept my distance and followed them through the winding streets.

They rounded a corner to a dead end, trapped between high walls. Vespera checked every place that could have hidden even a mouse before she allowed the person she was with to speak freely.

"No one will hear us here," the cloaked figure assured.

"You can't be sure of that," Vespera replied, her voice tight with worry.

The cloak hood was removed, and my jaw dropped with it, shock hitting me like cold water.

Sahir grabbed Vespera's face and kissed her as if they had done it for ages, with familiarity born of practice. Vespera backed up and put space between the two of them, her expression conflicted.

"I told you we can't do that anymore," Vespera protested.

Sahir reached for Vespera's hands with desperate fingers. "You can't be serious about ending this."

"I am! I told you that I love her. I really do want to be with Sage. I wasn't sure before, but I am now," Vespera declared with newfound certainty.

"What could have happened that changed your mind?" Sahir demanded, hurt and anger coloring her voice.

"It doesn't matter what changed. We can't keep seeing each other in secret. I don't want to keep lying to her anymore. I want things to work between Sage and me," Vespera explained with quiet determination.

"What if I told her? What if I went to her now and let her know that when you aren't with her, you sneak away with me, and we—" Sahir's voice turned threatening.

"Stop." Vespera pushed her further away, disgust and fear in her expression.

"If you do this, if you leave me, I promise you, she will regret it," Sahir pointed with menace, her words dripping with venom.

I was planted back in my own body, leaving the memory behind like waking from a nightmare.

That was why Sahir had played with Sage so cruelly, manipulating her with such precision. It was why she was so bitter, so set on destroying one of us specifically. It was revenge, pure and simple.

CHAPTER TWENTY-TWO
A WATERY RESCUE
PART TWO

SHIVANI

The world was burning around us, flames consuming everything we had built. So we all met where the fire felt normal, where the heat felt like it belonged naturally. It felt right to stay in Ashbell, surrounded by the familiar warmth of volcanic air. I was sure that Nikola was hiding in the mortal palace that he so longed to escape from, which meant we were an ocean away from our true enemy.

What was an ocean to a god?

The part of me that still only knew myself as a mortal whispered that it was comfort, that distance meant safety. The part of me that was also a goddess knew an ocean meant nothing—we could cross it in a heartbeat if we chose.

Alec, the land of water's mystery man who made deals with Hesperia, was the latest arrival to our sanctuary. Word spread quickly that Ruri was in Solaris, that she had tumbled the entire city down for Kyrell like a force of nature unleashed. No word had come since that devastating act, but an army did arrive in her wake. An army was free to choose its own commander and side, and Solaris' forces arrived with heavy hearts, swearing their blades to us in the name of Caym.

The army of sirens would have no choice but to lay tents down beside them, their songs of mourning mixing with the sound of clashing metal. I was supposed to help a demi-god that the sirens brought with them unlock their abilities in place of Hesperia and now Ruri, both gone when we needed them most.

I thought I should have been happy to have such a responsibility, honored to be trusted with something so important, but I wasn't. I could hardly focus on anything other than Fennic's lifeless form, the memory of his eyes pleading up at me.

"It's nice to meet you, Shivani," Alec offered, holding out his hand with practiced politeness.

I shook it, trying my best not to rush through the greeting.

"Have you ever done this before?" he asked with a small laugh, attempting to ease the tension.

I must have appeared less obvious than I truly felt. He tried to break the awkwardness with what seemed like a poor joke.

"Only a time or two," I answered, making the situation even more uncomfortable.

I sighed and rubbed my face before he stepped to the side. The girl, Nira, walked closer with hesitant steps.

"I have mostly clear instructions on how to do this, so… hopefully, it works, and you aren't stuck as a fish after," I managed, sounding foolish when I laughed at my own attempt at humor.

She only stared at me and blinked a few times, her expression flat and unimpressed.

"All right! That's enough," Queen Rina of the land of air declared, stepping forward with exasperation. "This is painful to watch. I have to step in. If we were in Brisa, I'd order you all cleaning duties for this awkwardness."

Queen Rina positioned herself beside me and placed a finger over the demi-god's heart with practiced precision. She pointed me to the girl's head, and I followed her lead without question.

"How do you know all of this again?" I questioned, curious about her confidence.

"I'm an original witch personally taught by Hesperia," Queen Rina whispered with pride. "Now, one, two, three." She counted down with military precision.

We both shot magic inside of her simultaneously, our energies combining and flowing together. Her life root, which sat inside of her heart, opened up and glowed golden like a small sun. We both removed our fingers carefully, and the girl looked at us with confusion clouding her features.

"Are you sure it worked? I don't feel any different," the girl complained, checking her hands for changes.

"I saw your root open," I assured her, though doubt crept into my voice.

"Maybe try to do something?" Queen Rina suggested helpfully.

"How am I supposed to do that?" Nira snapped, frustration evident in her tone.

"I don't know. I just kind of focus on it, and it happens," I explained weakly.

"Really helpful," Queen Rina laughed, though not unkindly.

Nira's face turned red instead of pink, skipping several phases of embarrassment and going straight to anger. She opened her mouth to speak, and out came a tunnel of water, powerful and uncontrolled. Rina and I met eyes instantly, understanding passing between us. She closed her mouth quickly, and her lip quivered with shock. She tested her lips a second time tentatively, and the same tunnel of water was released past us with even more force.

I saw tears form in her eyes, and although I wanted to feel

sympathy for her, I only felt afraid of what that uncontrolled power was going to cause.

"Queen Rina is going to help you. She is just so skilled, a natural leader, really," I announced, moving Rina in front of her by the shoulders and giving her an encouraging pat. "I have a few other things that I have to do, so…"

I walked with a quickened pace back to the main temple entrance, my heart racing. I nearly sprinted when I laid eyes on Vesim approaching. She had also been an invisible presence since our realms collided, a ghost among us. She spent all of her time with Juniper as the only mortal to step foot in the realm of the gods. I hadn't heard a whisper from her in days.

I jogged up the stairway, still unsure if she was truly there or if my grief-addled mind was playing tricks on me.

"Vesim?" I called out cautiously.

She turned and looked at me with a smile that caught me off guard. One that was filled with more joy than I had ever seen from her, genuine and bright. It held no sign of being forced or manufactured.

"Shivani! I was looking for you," she exclaimed, wrapping her arms around me in an unexpected embrace.

I embraced her back, but I struggled with its awkwardness. When had she become someone to hug so freely?

"What's wrong?" I asked, though her demeanor suggested the opposite.

"This time, I have good news for once. Ruri asked Juniper to find a way for us to guarantee the place of a god can be transferred into a dragon without having to pull a soul from the stars. She wanted assurance that no matter who died, their duty wasn't interrupted." Vesim's smile widened. "I'm happy to say we stabilized the dragons, and they can, without a doubt, become gods if needed."

"Ruri's plan is to give the place of gods to dragons?" I questioned, trying to process this revelation.

"I think it's a brilliant plan. They were created with the

God of Justice's help, after all. I've met temperamental dragons and stubborn dragons throughout my life. I haven't met a dragon willing to collapse and kill the entire realm for the sake of a title or personal glory," Vesim explained with conviction. "If you four can be created to hold the fate of us all, the dragons should be able to do the same if they were created nearly the same way."

I nodded slowly, though my mind reeled. I wouldn't pretend to understand Ruri's train of thought completely. I hardly understood what had happened before the realms collided, the history lost in fragments. It wasn't a subject openly discussed, and when I brought it up, an emptiness would wash over Koa like a shadow.

I would have to trust that my sister knew something that I didn't, that her plan had merit. Eventually, we would all have to start putting a little more trust in each other, or we'd never make it through this war alive.

CHAPTER TWENTY-THREE

KEEPING TIME HELD CLOSE

SHIVANI

I left Vesim to talk to the rest of the temple hands, her newfound enthusiasm infectious as she dove into learning every detail. She seemed genuinely interested in understanding the ins and outs of our operations. Seeing her, witnessing the transformation in her, made me reflect on myself with uncomfortable clarity. I hadn't changed enough—not for what I wanted, not for myself, and certainly not for my newfound family. The only part of Vesim that remained the same was the size of her big, brown eyes that had always held such depth.

I had fought myself for too long, trapped in my own hesitation and fear. I took for granted all of the things that I was spared while others suffered. Everyone lost so much—limbs, loved ones, entire worlds. I had a hard time feeling like I had lost anything when I knew, somewhere deep inside of myself, that my sisters would be fine. They'd be more than fine, because they had to be. They were strong in ways I was still learning to be.

I needed to do something to help, to really contribute in a meaningful way, too.

I marched through the doorway to the Timekeepers with renewed purpose. A separate temple was maintained where they all resided, their sanctuary of knowledge. The one I looked for sat at a long table with a thick, ancient book in his weathered hands. He peered over the edge of it at me, and even though the heavy pages stood between us, his eyes gave away his knowing smirk.

I took a seat at the other end of the table, the distance feeling both respectful and necessary. Like everything else in Ashbell, it was made of polished obsidian that reflected the light. The table was covered in crimson accents that caught the eye like drops of blood. Chandeliers hung from the vaulted ceiling, lighting up the room, and the space was bright enough to hardly notice the dark furniture that surrounded us.

"I've been waiting for one of you to visit me. I did not expect it to be you," Lui observed, his voice carrying years of patient wisdom.

"Who did you expect?" I asked, feeling oddly offended by his comment.

"Ruri," he answered without hesitation. "Have you noticed that you can speak freely now?" Lui asked, setting his book aside with careful reverence.

"I felt the shift, but I wasn't sure what it meant," I admitted, relief and uncertainty warring in my chest.

"So why have you come to me?" he asked with slight disappointment coloring his tone.

His voice was smooth but aged, like wine that had been stored for decades. He had a sense of ancient wisdom about him that made me feel like a child seeking guidance.

"There are a lot of problems to try to solve. Too many, really," I sighed, the weight of it all pressing down on my shoulders. "I thought that if anyone knew how to solve the biggest problem, it would be the people who had gathered information for years."

"You want to know if I know how to kill Nikola?" he asked, cutting straight to the heart of the matter.

"Yes."

"You cannot." He leaned forward, his expression grave. "He is older than you and I, older than the ground we walk on, even older than the sky we look at now. You can't kill the origins of life—not Nikola, not Yumi, not Dahlia. The four of you girls included. You can't die; you can only be contained, trapped like wild beasts in cages. It's why the plan was never to kill the four of you outright. It was always to place you inside of false gods, puppets who could be controlled. To siphon your power into a controlled container." He paused, letting the weight of his words settle. "Other gods, lesser deities—their vessel is temporary. A goddess of love may die, and lovers will tumble for a little while, but a new face will appear as the guide and guardian of all matters of the heart. The beginning, fate, these fundamental forces—they aren't that way. They're eternal."

"So, how do we find a way to trap him? How do you contain a god when gods seem so uncontainable? Dahlia split the realm, and that didn't work," I said, slouching in my seat as despair crept in.

"That's something the four of you will have to figure out together; I am still only a mortal man with mortal limitations," he answered honestly. "I learn everything I know from fragments of the age of moonlight, pieces of a puzzle I'll never see completed."

"What about Dahlia? Why is she powerless and alive, and why hasn't there been a shift in anything in the realm?" I pressed, needing to understand.

"She had to have handed her position to someone else, passed the torch. Whether that person is aware of their new rule or not, I don't know. You will have to speak to her directly." He watched me with unblinking eyes that seemed to see too much. "If not, then maybe she split herself, divided her essence."

"We will have to trap Yumi, too," I spoke out loud, though it was more of a realization than a plan. "Does this mean someone has Olexei's abilities as well?"

He nodded solemnly.

"How do we find out who? Is there a way to identify them?" I asked, desperation creeping into my voice.

"You would need to see them use a type of ability that didn't originally belong to them, something that betrays their true nature," he explained.

"Does anyone else know about this transfer of power?"

"No," Lui answered simply.

I sighed and looked at my fingernails, suddenly fascinated by their ordinary humanity while discussing such cosmic matters.

"You seem to have come just for someone to listen to your thoughts. I think you knew that even my answers only stretched so far," Lui observed with gentle understanding.

"I think a part of me held out hope that there would be a wild card, some secret weapon we hadn't considered," I admitted, feeling foolish but honest.

"We're all looking to the four of you now, placing our hopes on your shoulders."

"We need to hold a meeting and discuss this with the others here. If we can talk freely, we need to take advantage of it while we can," I declared, standing with newfound determination.

He rose without argument, only wearing a smile that suggested he had been waiting for exactly this moment, for someone to finally ask the right questions.

CHAPTER TWENTY-FOUR

A BLACK TIE EVENT

SAGE

I had felt strange ever since yesterday, an uncomfortable buzzing beneath my skin that I couldn't shake. I was fine when we arrived in Ashbell. I was fine when we left. When the wave of electricity washed over the land like a cleansing storm, I felt the same surge as I had when Nikola made me consume the heart that I had taken. He never explained to me who the man in the dungeon of Orest was or why I needed to eat his still-beating heart. It wouldn't have made a difference in my choice.

I would have listened to him regardless. I always listened to him with the devotion of a faithful dog. I just wished I could listen and understand the meaning behind his commands.

As I stood outside of the doorway to the throne room of Nikola's castle in Cylla, where he had been crowned king over mortals, I listened to Sahir and Nikola scream at each other like wild animals. Their voices echoed off stone walls, sharp with fury and desperation. I realized I had spent too much time blindly listening to others and not enough time listening to the voice inside my own head.

Sahir stormed out of the throne room like a hurricane and grabbed me by the collar with bruising force. She pulled me into the room and flung me across the polished floor, my body sliding until I hit the base of the throne.

"This is really worth it to you?" she screamed, spittle flying from her lips. "This useless thing is worth risking failure?"

"If I could have taken them all in one swift motion, do you not think that I would have?" Nikola yelled back from his elevated position, his voice carrying the weight of barely contained rage.

Sahir scoffed, a sound like breaking glass. She had thrown me into the middle of their conflict but had already forgotten that I was there, sprawled on the cold stone like a discarded doll.

"What is your plan then? Do you even have one anymore? You're locked out of Semper like a beggar at the gates. The curse of words was lifted, so now they can all speak freely about your secrets. The first to remember will be the first to spill anything you were holding close. The Fae you transformed are breaking down and dying like diseased animals. They can't handle all the power they hold," Sahir screamed at him without fear, her voice echoing off the vaulted ceiling.

"They served their purpose. I'll make more when I need them. Be content with your position—I spare you more than I spare anyone else," Nikola replied from his throne, his tone dismissive and cold.

"I won't be content until you give me what you promised me. Vespera is to be given back to me!" Sahir demanded, her voice cracking with desperation.

Nikola smiled, the expression sharp as a blade. "It's a common theme for you, isn't it? You claim Sage is nothing special, but everyone you love seems to love her more. I even have to admit she is quite special. There's something about her that even I find… compelling."

"You should know how it feels," Sahir's voice was still loud, but it trembled like a leaf in a storm. "Neither of your sisters wanted you, and even your brother would rather sit in an empty abyss than accept your hand! You're a lunatic, just like Dahlia always said! It's why she chose Olexei over you!"

Nikola stood and walked quietly toward her, each step deliberate and measured. His calm demeanor had me on edge more than his anger ever could. I hadn't been truly scared of him hurting me personally, but I had been terrified of what he would do to others. I was naïve for thinking that I would continue to be spared his violence with the way he treated everyone else around him.

Just as I knew he would, his full palm met her cheek in a thunderous clap of fury that echoed through the chamber.

"I am not a lunatic, and my ideals are not radical," he whispered to her with deadly calm. "When I create the perfect realm, my sister will have to come crawling back to me. When she regrets her choices and begs for my forgiveness, I'll give her your head as a homecoming gift."

"You wouldn't dare," she growled, but uncertainty flickered in her eyes.

"Are you sure about that?" he asked, his voice carrying the promise of violence.

"If you hurt me, I'll take her with me. She ruined my life once; I won't let her do it again and escape unpunished," Sahir threatened, pointing at me with a shaking finger.

"Stop before you embarrass yourself further," Nikola replied with dismissive cruelty.

Sahir stormed out of the room, her heels clicking across the ground in sharp staccato beats of discontent. Nikola held out a hand to me with false gentleness. I took it without hesitation, and he helped me get to my feet. I wouldn't deny his help

—I didn't want to be on the receiving end of the same treatment as Sahir.

"I'm sure you have questions, so ask them," he offered, his tone suddenly conversational.

He brushed my clothing down for me as if he were someone close to me, someone who cared. I stood tense but without resistance, afraid to move wrong.

"I don't have any questions," I answered, the lie falling from my lips automatically.

It was a stupid lie, and I couldn't explain why my body denied every truthful command it could have been given.

"Don't be shy. I'm sure you have questions about Vespera," he murmured, tucking my hair behind my ear before looking me over and taking a step back. "Sometimes mommy and daddy fight, but we will make up later, and things will be fine."

I was disgusted by the patronizing tone he used, speaking to me like a child who needed comfort.

"Vespera and Sahir were close once. I even met with her a time or two when they were together. Sometimes Sahir can be overly jealous and say things that she doesn't mean," he explained with false sympathy.

"Is Vespera okay?" I asked, the question burning in my throat.

I wanted to ask what he meant by them being close, wanted to understand the nature of their relationship.

I didn't dare push for more information. I didn't know where his boundaries lay, not well enough to test them like Sahir did with such reckless abandon.

"She is perfectly safe," he replied without hesitation.

His response gave me enough comfort that I nearly forgot about everything that had occurred, and my body relaxed slightly. He caught on to the change in my posture immediately, reading me like an open book.

"Where are your siblings?" I asked, curiosity getting the better of me.

His body tensed at my words, muscles coiling like a snake preparing to strike.

"That's not a topic for today or tomorrow. Go," he commanded, pointing toward the door with finality.

I was all too happy to obey. I took my leave, nearly running from the throne room. I took my first full breath outside of the doorway, relief flooding through me. I lost all that air in the same heartbeat when Sahir's hand met my face with the full force of her abilities, stars exploding across my vision.

My mind spun like a top, and so did my eyes, the world tilting dangerously. She took the opportunity to hit me again, the blow shaking something loose inside of me. I felt as though she and I had done something similar before, a memory trying to surface. The feeling took hold of me, and instinct drove me to place my hand over her mouth.

A thread of vines released from my palms and entered her mouth like living serpents. The sight terrified me, but when I tried to remove my hand, the vines were too far inside her, beyond my control. Her eyes turned to polished wood, but they still shifted back and forth in terror. Her feet transformed into tree stumps, roots digging into the stone floor. I felt somehow that there was justice in her becoming a tree, a fitting punishment.

When I pulled my hand back, the ends of the vines had sewn her lips shut with green thread. Nikola came through the doorway, and the only instinct I had left was to run as fast as my legs could carry me.

CHAPTER TWENTY-FIVE

THE HEART, THE ARTIFACT, AND THE KISS

SAGE

Nikola had not visited my room since the incident. He had not called on me or sent messages through servants. He had not disturbed me at all, as if I had done nothing worth his attention. I was grateful for this neglect because of the persistent feeling in my gut that told me I had fought with Sahir before, that this violence between us was an echo of something deeper.

The feeling that I had been in a similar situation before grew stronger with each passing hour, like a tide rising in my mind.

I felt exhausted in a way that no amount of sleep could cure, bone-deep weariness that seeped into my very soul. Somehow, I was also restless, like the day before an important event that would change everything. I had something important to do, but I couldn't recall what it was. The knowledge clawed at the back of my mind like a caged animal desperate for freedom.

No matter how exhausted I felt, I could not sleep because

the feeling that I was missing something crucial was more overwhelming than my body's need for rest.

I left my room to take a walk through the eerily quiet castle. There hadn't been the slightest sound for hours, and I took it as confirmation that Nikola and his followers had left. They should have departed, at least. Nikola had a world to conquer, and he needed to find a way to get himself back into the realm of the gods. I wondered how he would accomplish that when he had turned everyone with any kind of ability to help into a monster and sent the rest running to the opposing side.

He clearly couldn't get himself back into Semper with only Sahir at his side. The other gods, though they claimed allegiance to his cause, hadn't left the relative safety of Semper. The opposing side also had Onyx as their prisoner now.

Maybe Nikola had gone to retrieve him.

I walked through empty hallway after empty hallway, my footsteps echoing in the silence. There had once been many pictures and ornate candle holders spread throughout the corridors, but it looked as though the inhabitants had been in the middle of moving when they were all displaced. There were no staff members bustling about, no visitors seeking audience. There was nothing but hollow spaces and abandoned dreams.

Kyra had shown her face only once since the confrontation. Otherwise, she remained in her own land, surely recovering from the devastating losses at Ashbell like everyone else was attempting to do.

I stopped in front of the golden pedestal that held the still-beating hearts, their rhythmic pulsing visible through the glass. The urge to touch them was so strong it made my skin itch as if I were covered in hives. I shouldn't have given in to the impulse, but I was so certain that I was alone that my ability to resist dropped below zero.

I pushed open the knob and pulled the glass door open with trembling fingers. It confused me why Nikola made them out to be so precious but then left them so poorly guarded. He was portrayed as brilliant and powerful, but he was remarkably careless with his most valuable possessions.

He was so convinced that everything had to go according to his predetermined plans that I doubted he was as intelligent as he made himself out to be.

I reached up and touched the hearts with hesitant fingers, and one beat against my fingertip like a trapped bird. It was warm and had the same texture as the meat we consumed at dinner. I ran my finger over the next one and was instantly filled with white-hot rage before I was pulled into the depths of my own mind.

Hesperia and I sat in the middle of a garden so wide that I couldn't see any end to its verdant expanse. She picked at the grass with idle fingers, and I resisted the urge to scold her for the habit. Rina sat with a group of young girls nearby, teaching them the lessons that we had been passing on to her. She grew vines from a jar filled with broken-up bark, the magic flowing through her with natural grace. Together, Hesperia and I had taught her how to pull magic from the materials she had at her disposal.

"I'm sorry," Hesperia blurted out suddenly, her voice thick with emotion.

"No, I'm sorry," I countered quickly. "We shouldn't have let Sahir come between us like poison."

"She's just evil through and through. She is always scheming to turn everyone against each other, planting seeds of discord. We should have seen through her manipulations," Hesperia agreed with conviction.

"We can pretend it never happened," I offered, hope threading through my voice.

She nodded eagerly. "It never happened. I still love you, sister."

I hugged her tightly, and she threw away the blades of grass she had picked apart to embrace me properly.

"I don't want to fight with you again," Hesperia cried against my shoulder.

"Me either," I agreed, feeling the rightness of reconciliation.

"If anyone is going to fight, it should be because Ruri ate the last of the chocolate," Hesperia mumbled through my hair, and I could hear the smile in her voice.

I blinked multiple times, and the rage I had felt before transformed into overwhelming sadness. I stood there, fully back inside of my body, in front of a glass cabinet of stolen hearts. In the home that belonged to my enemy, after I had abandoned my sisters to crumble under the weight of war.

I ground my teeth against each other until they caused sharp pain, the physical discomfort grounding me in reality.

I ripped fabric from my dress and used it to scoop the hearts up carefully, placing them inside so that I could take them all with me. I didn't know who they all belonged to, but I knew with certainty that Sahir and Nikola did not deserve to possess them. Once all of the hearts were secured on the fabric, the only thing left was a small box that I recognized from Yumi's private room in Semper. I opened it with shaking hands, and inside was the small golden artifact that my father had crafted for Shivani so that she could identify the traitor among us.

Yumi had kept it all along, hidden away like a guilty secret. It was never lost.

I tucked it inside with the hearts before I folded the fabric carefully so that everything was protected together. Then I stormed with renewed purpose out of the mortal castle, leaving behind the lies and manipulation.

I paused for a moment outside to take a deep breath of free air. At first, my mind felt as if it were being flooded with returning memories, but once it calmed, I felt a little more complete than I had in months. I felt a little more like my true self. I remembered so much more now—the love, the laughter, the bonds that had been twisted into chains.

I was going where I belonged at last. I was going to find my sisters, and then I was going to kill Sahir properly this time. This time, she would stay dead and never hurt anyone I loved again.

CHAPTER TWENTY-SIX

THE DREAM WALKER

DEIMOS

I had considered for many sleepless nights what my best course of action would be. I poured cup after cup of poorly made wine to calm my gnawing anxiousness, the bitter liquid doing little to quiet my racing thoughts. I did not enjoy the concept of secrets—they were fundamentally illogical to me. The thought process, no, the immense effort that needed to be put forth in order to lie and cover tracks felt like wasted energy.

My body shivered and prickled at the very thought of such deception.

If one were to spend their time with someone, to invest in the sacred bond of friendship, then why not be completely honest? If one were to believe that they were a true partner, wouldn't one expect all cards to be face up on the table, laid bare for examination?

I had begun to understand that what I thought to be true was nowhere near what some others considered reality. Nikola had convinced me thoroughly that the two of us shared a common side, that even if our final goals could not perfectly

align, until those crucial moments arrived, we would work as one unified force.

I never kept a single secret from him.

Every kiss I laid upon Ruri's soft lips, every strand of her silken hair I stroked, every whisper she weaved through my ears late at night like music—I reported it all back to him with faithful devotion. I spoon-fed every move I made straight into his disgusting, manipulative mouth. He held no respect for me, no regard for my position in his grand scheme. He cared not for our working promise or the trust I had placed in him.

If he were not to be held by his words, what was he to be held by?

His ankles, his throat?

I felt the veins in my forehead throb against the quickening of my heartbeat, pressure building like a dam about to burst.

I despised the feeling that arose inside of me when I knew someone was lying to me, the sick twist in my gut that came with betrayal.

Nikola had many extraordinary skills—that could not be denied by anyone. He sang a song like no other being in existence, his voice crafted for enchantment. He was destined for a stage, born to command attention. He carried a curse with his melodic sing-song voice, or perhaps it was a blessing, depending on one's perspective. No one refused him once a note came from his lips, their wills bending like reeds in the wind. He hardly needed to sing at all—he had a natural gravitational pull about him. One might have said he worked the same way as the universe itself, drawing objects into his orbit where they spun around him, desperate to stay close.

They spun until they felt sick and dizzy, all for the chance at a smile from his perfect lips.

I had talents, too—talents that he seemed to have conveniently forgotten.

If he would not speak with me honestly, then I would walk

through the dreams of someone who would. Someone who was unprotected from such an intrusion, someone who indeed held all of the answers I sought, but no longer held a substantial advantage of power to resist me.

I would walk through Olexei's dreams like an uninvited guest. I would force him to relive the events of the past, make him show me every detail. He would reveal the truth to me, even if unwillingly, and I would finally know whom I should assist in this cosmic game.

In the end, I wanted the final say in my own destiny. Semper's throne was mine by right, and I could not fight both the sisters and Nikola simultaneously to claim it. It had to be conquered one enemy at a time.

I couldn't imagine that Nikola had been the best choice of sides if I had already assisted him and yet still found myself with memory blocks on certain crucial subjects.

I pulled a locket from the inside of my burgundy vest and twirled it until the miniature picture of Olexei faced me, his painted eyes seeming to watch.

The dreams of anyone ever born sit captured inside of simple necklaces like these. I possessed millions of them, collected over eons, but deities had been blocked to me until the wave swept over the realms. I had questioned Yumi about this limitation, and she assured me it must have been a symptom of the realm settling, like a bucket of rice that required a light shake to condense properly.

If Nikola had been the one on our side of the realm shatter, I was certain events would have carried out in his favor. Yumi was utterly unfit for the task of leadership. She was suspicious and paranoid, lacking the proper wisdom to convince the other divine beings of even the simplest subjects.

I placed the locket on the cold floor and stepped inside its magical confines. I was immediately transported into Olexei's dream, reality shifting around me like liquid. He sat with Dahlia on a checkered blanket, peaceful and content. They ate a leisurely meal in the garden of the golden city, surrounded by everything one might imagine would inhabit such a picture-perfect scene. Tiny wildlife chirped melodious songs, and their daughters laughed together ahead of them, their joy infectious.

I felt the contents of my stomach twist to life and beg to be expelled.

I shifted his dream into something more useful to my purposes, exerting my will over his subconscious. I waved Dahlia away like smoke and whispered to him, compelling him to take me to an event he thought too important to forget. I whispered to him to show me a moment when he considered a turning point in our old timeline, and he responded without resistance, like a puppet on strings.

Dreams were delicate things, fragile as spun glass. If he became aware of my presence, he could resist me with conscious effort. He could struggle against my will and create difficulties. He would not win such a battle, but he would make my task infinitely harder. If he realized that we were inside of his mind, if he wanted to twist the view in front of him to work for his advantage, he could accomplish such deception.

My suspicions about his level of alertness rose when he simply allowed me into his dreams without any struggle.

Olexei sat at a desk engraved with the intricate symbol of the sun, its rays carved deep into the golden wood. In front of him stood Ruri, and my breath caught at the sight of her. She was covered from head to toe in emerald fabric that complemented her natural beauty. The corset was colored a shade brighter than the flowing gown, but it still matched her long, lustrous hair perfectly.

"It's important that you guard this magic and keep it safe at all costs. If you cannot hold it yourself, then keep it somewhere that you can trust without a doubt. It will be a tool not to change the tides of battle, but to help heal the realm afterward. It has the potential to cleanse what has been corrupted," Olexei told her with grave seriousness.

"What will I be cleansing?" Ruri asked him, concern evident in her melodious voice.

My presence was covered in shadow, and it was only a dream, but I hardly resisted the overwhelming urge to reach out and touch her.

"We cannot fully know the future—the smallest choice may change the largest of outcomes. What your mother and I do know is that our place in the realm of mortals and gods is coming to an end. We have already fought this battle and lost decisively. It's time for us to step aside and pass the torch. Trust in your sisters above all else. The four of you are capable of much more than Nikola is, if you work together in harmony," Olexei explained, though he still only spoke around the crucial points.

"What of the rest of them? Sahir? Deimos?" Ruri's voice was distressed, worry creasing her beautiful features.

Olexei shifted his knowing gaze to where I stood hidden in the shadow. "Nikola is currently planning how he will lock Deimos up with the rest of the disobedient or untrustworthy deities. Deimos will sit beside any other deity that Nikola feels threatened by. He is not an equal or superior. He is merely a fool being used."

"If you wish to speak to me directly, old man, then you should do so," I chuckled, stepping forward from my concealment.

"Did you think that I would not know you were here, invading my private thoughts?" Olexei asked with knowing eyes.

"It matters not," I replied with false bravado. "Why did you bring me here to witness this?"

Olexei stood from his desk and moved toward me with deliberate steps. "This was the last moment that I had with her before you aided in ending our life as we knew it. I saw the way you looked at her then, just as I see the way you look at her now with that same hungry expression. Are you searching for an answer to assist in our cause, or are you searching for a way to win her affections?"

"You've not changed at all," I observed simply. "All of this time later, you still refuse a direct path to truth. I sought you out to simply fill in a gap in my own memory. I have no recollection of what my position was before the shattering occurred."

"You wouldn't recall those events—they were taken from you deliberately. You were placed beside the rest of us deemed unworthy of Nikola's trust. He used you thoroughly, as indeed you were using him, and then tossed you away like garbage. The two of you played the same manipulative game, and it had to have a loser. You attempted to play both sides then as well, in the hopes that you might get your claws on her." He paused, his expression hardening. "You won't succeed in changing anything here. If you are to be a villain, then be one with conviction. Do it with your full potential like Nikola does. She will hate you no matter what choice you make."

Olexei shoved me out of his dream with supernatural force, and I tumbled out of the locket onto the rocky ground of the realm of dreams, gasping and disoriented.

He had not changed, and apparently, neither had I—still chasing the same impossible dream.

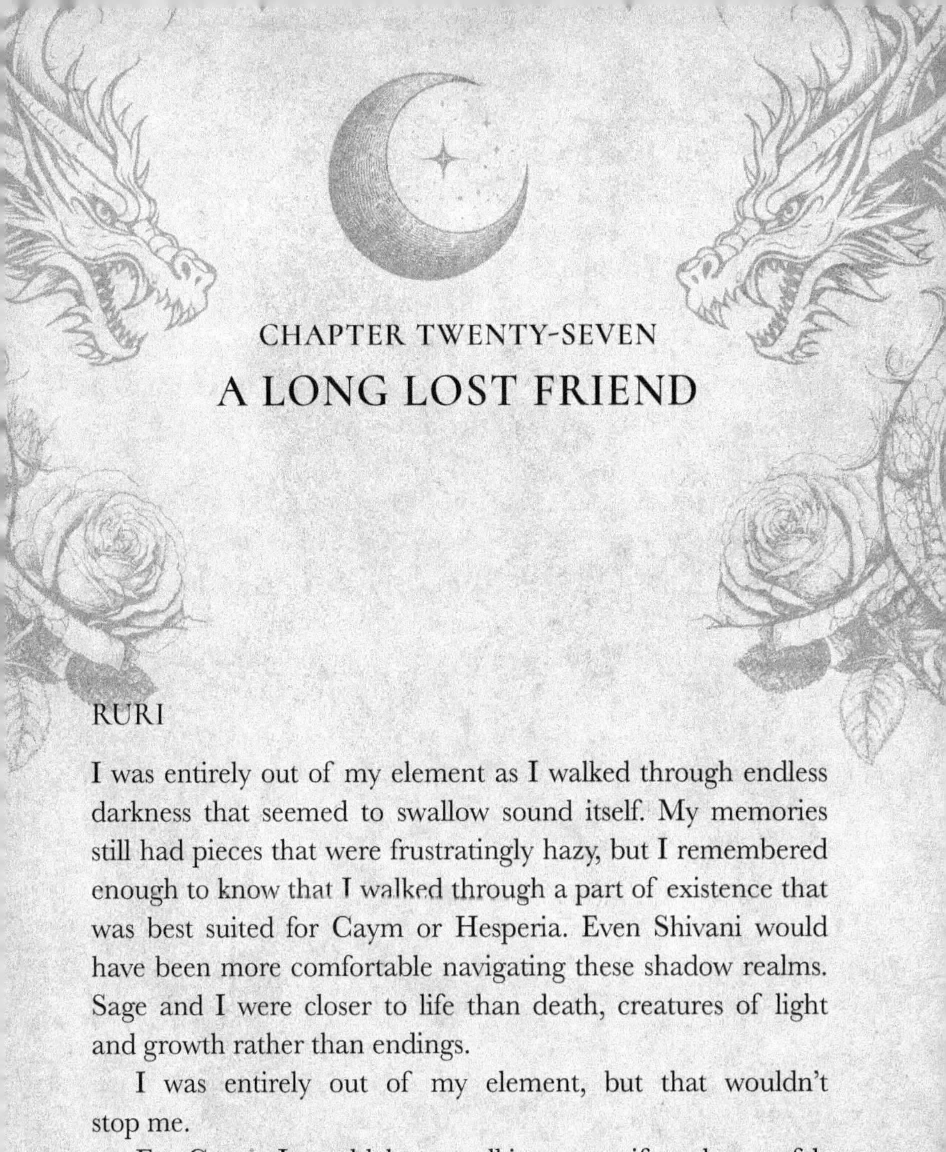

<h2 style="text-align:center">CHAPTER TWENTY-SEVEN
A LONG LOST FRIEND</h2>

RURI

I was entirely out of my element as I walked through endless darkness that seemed to swallow sound itself. My memories still had pieces that were frustratingly hazy, but I remembered enough to know that I walked through a part of existence that was best suited for Caym or Hesperia. Even Shivani would have been more comfortable navigating these shadow realms. Sage and I were closer to life than death, creatures of light and growth rather than endings.

I was entirely out of my element, but that wouldn't stop me.

For Caym, I would keep walking, even if each step felt heavy as lead. Even if it drained me of strength I could barely spare. I'd take him home, piece by piece until I put him back together again, because without him, I'd never be whole again. I only knew life with him by my side, and I had no desire to learn what existence meant without him.

I settled into the comforting idea that he was only on vacation, that he would come home soon and we would embrace like we always had. I swam through the fantasy that he needed to leave to handle a few urgent matters and that he would indeed be home soon, whole and warm in my arms.

Any other possibility sent me into a spiral of emotions that were too overwhelming to be processed without breaking apart completely. I felt decent for the first time in days while holding him, even if he wasn't moving, even if he was only a dead soul trapped between worlds. It was at least hope, fragile as spun glass.

"You lie. You sneak. You need chain," Jeb accused, pointing his bony finger dangerously close to my face.

I halted just in time to avoid being stabbed by his sharp, accusatory digit.

"You not wait like ask. You not listen. You not follow rule. You not—"

"Okay!" I interrupted, guilt washing over me. "I'm sorry, Jeb. You were helping in Ashbell. They need more help than I do right now."

"No," he protested, stabbing his finger toward me again with indignation. "You say trust means honest. You not trust?"

"I trust you," I relented, my voice soft with genuine affection.

"Then stop lie!" Jeb demanded with the fierce loyalty that had always defined him.

He held a torch in front of us, its flame dancing in the otherworldly darkness, and guided me in a different direction than I had been walking. I was relieved to have him as my compass. I didn't want to take resources from a place that needed every hand it could get just because I was being selfish. I knew I was being selfish, abandoning them all to struggle like fish out of water. I didn't regret it, either. Even if I somehow fixed the entire realm and brought lasting peace, it would mean nothing to me in the end without Caym.

I cracked a small smile, because Jeb was my close second

in importance. He had come to guide both of us home, loyal to the end.

He stopped abruptly, and I followed his example just as quickly. Two men approached us with their hands held in plain sight, a gesture of peace.

"Who are you?" I asked, protective instincts flaring.

"My name is Ekron, but you would only know me as Sin," the smaller figure replied.

I nearly dropped Caym at those words, shock running through me like lightning.

"This is Quade," he added, pointing to his companion.

"This is where you've been the whole time? You've gotten so big," my voice cracked with emotion. "You grew up all alone? In the dark?"

"When you say it that way, it does sound rather tragic. However, I assure you that it wasn't as bad as it seems. Quade kept me excellent company. He taught me many things, and we watched you all from here," Ekron explained with maturity beyond his apparent years.

"Who is Quade to be teaching you? I'm unaware of anything good that could lurk in the shadows between life and death. This isn't a place that anything is supposed to dwell permanently," I couldn't resist the urge to lecture, maternal instincts awakening.

"Who I am is a long story better suited for another time— it's boring compared to how much you have yet to take in. I have learned that talking isn't something most of you enjoy doing with each other openly. I think you may be able to complete a full puzzle if you all gave each other the pieces you've been hoarding," Quade observed with irritating wisdom.

His casual attitude made my blood boil, and Jeb must have sensed it because he backed up closer to me protectively.

"I mean no harm—the opposite, in fact. I know that you

long to bring Ekron back to the realm of the living, and I know that you can accomplish it the same way Nikola did. You can make him whole again with the use of your dragon eggs. It takes time and patience, but it can work. You truly did create something unique with them," Quade explained with an encouraging smile.

"I wouldn't trust any words or ideas from anyone who refused to tell me something so simple as who they are," I demanded firmly.

"I don't refuse—I simply said that you had much to take in before concerning yourself with my identity. If it helps Ekron get back to Astra, so that he may have a mother again, then I am an open book," he offered with spread hands.

I nodded my head while I cradled Caym closer to my chest, his weight both comforting and heartbreaking.

"Very well," he relented with a sigh. "I am your uncle. You could also say I'm the one Astra replaced in the cosmic order. Your mother wanted four of you girls because it reminded her of the four of us originally. She has a way of rewriting history the way she likes it best. It doesn't always align with the truth."

"Why would I believe such a claim?" I asked, skepticism warring with desperate hope.

"I don't require you to believe me for you to bring him back," he shrugged with maddening casualness.

He was so nonchalant, but my mind raced with implications.

My uncle? Uncle?

I was taught the world started with my mother. Then, I was taught it started with Yumi. Now I was supposed to believe there was not just one, but two buried souls hidden from history?

"Take your time and consider it carefully," he suggested, stepping backward into the shadows. "As an offering of my good will, I'll help you leave with Caym. If you should decide that you want Ekron to be reunited with Astra, you only need to put the pieces of his heart together with Sahir's inside of a dragon egg and let it grow."

Before I could respond, Quade shoved us out of the shadow realm and into the blazing light of the temple of Ashbell, reality crashing around us like waves.

CHAPTER TWENTY-EIGHT
A FULL HEART

RURI

Olexei stood beside me in respectful silence while Seere did what they could for Caym, their healing hands moving with practiced precision. He lay in a bed beside Vespera and Coy, all three forms eerily still. None of them held any sign of life, their chests unmoving as stone.

I knew there had to be hope because I had heard no whisper of a new deity taking their positions. It meant that their hearts had to be intact somewhere, waiting for me to find and reclaim them.

I forced a group of clerics to work on all three of them, even though I knew it wouldn't make a difference in their current state. It wasn't going to change the fact that they were dead, their souls separated from their bodies. Nothing that they could have done would suddenly replace their missing hearts. I wasted their time anyway, desperate for any action that felt like progress.

I wanted to tell them to stop their futile efforts. I wanted to let them do something truly useful with their skills. I wouldn't give that order. I didn't have the strength.

I couldn't.

Even if it was useless and I knew it deep in my bones, it still somehow made me feel better to see them trying.

"I do think that it is fitting you gave Caym the sun gifts," Olexei whispered, his voice warm with memory.

"Why?" I asked, though part of me already knew.

"I always believed that he was the lightest thing to ever sit in the dark," Olexei smiled with genuine affection.

It did feel fitting. He was the brightest thing to ever enter my life, too, bringing warmth to corners I didn't know were cold. I wished that I could have taken his light conversation as just that—simple comfort. I couldn't manage that either. I still felt as much rage as I had before I rescued him from the shadow realm. I still felt restless, like a caged animal pacing.

I couldn't get Astra's son out of my head, and I could not move past the betrayal that I felt from the revelations that had been forced upon me.

"Can we talk privately?" I leaned in to ask, needing answers.

"Of course," Olexei nodded, his expression growing serious.

"Is there a way to bring Astra back to us?"

Olexei looked at me with a deeply furrowed brow. "Well, you girls were made to bend the rules of existence itself. If all four of you were together and working in harmony, I suppose anything could be possible. I don't think that's what you really wanted to ask me, though."

He was right, as he usually was.

I sighed heavily. "Who is Quade?"

I wasn't afraid of the man himself, but I was terrified of the confirmation that the question might bring.

"I haven't heard that name since my creation, since your mother spoke of him in profound sadness. I do wonder how you heard it, but I won't pry into your business. You seem to be one of several to bring up his name recently. All I know is that he was their eldest brother and he was murdered long ago. I didn't press Dahlia for details because it never seemed to matter to me personally. He fell into distant memory at first, then he was all but forgotten by everyone. I don't think I ever would have remembered him myself if you hadn't brought him up," Olexei explained with careful honesty.

"So, you know nothing useful? You can't tell me if he's good or bad? Worse than Nikola? If my mother is a serial murderer hiding behind good intentions? If I get too mouthy, will I be next on her list? I don't think you're being completely honest with me," my voice began to grow louder with each accusation.

Olexei turned me to face him and placed both of his warm hands on my shoulders, grounding me. "Who put these dark thoughts into your head? Your mother would never hurt you. The four of you are her greatest treasure—"

"We aren't trophies to be displayed," I interrupted sharply. "Saying this doesn't make anyone feel better. The truth would make all of us feel better, and I'm not sure if I believe that she would keep such important secrets from you."

The room grew silent as death, and all movement stopped. The Seere that were supposed to be bringing our guardians back to life looked as if they were ready to crawl out of the room if it meant they weren't around for any further conflict. I heard the water from their rags drip into bowls with echoing plops, and the group of them did their best to silence their breathing while mine fell heavily in ragged gasps.

"I am comfortable with her keeping secrets because I trust that she has good reason for it, if she does," he replied with quiet conviction.

"Ruri!" a voice screamed from outside, sharp with urgency.

A guard ran inside and pointed behind them with shaking hands. They were too flustered to speak coherently, only shaking their finger at the entrance like a warning. When Sage walked inside, I didn't hesitate to pull my magic to the front and let it spark dangerously from my fingertips.

She lifted the cloth that she carried and showed me the hearts that she held, and I nearly collapsed from the shock. My legs shook like leaves in a storm, and a wave of overwhelming emotion rushed over me. Dahlia stood behind Sage, but I nearly forgot that I was angry with her. The small bits of me that remembered our conflict were too insignificant to stop my joy, my relief at the sight in front of me.

I knew those hearts had to be theirs—Caym's, Vespera's, Coy's. I knew he couldn't have been gone forever. I allowed myself the moment of release, and it nearly brought tears of pure relief.

There was a sparkle in Sage's eyes that I wouldn't acknowledge out loud. It showed me that she was herself again, her true self. I was happy to have her cobalt eyes looking at me with the familiar glimmer they carried again. I wouldn't say it out loud, though. She had put us through too much suffering to be praised so soon. She needed to feel the pain the rest of us had been forced to carry, and I didn't care if it made me a horrible sister. I wanted to see hurt in her eyes before I could even consider forgiveness.

"I'm sorry," Sage whispered, her voice barely above a breath.

I nearly broke from the sound of her genuine remorse. Nearly wasn't fully, and I would hold strong that she could not walk into the devastation we'd been desperately fending off and get to pretend as though she didn't help cause most of it.

I grabbed the cloth from her hands and gave it to the clerics without ceremony.

My husband's heart was with him again, and I'd soon have my world restored. Despite this miracle, I felt only bitterness and betrayal when I looked at Sage.

I needed Caym to ground me, to remind me how to feel something other than rage.

CHAPTER TWENTY-NINE

A GREAT GATHERING

RURI

Things had become completely reversed. I was on the receiving end of an embrace that might have broken me if it had been any tighter. Hesperia held me so fiercely that I was certain she meant to crush me into dust. She had to have that intention—I couldn't have protested even if I truly wanted to. I was completely at her mercy. I wiggled and pulled against her grip, but it meant nothing against her desperate strength.

"I missed you so much, I thought that I'd never see you again! I thought that you hated me, blamed me for the way things turned out, but then I realized it was just my imagination running wild!" She laughed with manic relief. "It was just my own mind creating something to torture me. You would never have blamed me for all of this chaos. When I realized that truth, I dug through a barrier with a fake version of you helping me."

Juniper leaned out from behind her and stared at me with concerned eyes. "You may want to let her breathe."

"Oh, yes," Hesperia released her crushing grip immediately.

"Nothing you just said made any sense, but it is nice to see you again," I gasped, filling my lungs with precious air.

"Eventually, we will have to sit down and talk through everything that happened, but now isn't that time," she replied.

She spoke with apparent responsibility, but the wild gleam in her eyes suggested that she didn't mean a word of it.

I didn't engage further because I knew if she was allowed to start up again, it would be quite some time before we entered the hall waiting for us. We were expected to attend a crucial meeting filled with all commanders and rulers on our side. We had a mountain of issues to discuss while the enemy hammered against our doorway like thunder.

The fighting on the outskirts of Ashbell hadn't stopped since Kyra and Sage brought their forces the first time. We were surrounded by the dead and the desperately fighting. Nikola was able to create horde after horde of his twisted creatures, and we could battle them over and over in endless cycles, but it would accomplish nothing if we couldn't reach him directly.

I walked into the hall and immediately felt all eyes on me like physical weight. The walk through the great hall wasn't that long in reality, but the distance felt doubled with how intensely the stares fell on us. I knew it wasn't only me they watched with such scrutiny—it was Hesperia, too. Shivani and Sage already stood at the war table in the center of the gathering hall, their postures tense with anticipation.

Ashbell's castle was equipped for everything I could have imagined and even things that I hadn't considered. Things that they had desperately needed after I abandoned them.

I took a spot beside Sage and we all sat in our designated places. Sage looked excited but nervous, but I only sat where I did because I didn't fully trust her yet.

"Let us not waste precious time," an angel spoke with clipped efficiency.

"Agreed, what are you four going to do against this threat?" a lesser God demanded impatiently.

"We were told you all needed to be together and we would be safe!" another voice called out.

"I want to know about the prisoners you took!"

"I want to know why we are here talking and not out there fighting!"

The voices overlapped in a cacophony of fear and frustration.

"First, if I had gained anything useful from any prisoners, you'd know by now," I declared, cutting through the noise.

"Yes, you are not our enemies, just as we aren't yours," Hesperia agreed with firm conviction.

"I only just arrived here. We aren't wasting time—we called this meeting as soon as we sorted out another critical matter. It hasn't even been a full day," Sage inserted defensively.

"We called you here to make a solid plan and to ask for your agreement on necessary alterations," Shivani paused dramatically before continuing.

"What does that mean exactly?" an army leader asked with suspicion.

Lui cleared his throat before he spoke with the authority of ancient knowledge. "A primordial being cannot be killed through conventional means. They can only be absorbed and kept under control. We can separate them, we can lock them away in prisons of our making. We can never truly destroy them. You will have to forgive the sisters of fate if they do not have a perfect plan immediately for such an unprecedented task."

"My name is Dominic, and I am from the vampire temple. I think I can speak for many of your thoughts as well," a composed voice interjected. "I, too, doubted the four of them for far too long. I carried that doubt so persistently that I'm sure I aided in bringing us to where we are now. I doubted long enough that it wasted valuable time and cost lives. I can tell you firsthand that starting things out this way will not help anything. I urge you to be silent and listen to what they have to say."

"I want permission to bring you back from the dead," Hesperia interjected with startling directness. "If quick results are what you want, then I won't beat around the bush. You can't help us find a way to cage Nikola while you're alive and vulnerable. But we decided together that we can't become like him either. We want your consent before we proceed with this plan."

"Things won't be easy for any of us," I agreed grimly. "Most of you will die in the coming battle. Hesperia has the ability to change the permanence of that fate. She can raise you from the dead as bodyless souls. You will be nearly impossible to kill for the average mortal enemy. It will create a second wave army. It is one of the few advantages that we still hold."

"Nikola cannot do this same thing?" someone asked with hope creeping into their voice.

"He cannot," I confirmed.

"Can we be brought back in our bodies after victory is achieved?"

"I cannot guarantee that outcome," Hesperia admitted with painful honesty.

"What choice do we have left?"

"We agree to these terms," the speaker for the Angels declared solemnly.

"Good." I slammed my hands on the table with finality. "I'll be going then."

"What?" several voices called out in confusion and alarm.

"You wanted progress, did you not? There's nothing else that I can contribute by simply sitting here talking in circles," I replied with sharp sarcasm.

I didn't listen to any other words spoken, their protests

falling on deaf ears. My sisters would gain control of the situation or they wouldn't—it was as simple as that. I had somewhere else to be, somewhere I wanted to be more than trapped in endless meetings.

I jogged down to the castle dungeons and flung the heavy metal gate open with more force than necessary.

"Finally," Onyx groaned from his chains, the sound echoing off stone walls.

"Don't get too excited. I'm not here to free you," I snapped, crushing any hope he might have harbored.

"Disappointing. I'm sure your sister would love to see me," he smirked with infuriating confidence.

"I doubt it. I'm here to see what you've learned from Nikola that might be useful," I declared, crossing my arms defensively.

"You want me to turn against him?" Onyx laughed, the sound bitter and mocking.

"I want you to give me information in exchange for your life," I stated plainly.

"I am confident that I will get out of here soon enough," he replied with maddening certainty.

"Why would you think that?"

"You truly think that you've uncovered everything and you're on the direct path to victory, don't you," he observed with cruel amusement.

"I think that I'm closer to success than you are. You mean to tell me that we spent all of that time together, for years we have all considered you not just friends but family, and you have nothing to offer to help us survive?"

Onyx nodded with cold finality. "That's exactly what I'm telling you. You took up the most miserable years of my existence. I'm glad to be free of that suffocating lie."

A part of me was genuinely disappointed. I had considered him family, had trusted him with my life.

"That's disappointing to hear, but I won't have a problem giving you exactly what you gave me—nothing."

I turned to leave, filled with rage and jumbled thoughts swirling like a storm. I ran straight into someone and nearly exploded in emotions until I looked up and saw his face.

"You're awake?" I nearly screamed with disbelief and joy.

"Hello, wife," Caym smiled, his voice the most beautiful sound I'd ever heard.

I felt tears well behind my eyelids, threatening to spill over.

"I'm awake and whole again. I also found Sin while I was in the shadow realm. His name is Ekron and I think that we can bring him back with a dragon egg," he explained, kissing each of my hands with tender reverence.

"We haven't even brought Astra back yet," I sighed, though hope bloomed in my chest.

I wanted to believe completely, but he was only back because of Sage's intervention, and that complicated everything.

CHAPTER THIRTY
THE WOLF

KOA

I watched Shivani's thin fingers push around her dinner with listless movements, the food growing cold and untouched. She was a far cry from the shape she used to be when we first met. Once she had possessed defined muscles that spoke of strength and vitality. At her meal now, she appeared tired and worn thin by the weight of responsibility. She was still gorgeous—her red hair had grown to double the length it once was when it was cut to her chin, flowing like liquid fire. Her smile still sent me into a frenzy when I was blessed to see it. She was perfect in my eyes, but she also carried the weight of all of our collective emotions on her increasingly fragile body.

Did she see me the same way I saw her?

I supposed we all probably wore our burdens visibly, but we didn't see ourselves the same way others perceived us.

"Do you think it's a trick?" she asked suddenly, breaking the comfortable silence.

"Hmm?" I looked up from my own untouched plate.

"There's been so much emphasis on the four of us

needing to be together and how it needed to happen urgently." She paused and considered her next words carefully. "Do you think that Sage showing up with the hearts—I don't know, it feels too easy? Do you think it's some kind of elaborate trick?"

"Like it's exactly what Nikola wanted to happen," I agreed, understanding immediately.

"Right! Like it's precisely what he orchestrated. What if there was something wrong with the hearts? Or with Sage herself?" She hit her fist on the table with frustration, making the dishes rattle.

I wasn't certain that I believed there was anything sinister beyond Sage getting her mind back, but every small victory felt as if it were a trap the longer Nikola remained at large.

"If there were something wrong, I'd protect you against it," I promised with quiet conviction.

"I know you would," she replied, looking back down to her dinner plate with tired eyes. "I just wish that I could protect everyone else as well."

There was always distance between us—thick air heavy with unspoken words and missed opportunities. Eyes always focused on the floor instead of each other. There were no sweet touches or longing looks anymore, just distance and anxiety that neither of us knew how to bridge.

"You don't give yourself enough credit. You've achieved so much more than you realize," I said, reaching for her hand across the table.

"That list is not as long as I wished it would be by now," she murmured, her voice barely above a whisper.

"You need to give yourself some credit, some grace. A break from all this pressure. All of this stress isn't good for you," I pleaded, squeezing her fingers gently.

Shivani met my concern with a forced smile that didn't reach her eyes. "I'm going to get some rest while I can. I know you have patrol for the inner city tonight. Be safe out there."

I kissed her hand before she could stand from the table, savoring the brief contact. The crimson train of her dress followed her out of the room in the way that I wished I could have, too, but knew I shouldn't.

When she was out of sight and the sound of her shoes had faded into silence, I stood to leave my own meal untouched. She would have only continued to feel uncomfortable if I lingered around her when she clearly needed space.

I marched with determined haste to the dungeon, my footsteps echoing in the empty corridors. There hadn't been much opportunity to make this stop recently. It had quickly become the most heavily guarded place in Ashbell. It was my own shifters guarding it, loyal to me above all else. I sent them all on their meal break to create a small enough window for me to get inside unobserved.

I checked every corner and shadow on my way down, scanning for any potential witnesses. I couldn't risk any eyes on me for what I was about to do.

"Took you long enough. Still, I'm ready for my release," Onyx declared as he wiggled his hands beneath the heavy chains that bound him.

"No, no. Whatever brotherhood we once shared, it's gone forever. Do you think anyone kept your secrets after what you've done? I trusted you to keep Ruri safe and protect Sage. I trusted you to come with me to the shattered realm to rescue Shivani from certain death. I left you in charge of my own lands because you were my brother, because I trusted you with everything. Instead of being honest with me, you handed Ruri to Deimos on a silver platter. You violated Sage's trust. No, you were responsible for her death more than once. You killed our brothers!" I pointed at his face with accusatory fury. "Why would I help you escape?"

"Koa! You can't expect me to have told Nikola that I refused to kill Caym. It was you or him—I had to choose!"

Onyx yelled, desperation creeping into his voice. "I did what I had to do to protect our brotherhood, our sacred bond!"

"You should have chosen yourself then! I would have ensured you came back and you'd still have allies fighting beside you," I replied, my voice cold as winter. "If you had been honest from the start, I would have defended you to the death. You need to find another tactic because I understand now that we were never truly brothers."

Onyx stared at me with his jaw hanging open and his golden eyes widened in shock and disbelief.

"The only thing you can do now is hope that you have information worth keeping you alive," I demanded.

"As you can see, I've been chained up here like an animal. Last I heard, it was Nikola's plan to imbue the hearts with some kind of dark magic so that he could have fighters operating from the inside. He hadn't succeeded in the process when I was brought here because Sage hardly had use of her magic then." Onyx laughed bitterly. "I think it would mark his first significant failure if she got the hearts out before he could possess them."

"That's all you have to tell me?" I asked, disappointment heavy in my voice.

"That's all I have to tell you, brother," Onyx mocked with venom.

I stared into his golden eyes and searched desperately for any sign that maybe he felt genuine regret. Any hint of remorse or acknowledgment of the pain he had caused. I only needed to see one small sign that he wanted to take it all back and I would have spared him.

I saw nothing but cruel enjoyment reflected back at me.

I pulled my sword from its resting place on my side and swung it with decisive force. I felt the blade slide through flesh and muscle until it met bone, and I applied more pressure until the job was complete. His head hung from his body by only a thread of muscle and sinew. If I left him that way, he'd eventually return. There was hardly any finality in death unless the hearts that held the life root were completely destroyed.

I was certain I still had time for that final step. I didn't want him coming back to torment us again. He had put us through so much more suffering than we needed to endure. I hesitated for a moment when I held his still-warm heart in my hands. The thought that Shivani, or the others, would be upset at what I had done flashed through my mind briefly.

I'd deal with the consequences if they were truly angry, but if Onyx had nothing valuable to offer us, if he refused to share information or change sides, what use was there in keeping him alive?

I pulled out a box of matches from my pocket and struck one, the flame dancing in the dim dungeon light. I held it against Onyx's heart and watched as it began to burn.

I would destroy every piece of his heart before I left this place.

CHAPTER THIRTY-ONE

THE TALLEST POINT

HESPERIA

I had imagined for such a long time what it would have been like to have my mother and my sisters back together again. I had dreamed of how much better things would have been, painting perfect pictures in my mind. I convinced myself that it would have been like old times again, that we all would just reconnect like nothing had ever changed between us.

I was wrong about everything.

The tension in the room was so thick, I could hardly draw breath into my lungs. Mother sat in the middle and watched all four of us with unconditional love shining in her eyes. My sisters did not return the same warm gaze. They sat somewhere between deep hurt and profound confusion, their faces masks of carefully controlled emotion. I was probably too hopeful in my expectations, and they sat on a very different emotional spectrum. In my mind, we were going to eventually just click back into place like pieces of a puzzle.

We just waited on a single puzzle piece to slide into the right position. When that one piece finally sat where it belonged, we'd laugh together again like we used to.

"I find it appropriate that I ask if anyone else has words to speak before I do," Mother announced, her voice carrying the weight of unspoken history.

Sage only watched her fingers fiddle nervously with her dress, unable to meet anyone's eyes. Ruri communicated everything with her facial expressions while she held her lips firmly closed in a thin line. She was filled with barely contained rage that simmered beneath the surface. Shivani, although her face was softer than Ruri's, still adjusted uncomfortably in her seat as if the chair itself burned her.

"There is a place that once aided me in my darkest hour. It is well hidden from prying eyes, but filled with power that I can no longer give. It is a point so close to the raw energy of the universe that it can even enhance deities beyond their natural limits. It's the last thing that I can offer you," Mother explained with quiet desperation.

"You've handed us so much already. How can we possibly thank you for all your generosity?" Ruri replied with cutting sarcasm as she stood and made no effort to quietly leave the room.

"Sit down, Hesperia," Mother commanded firmly.

I looked to Mother and back to my own body in confusion. I hadn't realized that I was on my feet, ready to chase after Ruri and drag her back to this conversation by force if necessary.

"Are you sure it will actually help? You're asking us to abandon our posts when we are the only things helping keep Nikola's constant stream of attacks at bay?" Shivani questioned with practical concern.

"I do admit that I cannot guarantee anything will come of it. The alternative is to continue the same futile attempts until Nikola has decided that he's strong enough to make his final move," Mother added with grim honesty.

"He's consuming souls like a glutton, and I think that's why he hasn't come himself yet," I observed. "I'm not sure what's worse—letting Nikola gain power unchecked or leaving everything unprotected against his eventual appearance."

I didn't know anything concrete about where we were supposed to be going or if it would actually work. I did know that if Mother thought it was a worthwhile enough idea to bring it up, it had to be worth attempting. I had to try my best to convince them, despite my own doubts. The effort didn't come without the gnawing fear of what might happen while we were away.

Shivani sighed heavily. "I'm not going to try and argue this any further. If Hesperia has it fixed in her head that this is what we have to do, then we won't win this debate."

"Then we will leave at first light," I declared with more confidence than I felt.

Sage nodded in agreement with Shivani, and I didn't wait for any more words of protest. I jogged out of the room to find Ruri, knowing she would need the most convincing. She wasn't as likely to give me what I wanted simply because I wanted it—she required actual reasoning.

My mood quickly tumbled into despair when I realized that instead of looking for my sister in the comfort of her temple, instead of being in the place where I felt comfortable with my family again, I was being shoved back into the mind games that Nikola loved to trap me in.

I was physically far from Nikola, but he was always mentally close, like a parasite in my thoughts.

I knew the realm was crumbling around us, but I almost didn't care since we were all back together and Coy's heart was beating in his chest again.

"My sweet girl, you didn't really think that I was going to let you just abandon me like that," Nikola frowned with mock disappointment.

"I had hoped for exactly that," I mumbled, not bothering to hide my contempt.

"Hesperia," he replied, shaking his head and flicking his

finger at me dismissively. "That's no way to speak to me. We've spent more time together than you've spent with Coy or Dahlia. We should be closer than this by now, shouldn't we? You didn't even try to say goodbye before you broke out and ran away. It seems to be a troubling trend with you girls."

"Maybe you just aren't worth losing time over," I retorted with venom.

"Don't be rude to me. You left me without so much as a farewell, but I left you with a special surprise," he announced with predatory satisfaction.

Nikola moved the fog from around us and released me from his mental cage. I was placed back in the middle of the temple hallway, reality crashing around me. This time, Coy stood in front of me with a presence that made my heart leap. He had a smile stretched across his face—the first full smile that I had seen on him since before anything had begun to pull us out of the Golden City.

He wrapped his strong arms around my waist and lifted me into the air with ease. His embrace was as warm as it had felt in our happiest days, familiar and safe.

"I'm so sorry," he whispered through my hair, his face buried as deeply as possible in my locks. "I can't believe there was anything that could have ever made me forget you."

I felt tears gathering in my eyes, but there was a large part of me that didn't allow myself to enjoy anything in front of me after Nikola's ominous words.

What was his surprise? He wasn't kind enough to give me the love of my life back without some sort of terrible string attached to it.

CHAPTER THIRTY-TWO

THE HOME THAT SHOULD HAVE BEEN

SAGE

Vespera and I hadn't gotten a chance to really speak since we had both returned from the brink. Since our memories began snapping into place like puzzle pieces, each one bringing both clarity and pain.

I wished it could have been joyful and exciting. I remembered too much for it to be a happy reunion.

Dahlia had hoped that when she created guardians, she would also forge soul bonds that would outlast anything the universe could throw at us. I wasn't sure that Dahlia had accounted for the possibility that one of us would end up wanting someone else more than their destined partner.

I remembered seeing Vespera and Sahir together with perfect, heartbreaking clarity. I remembered the way the two of them sounded so utterly in love, their voices intertwining like music. I didn't think that I would ever get that sound out of my head, the melody of their affection haunting me.

I didn't know where to meet her for this inevitable conversation. I felt as if I hadn't gotten much time in the realm as my true self. I recalled my life under Yumi's control, and the calculated way that Sahir chose to get close to me. I knew now it was to seek revenge against Vespera. I remembered my life after I was banished from Semper, every moment of it. It all felt so fake and manufactured.

It was my body, my mind, but it wasn't truly me living those experiences. It was like watching a hazy dream unfold through someone else's eyes.

Even with the fog that felt as if it sat over my memories like morning mist, I knew that the home Ruri built for us over-looking the volcano was a safe place. It had slight differences from what I recalled from before—new furniture, different arrangements—but it still felt the closest to home as any place I had been since I felt like myself again.

"Knock, knock," came a familiar voice from outside.

My smile was only half fake as warmth bloomed in my chest. "I'm inside."

Vespera walked in, and the hurt I felt still beat inside of my chest like a second heart, but I couldn't deny the weakness in my knees at seeing her. It was strange to me, when I thought about it rationally, that I ever found it hard to choose between her and someone else.

"It's hard for me to believe that it's truly you," Vespera confessed, her voice soft with wonder.

"It's hard for me to believe that it never was truly me," I replied, the weight of lost time heavy in my words.

I wasn't sure if she felt the tension crackling in the air, but I knew that I felt it like electricity. I felt it stab at me when she tried to hug me with familiar affection. I wanted to lovingly hug her back, but I couldn't make my body cooperate. The thumping in my chest was louder than anything else in the room.

"What's wrong?" Vespera asked, concern creasing her beautiful features.

"Do you remember the Golden City?" I asked, needing to face this head-on.

"Of course I do," she nodded, confusion flickering in her eyes.

"One of the last memories I have before I died is looking for you desperately. I just knew that I was going to die and that I couldn't do it without saying goodbye to you first. I found you, but I found you with Sahir," I admitted, the words tasting like ashes.

"Stop," Vespera interjected, pain flashing across her face. "I regret every single minute that I was around her. I won't make excuses for my actions. It was wrong, and I want you to know that no matter the reason for what I did, I'm sorry."

If we were about to die again in this endless war, I didn't want to die thinking that I wasn't good enough for her.

Another knock sounded at the door before I could let out a full and deep breath. Relief washed over me like cool water.

"Sage!" Hesperia squealed with pure joy.

She ran into the room and barreled into me with enough force that I lost my breath, her enthusiasm knocking the air from my lungs.

"Hi," I grunted, trying to breathe again.

"I thought you'd never wake up. It took so long, and you missed so much! So many things needed to be done every time I tried to come speak to you!" Hesperia took a deep breath to continue her rapid-fire speech. "How could you become best friends with Sahir? Sahir!" She shivered with disgust. "A pile of feces would have been better company. What was it like to live under Yumi's rule? Ruri is so tight-lipped about it all. She never wants to discuss anything important. I never imagined Yumi was smart enough to convince anyone she could rule effectively."

"Hesperia!" Shivani snapped from the doorway.

Hesperia grimaced and stepped back sheepishly. "Another time, then."

"Were we interrupting something important?" Shivani asked with careful diplomacy.

"No," I replied quickly, perhaps too quickly.

Ruri stood with arms crossed defensively in the background. Her emerald hair was tied with a simple string into a ponytail, and it allowed me to see every wrinkle of disapproval etched on her face.

"Hi, Ru," I murmured, my voice barely above a whisper.

She deepened her frown, her expression growing darker.

Hesperia grabbed Ruri by the arm and pulled her forward, despite Ruri's attempt to keep her body stone-heavy and immovable. Ruri did not want to be moved, but Hesperia did not seem to care about resistance. She stopped when Ruri and I were face-to-face, close enough to see the hurt in each other's eyes.

"Now hug!" Hesperia commanded with sisterly authority.

Vespera and I might have had a long way to go, and I might not have been sure what direction I wanted our relationship to take. I did know with certainty that I wanted Ruri and me to be okay. I hugged her like Hesperia requested, but Ruri remained reluctant and stiff in my arms.

"I'm sorry. I truly was awful to all of you. You went through so much suffering, and I was trying to prove something to Sahir while you endured hell," I choked out, the words scraping my throat raw.

I felt the hitch in Ruri's chest at my words, her breath catching. She hugged me back tentatively, but she didn't speak immediately. She didn't need to—I felt her body struggle to hold back tears that threatened to spill over.

"It doesn't matter now," Ruri declared as she moved backward away from me, rebuilding her emotional walls. "I only came to see if there were any plans that still needed to be made before we left. I'm not staying for this. This is no time to sit around and cry over the past."

"And if we die in the next few days?" Shivani asked, crossing her arms with practical concern.

"Then we will have plenty of time to cry while Deimos holds us in his realm," Ruri answered with dark humor.

Hesperia laughed despite the grim sentiment, "I guess that was the final planning that needed to be done, then."

Something about the emotions that had passed between us all made me feel a little more forgiving toward Vespera, too. If only because I didn't want to die dwelling on what had been when I could have had a few precious what-could-be moments instead.

CHAPTER THIRTY-THREE

THE GROTTO

SHIVANI

The four of us stood before what was the most beautiful hot spring I had ever seen, tucked away inside of a hidden grotto at Orest. I didn't understand how they had possessed something with such obvious power in front of them for years and had no idea of its true nature. I had heard many stories of not just their time in these springs, but of others who had wandered inside as well, seeking relaxation or healing.

None of them had ever considered what would have happened if the wrong person stepped inside.

"Are you ready?" Hesperia asked, her voice echoing off the grotto walls.

"No," the three of us answered in perfect unison.

Hesperia shoved me into the water without saying another word, her push forceful and decisive. I was certain that I wouldn't have had a deep enough breath to make it far when, like a drain, I was pulled down and into the pitch black depths.

"Hello, keeper of time," a masculine voice murmured from the darkness.

"Who are you?" I asked, my voice somehow carrying clearly despite being underwater.

I felt as if I still floated in water, but I was able to take in breaths like I was on land, the sensation disorienting and impossible.

"The universe may have started with Dahlia, but there are many other powerful forces that make the universe continue spinning. You should focus on who you are, instead. After all, you are the one meant to make the realm stable and just," the voice explained with ancient authority.

"I don't need you to tell me how I'm supposed to be. Can you help me or not?" I demanded, impatience flaring in my chest.

"If you can do a few simple things, then I may be convinced to help you," the voice responded with amusement.

"Get on with it then," I snapped.

"You will need to admit to me a fear, and a regret. You will need to give them away so that they no longer hold you back from your true potential. Then you must present a sacrifice."

"A sacrifice?" I asked, unease crawling up my spine.

"This is not a place for lies or half-truths. This is a place for an honest exchange."

"Fine. My biggest fear is letting someone take control of me again. I never want to be so out of control that my body is used to hurt innocent people again," I admitted, the words scraping my throat raw.

"Mm. Like this?" the voice questioned with cruel curiosity.

My limbs moved against my will with terrifying precision, and blood orbs shot from my hands into the chest of a child —a child that I hadn't seen before that moment. Her small body dropped to the blackened ground like a broken doll. My legs refused to move toward her despite my desperate attempts.

"Stop it!" I screamed, my voice breaking with horror.

"It is only an image," the voice laughed before it released

me from its control. "Do you think that this, too, is your biggest regret?"

My heart pounded in my throat like a caged bird, and when I was back in control of my body, the girl had also vanished.

"Yes," I answered, though the word felt inadequate.

"I think this is a lie," the voice observed with disappointing certainty.

I swallowed hard, forcing myself to dig deeper. "My biggest regret is letting Fennic and Mori die when I could have saved them."

"You were quite useless in the shattered realm and hardly became of use in this realm either. I would regret it, too, if I were you. He thought he would at least remain your friend, but you never had the courage to speak to him honestly. He died wishing that you had reached out."

"What is this supposed to help!" I screamed, fury and pain mixing in my voice.

"To be just, and powerful, you must not hold these burdens. It is simple logic. You want me to give you the power to hurt the oldest primordial? You must prove that you will not fall to such trivial mortal concerns. These are the worries of mortals, not of gods. Fennic's body may be gone, but will you ruin more lives because of your grief? If you would, then for how long? Would you still place yourself above Nikola if grief drove you to madness?"

I didn't know who this entity was supposed to be, but I despised everything about it.

"The next step, sister of time, is your sacrifice. What will you give me in exchange for power? It must mean something significant to you. It should be something that you cared for deeply."

I didn't come prepared to make an offering. I hadn't considered it an option in my planning. I hadn't considered much on the trip, honestly. I had kept myself in an automatic mode, functioning purely on necessity. I did what I needed to, as I needed to, simply because it needed to be done.

"I'll give you my word that I will come back and let you free," I offered desperately.

"Who said that I did not like it here?" came the amused response.

"I'll bring you food?" I offered weakly.

"Sister of time. Think deeply. I want you to give up something that you both long for, but feel held back by."

Koa's memories of me from the Golden City floated unbidden into my mind.

"Yes, exactly what I want you to dig into," the voice confirmed.

I was startled by the realization that it could hear my thoughts.

"Is that what you want?" I asked hesitantly.

"Is that what you feel held back by?"

"The idea of living up to the version of me that Koa remembers from a time that I don't feel connected to anymore does weigh on me," I answered honestly.

"Why does it burden you?"

"I'm not that person anymore. I don't feel connected to the gods or their ways. I hardly remember to call myself one. I still feel closer to the mortals I was raised among." I paused, forcing myself not to stutter. "I feel closer to the girl raised thinking she was cast out by the gods, than I do to the girl who is supposed to be one of the most just of them all. I find it hard to be close to him when I have such a large shadow of perfection to stand in."

"I will accept your offer. His memories of the Golden City, in exchange for the last strand of power you will need to defeat Nikola," the voice declared with finality.

Hot spikes of energy ran through me before I could protest, burning like molten metal in my veins. They lit me up like a blacksmith readying his forge for battle. My body was shot out of the darkness, out of the warm water, and slammed onto the rough rocks of the grotto in an instant.

I gasped for air and coughed up water, my lungs burning, but I was completely alone. My sisters were not in the grotto with me—they had vanished as if they had never been there at all.

CHAPTER THIRTY-FOUR

SINKING INTO THE DARKNESS

SAGE

"Hello?" I called out into the void.

The space around me glowed with brilliant white light, but it was completely empty—nothing but a square box of blinding luminescence. I was certain that if I reached out in any direction, I would have touched all four sides within arm's length.

"Can anybody hear me?"

I yelled again, but my voice only echoed back to me in hollow mockery. I tried to walk, but my feet didn't move no matter how much I willed them to. I didn't enjoy the idea of being trapped in a tiny box like a caged animal, but it didn't matter in the end whether my feet moved or not. I had nowhere to go, no escape route to pursue.

"Can anyone hear me?" I yelled again, desperation creeping into my voice.

"Are you willing to share with me your greatest fear, Sage?" a man's voice suddenly responded.

The masculine voice echoed back to me and confirmed my growing feeling of being completely trapped.

"Why would I do that?" I asked, suspicion flaring.

"We can call it a budding friendship or an exchange of valuable information," he replied with amusement.

"I can't be friends with someone if I don't even know their name," I called out into the brightness.

I felt like a fool, not knowing which direction to speak toward in this featureless prison.

"You can call me the Blood Weaver while you are here, but you must not repeat that name once you leave this place," he instructed.

"That name sounds like something I should not trust, especially if the person behind the name is asking me to keep secrets," I declared with growing wariness.

"I'm sure you've encountered much worse than I could ever be. I'm only a soul, watching and waiting for purpose," he explained with casual indifference.

"How do you help me, then?" I asked, needing to understand.

"An exchange of sorts, nothing more complex. You're going to tell me your biggest fear and regret with complete honesty. Then you're going to offer me a sacrifice of something meaningful. If you are truthful, if you are genuinely open, then I will deem you worthy and give you the last bit of power that you desperately seek," he explained methodically.

If I were anywhere else, if I were with anyone else, I might have struggled against the idea, but I had hoped for some time that I would find a place to spill those kinds of thoughts. I wanted desperately to have a safe space to confess the things that I should voice in the midst of all the chaos surrounding us.

"My regret is being weak, and so is my fear," I whispered, my voice barely audible. "I'm afraid that I won't be strong enough to stand up for what's right or protect my sisters. I'm afraid that I'll let them down again or stand helplessly on the sidelines while they're hurt."

"Like you did while Yumi beat your sister mercilessly? While she begged in front of your mother for relief from her suffering?" he asked with casual cruelty.

I bit the inside of my lip when I felt it quiver with shame and pain.

"I wasn't in my right mind," I defended weakly.

"Neither was your sister, but she held strong under a much harsher environment than you faced," he spoke with a matter-of-fact tone that cut like a blade.

"I'm not proud of it. I wish I could change everything that happened. I'm terrified of repeating those failures," my voice shook with emotion.

"What would you be willing to sacrifice to ensure you don't disappoint them again, then?" he asked with renewed interest.

"I can offer you my legacy—my ability to create a child and continue anything to do with my bloodline. I'm just as afraid to create a child who would allow things like I did," I confessed.

"Interesting," he murmured.

The way he said that single word sent chills down my spine like ice water.

"I'll accept your offer," he declared. "You understand that once you make this sacrifice, you cannot change your mind. You will be bound to your word for as long as your eternity lasts. You will be the only one left with your blood."

"I understand completely. I think it's for the best," I agreed without hesitation.

I was too afraid that my blood was already tainted with my inherent weakness. I would rather spend forever making up for my choices than live knowing that not only did I make mistake after mistake, but that any children I created would follow that same destructive path.

I was afraid that it would be worse than that—that they would end up so deep in darkness that they would end up like

Sahir. That maybe Sahir's cruelty kept manifesting generation after generation, and her lifelong mission of making me suffer would extend to my innocent children.

I was fine with being the end of my line. I wanted to be the final chapter of my bloodline.

Hands reached down from the top of the white box like descending nightmares. They were gray as ash, with nails long enough to dig out an entire garden. I tucked myself closer to the ground in a futile attempt to escape, but the claws dug into my skull anyway with vicious precision. Pulses worked their way down through my mind over and over like waves of invasive water, each one more painful than the last.

He retracted his nails and threw me out of the box with supernatural force. I felt my skin tear when my body skidded against rough rock, pain flaring across every nerve. I stopped rolling next to Shivani, who looked as pale and shaken as I felt.

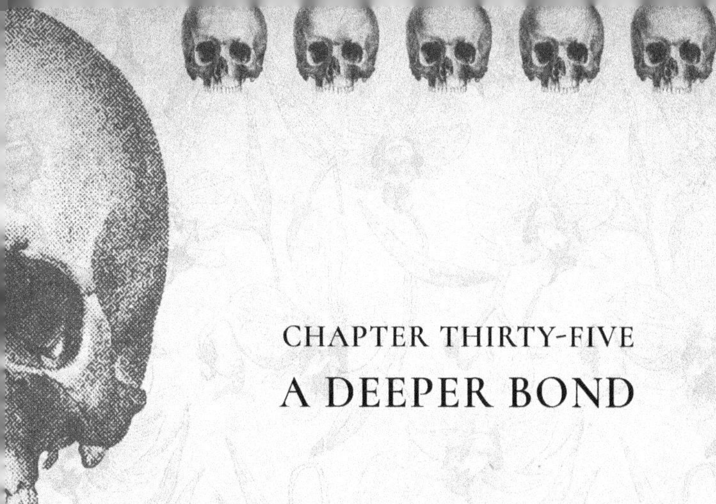

CHAPTER THIRTY-FIVE
A DEEPER BOND

CAYM

I took advantage of the girls being away and called an urgent meeting. I wanted all of the guardians present, the season deities, everyone who could make a difference. I called them to a small, private room inside the temple of magic where we could speak without being overheard.

"I know that it's sudden, but I wanted to meet while they were gone," I began, clearing my throat nervously. "We have what feels like an endless wave of enemies battering at our door. The other lands across the realm are burning, consumed by Nikola's forces. The only safe place to be is here in Ashbell or in Brontide, where Kyra has lost her mind to grief. The heat hasn't even been turned all the way up yet—this is just the beginning. That scares me more than anything. What's on the horizon for us when Nikola decides that he's ready to show his face and unleash his full power?" I asked, letting the weight of the question settle over them.

Vespera and Koa nodded in understanding, but didn't speak, their expressions grim.

"Do you have a plan?" Coy asked, leaning forward with interest.

"I have been thinking deeply on it," I replied with determination.

"Is that why you called us here?" Inola questioned.

"It is." I nodded firmly. "I think no matter how good the first plan we devise is, a backup plan is going to be the best way to move forward safely. I think that we should bond our lives to the girls."

"Like a cat and its nine lives?" Koa posed his words as a question, understanding dawning in his eyes.

"If Nikola were to kill them, we would die first and they would keep going," I explained with quiet conviction.

"I'd rather die than them," Coy agreed without hesitation.

"Nikola wouldn't expect it," Vespera added with growing enthusiasm. "He'd think they were dead and move on to other targets. They'd recover and have a second, secret chance."

"I've felt strange since I came back from the shadow realm," I admitted, vulnerability creeping into my voice. "Like there's something fundamentally wrong with me. I don't want to hurt anyone, but I get this persistent feeling inside my mind that tells me I will." I looked up to see every eye in the room focused on me with concern. "I'd rather die so that they can live than risk this feeling being prophetic."

"Should we be keeping this from them?" Cyrus, God of Summer, asked with moral uncertainty.

"I think it would be best," I replied, though the decision weighed heavily on me.

"It's funny that this should be your idea and I have to use forbidden old magic to help," Inola chuckled, though there was no humor in her eyes.

Her gaze became distant for a moment, as if she weren't with us but replaying lost memories from ages past.

"The last time there was something close to this was bone binding. A lot of witches paid for it with their lives when it went wrong. Hesperia was deeply displeased when she learned of it." Inola, Goddess of spring, paused again, gathering her thoughts. "It's liberating to speak freely again. It feels irrelevant now, but I learned some time ago that Sahir taught Helia old magic, too. They used it in another realm for binding souls and transforming people into hybrids against their will. It was Nikola who originally taught it to Sahir." Inola shook her head with disgust. "Maybe another time we can finally sit down and put all of the pieces of information we have together into a complete picture."

Eyes glanced around the room as if they were bursting to spill secrets too, but no one spoke up. There was a silent agreement that maybe one day we would share everything, but today wasn't that day.

Everyone had made clear agreement on many things during our quick meeting—everyone except Sina, the Goddess of Winter. She looked uncomfortable and less enthusiastic than everyone else, her ice-blue eyes troubled.

I knew that I had asked for something monumental. That I asked my brothers and sisters to be okay with dying for love. I didn't understand why, of all the deities to look unaccepting, Sina was the one. It should have made me uncomfortable, but instead, it made me hopeful that if I had only followed her instincts, I might have learned something useful.

Inola, the Goddess of Spring, was on the ground on her knees, her green robes pooling around her. She drew intricate shapes onto the ground with dirt in preparation for the dangerous ritual. I don't know why I expected pushback from anyone over my idea, but I did expect some resistance. I wouldn't have let anyone talk me out of it, though. I would not have changed my mind under any circumstances. I had expected to have to defend myself at the very least, to argue for the necessity of such a sacrifice.

CHAPTER THIRTY-SIX
A MOTHER'S LOVE

RURI

I stared at the grotto's shimmering surface, mesmerized by the gentle movement of the water. I watched the ripples and thought about how I had been there before, standing just a few feet from a wealth of answers and yet never quite making it deep enough to touch them.

I stared at the grotto, but then I was shoved into the warm water without warning. When I swam to the other side, I found myself in Merripen, the familiar landscape of home spreading before me. Caym was nowhere to be seen, but my children were there—alive and whole and beautiful.

A little boy with pink eyes, the same striking shade as Astra's, played with two little girls in the afternoon sunlight. They both had short green hair and small, perfect noses, the same delicate features as Caym. I sat on the worn stone steps of Caym's castle and watched in reverent silence. Nola helped them with their game of tag, and they giggled with pure joy every time they dodged a bony finger, their laughter like music in the air.

I didn't know where I was or why I was there, but a part of

me didn't want to leave this perfect moment. I didn't even know if their graves were still intact in Cylla after all the destruction. I hadn't been able to go and see since I fully gathered my memories, too afraid of what I might find. I didn't know what words I could possibly say to them to explain why I hadn't done more, sooner, to protect them.

The list of children that I needed to try and bring back grew too quickly, an impossible burden.

"The two of you do make beautiful children. Does it weigh on you that you robbed Caym of that kind of happiness the first time? Or that you may never have a relationship with your first child?" a voice asked from the air itself.

There was no visible form to accompany the voice, just words floating on the breeze.

"I asked your sisters to tell me their biggest fear and regret as a start to our conversation about granting you your wish. I don't need to ask yours—it is the clearest thing I've ever seen. You regret the choices that you made with Kyra, and your fear overlaps with that regret. You fear never being able to experience life with Caym and children."

"Enough. Who are you to demand something so private?" I responded with rising anger.

"I am the one that holds what you desperately need. No one will know what we discuss here—this place is beyond such concerns. I require you to face these truths and put them to rest. Even if I hand you what you've come for, if you do not leave with a clear mind and stop holding yourself back, it won't matter."

A shiver ran through me like ice water. His voice was so carefree and casual. He knew that he held all the cards in his favor and he made no attempt at hiding it in the way he spoke to me.

"You want me to admit I failed, in order to save things outside of wherever we are?" I asked, steel creeping into my voice.

"Exactly. Then I will ask you for a sacrifice," he answered with satisfaction.

"Fine." I took a deep breath, steeling myself. "I thought that by hiding Kyra from everyone, I was protecting her from a cruel world. I knew that Yumi would want to use her if she discovered her existence. I knew that Astra would be devastated if she knew the truth. I was certain that Caym would not be able to keep it secret if he saw her hurt. I never imagined that making what I considered the best choice for her would make me her biggest enemy. That it would hurt her so deeply or cause such an irreparable rift between us. I stepped as carefully as I could, and I endured so many painful nights with my head held high to bring us all to a point of peace. I regret it all. I'd rather have fought and died one hundred times than watch my own flesh and blood fight on the wrong side."

"Then do you regret it because you think you made the wrong choice, or because of the side that she ultimately picked?"

"Can't it be both?" I asked, frustration bleeding through. "Can't I say that the side she decided to align with is what feeds the regret I can't seem to shake? That my disappointment in her keeps me from finding a way to look at her as anything but a failure?"

"You can say whatever you'd like," he responded with indifference.

"What is your biggest regret?" I countered, turning the interrogation back on him.

"Like you, I once thought that if I played the game of the gods and held my head high, it would matter in the end. I once stood in the middle playing peacemaker, too. I did things that I didn't agree with for the sake of my own siblings. In the end, it only placed me in a position to fail spectacularly." The voice responded with bitter experience.

"I thought you said that our conversation went nowhere,

Why are you being so deliberately broad?" I asked, pressing for details.

"My eldest sister wanted to hand out the world to our baby sister like gifts. My eldest brother wanted only for our eldest sister to see him and love him. I was the peacekeeper between the two of them, trying to hold everything together. Peace was brief and came at the cost of my sanity. Then my power, then my position, then the very memory of my existence. Eventually, the cost was my life. They still do not live in peace. They still hardly consider my sacrifice relevant."

"Do you want revenge?" I asked, understanding his pain.

"It is time we move on to your sacrifice," he deflected instead of answering.

"Kyra," I blurted without hesitation.

"Your daughter?" His tone became more curious than bland for the first time.

"Yes. I'll offer her," I repeated with conviction.

"I won't give her back to you. She won't wake up one day and look at you as a mother," he warned with gravity.

"I know," I replied without flinching.

It was exactly what I wanted—my mistake erased, and the ability to move forward and try again with a clean slate.

"Then I accept your sacrifice," he declared with finality.

The grass around me died instantly, withering to brown. The bodies of everyone in front of me dropped to the ground like puppets with severed strings. The once-perfect vision in front of me crumbled until I, too, turned to ash and dust. I felt myself float into the wind, weightless and free. The breeze carried me back to the grotto where two of my sisters waited with concern etched on their faces.

I felt truly free instead of filled with poisonous resentment for the first time since I had returned from the dead.

CHAPTER THIRTY-SEVEN

THE FABRIC OF FATE

HESPERIA

The darkness that surrounded me felt achingly familiar. It was the same endless abyss that I had inhabited for so long while under Nikola's control, a prison I knew intimately. The air was just as cold and suffocating, and I felt that old sense of hopelessness creeping back into my bones.

"Hello, Hesperia," a dark voice called out from the void.

It was eerily similar to Nikola's melodic tone, yet there were unmistakable hints of Mother's warmth woven through it, creating an unsettling combination.

"Hello, voice," I replied with practiced calm.

I had stopped questioning the things that happened in the darkness a long time ago—resistance was futile in places like this.

"Are you scared here?" it asked with curious interest.

"Should I be?" I asked in return, genuinely curious.

"Your sisters were terrified. They hardly wanted to admit it, but I could see their trembling fingers and hear their shaky breath betraying their fear."

"Did they succeed in their trials?" I asked, concern for them overriding my own situation.

"What would you do if I told you they all succeeded?" he asked, deflecting my question.

"I'm not sure," I shrugged honestly.

"There's no tremble in you at all. Is that because you think this is not real?" he questioned with growing fascination.

"Yes."

He laughed, the sound echoing strangely in the void. "I anticipated you to be the one that was the most comfortable with me. Let me get to the meat of things without delay. You must offer me a sacrifice—an exchange of something mean-ingful. I want you to think of it as assurance that I'm gifting a power so strong to someone who can keep it with a clear mind. We will start smaller, with a fear and a regret."

"It seems my closest friends have been the voices I've met in the darkness of my own mind. It makes it simple to answer you." I paused, gathering my thoughts. "I regret lying to my sisters for the sake of my mother. I can't seem to stop it, though." I shook my head in frustration. "I'm sure that I could stop if I truly wanted to. I don't stop because I see her, and I know that she loves us with everything she has. That anything she does is for our protection. I have so much confidence in her choices being in our best interest that I'm willing to lie for her, to hide crucial things for her if she says that it must be done. I don't think that my sisters will see it the same way I do. In fact, I know they wouldn't understand. Ruri and her daughter are alike in the way they feel about their mothers— they demand honesty above all else. Ruri would never under-stand why I hid so many important things from her. I regret it because I know that if I don't keep my mother's secrets held tight, I risk losing my sister forever."

"You fear losing them," he stated as if he needed clari-fication.

"I do. I fear that if I slip, even a little, they will run from me like I'm poison. I've done everything that I can to keep Mother's secrets close to my heart. I'm sure there's no way for them to come out naturally, but I'm haunted by the idea that they will surface in some way that I can't foresee. That there may be someone who knows something that I'm unaware of, someone who could expose everything."

"If there was such a person, would you kill them to keep her secrets safe?" he asked with deadly seriousness.

"Yes," I replied aloud without hesitation.

"You didn't even pause to consider it."

"I don't need to think about it now. I have thought about it for a long time, during every moment of my imprisonment. While my sisters lived, even if it was painfully, I was left in the darkness with nothing but my thoughts. The only thing that I had to occupy my mind was them. If it wasn't them consuming my thoughts, it was Coy. My life was put on pause for so long that I nearly gave up hope entirely. I'd do anything, even if it made me an awful person, to have a future where all of us were together and happy."

"If I could guarantee that future, what would you give up for it?" he asked with renewed interest.

"The fate of Nikola's soul in the afterlife," I answered without missing a beat.

"Why is that your choice?" he asked, though the smile was clear in the way that he spoke.

It was the best guess I had, but it worked in my favor, confirming my suspicions.

"It is only my choice to make. Fate and the crossroads are mine to control. There are only two gods that I know who enjoy locking people in darkness for eternity. If this is the kind of place that you inhabit, then you must be connected to something involving one of them. As the Goddess of Fate, I would be willing to hand over Nikola or Deimos to you for judgment. I feel confident in saying that you want Nikola specifically. If you have the kind of power to help my sisters and me, then you wouldn't be concerned with someone as relatively powerless as Deimos."

"I accept your offer," he answered with simple finality.

I heard a sharp snap echo through the darkness, and I had to blink more times than I could count to adjust to the brilliant amount of light suddenly shining around me. My eyes watered from the intensity as they slowly adapted.

I was the last one back in the grotto, my sisters already waiting with expressions of concern and curiosity etched on their faces.

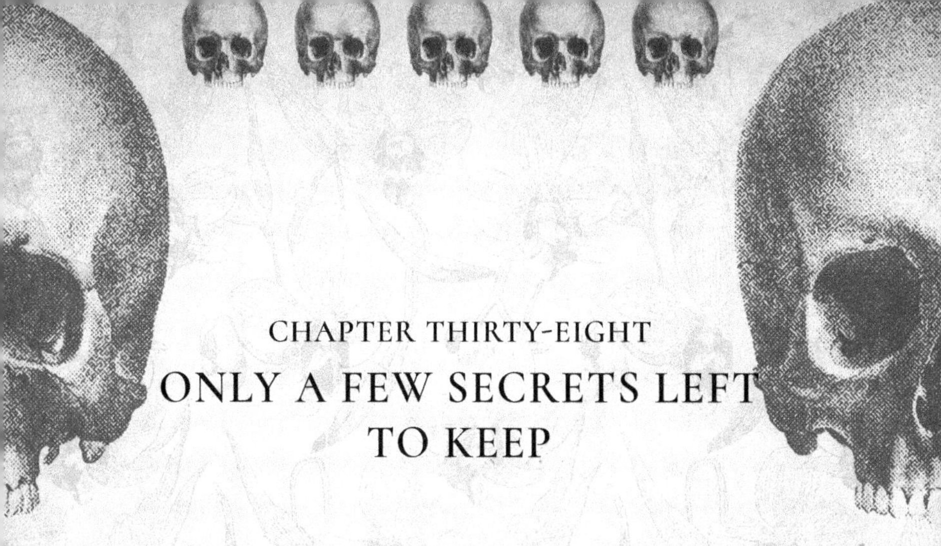

CHAPTER THIRTY-EIGHT

ONLY A FEW SECRETS LEFT TO KEEP

CAYM

I followed Sina, the Goddess of Winter, for the entire afternoon like a shadow tracking its target. Hesperia considered her a mentor and looked up to her with genuine admiration. Hesperia was a smart girl, but if she had her mind set on Sina being innocent, she'd find a way to talk herself out of anything she witnessed. I didn't care for Sina in either direction—I had no personal attachment. I'd clear Sina's name myself, or kill her myself if necessary.

I had nearly given up my surveillance when Sina left the safety of the temples. We had fortified the inner city and the temples with everything we could manage. They were as safe as they could have been under the circumstances. Outside of what we had carefully set up, the lands were nothing but chaos and destruction. When the land finally had time to breathe, Nikola sent another wave of his twisted creatures after us like clockwork.

Sina was still a dragon, her massive form imposing against the landscape. She was the last seasonal deity to maintain her dragon form. She was the only deity to be a dragon that actively wanted to remain one. Every other deity was fond of the idea of returning to their original bodies, but not Sina.

Sina took off in a sprint toward the tree line, her powerful legs eating up the distance.

Flaming trees did their best to block her path, and if I hadn't been directly on her tail, I might have lost her completely. The trees gave me the same opportunity for concealment. They granted me more grace, because they hid me better than they concealed anything else. When she stopped in front of Sahir, I felt my insides turn to liquid fire.

"Nikola says that he is bound to the land of the mortals by the Blood Weaver. He wants you to find where he is hiding and bring him to Nikola," Sahir whispered with urgent conspiracy.

"All four of the girls are gone on their mission. We've received no word on when they will return. Now is the best time to launch the full-scale assault," Sina replied without hesitation. "We will need to eliminate the guards standing watch here, then it will be free movement inside the defenses."

"Then go do it," Sahir commanded with cold authority.

I watched Sina charge forward without even the slightest second thought or moral hesitation. She was the perfect picture of willing obedience to a cause she believed in. Nikola hardly faced any challenges in enacting his desires—his manipulation was frighteningly effective. He had Onyx to control my side of things and report back intelligence. Sina was positioned on the other side. Anything he could have dreamt of needing to know, one or the other received and transmitted to him.

I could hardly imagine who else Nikola had managed to shift onto his side through persuasion or coercion.

I pulled out the shell I kept secured on my hip. Instead of using it to try and communicate with anyone, I blew into it to alert everyone of the impending danger. I blew as hard as I could, and an alarm sounded from the other end of the shell, piercing the air.

Everyone that could have held a weapon would gather their strength and be at my side before I counted to twenty. Sina killed the second guard with ruthless efficiency, and Sahir pointed in a horde of creatures that made my stomach churn. They looked worse than they had in previous attacks. Nikola seemed to be reanimating the hordes we had killed, but it didn't do them any favors in strength or appearance.

The sight, the very idea of recycled death, made me nauseous. I knew he wasn't stupid or careless. He had to have had something more sinister up his sleeve, something that I genuinely feared.

I needed to find Coy immediately. I needed to let them know that Sina was a traitor before more damage was done.

I moved through soldier after soldier and waved them into the crowd of monsters, directing the defense. I knew I should have stayed and fought alongside them, but I wouldn't. I needed to find Coy, and once I saw that he was nowhere in sight, I pulled out my own blade with grim determination.

"Coy!" I yelled across the battlefield.

I found the end of the crowd of soldiers and still did not see the other guardians anywhere. My heart sank like a stone, and I had to take a deep breath to steady myself. The way things were developing had begun to mess with my mind in dangerous ways. I couldn't guarantee any safety or even predict a next move on any front.

I was haunted by the persistent idea that I'd blink with too much confidence and my friends would be dead when I opened my eyes, too.

"Caym!" Coy yelled as he ran toward me through the chaos.

I sighed with profound relief. "I thought something terrible had happened to you."

"I won't go down that easily, brother. Nikola sent a wave at us from both directions simultaneously. When your shell went off, we were already knee-deep in creatures," Coy explained, breathing heavily.

He was out of breath, but I thought it had to have been from running rather than injury.

"Sina is a traitor. She sold us out to Sahir and Nikola without hesitation. I'm worried about the ritual we performed to bond our lives to the girls. I'm concerned that yours and Hesperia's bond didn't work properly. If Sina were a traitor during the ceremony, she never would have bonded correctly with her sister. If she told Nikola about our plan, you can be sure Nikola will try harder to kill the girls in the most brutal way possible the first time around to eliminate us as obstacles."

Coy nodded with understanding. "I will go find Inola and see what she can do to fix this."

"I'll hold things here until you get back," I promised, gripping my weapon tighter.

I could see Koa and Vespera fighting in the distance, their forms barely visible through the smoke and chaos. The three of us would hold the last of our safety together, no matter the cost.

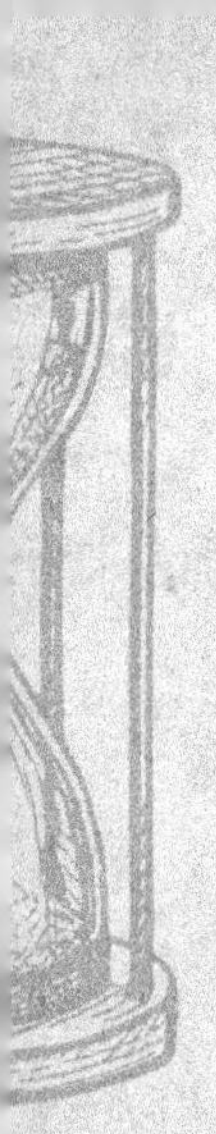

CHAPTER THIRTY-NINE
THE FIRST STRIKE

SHIVANI

A Fiia sent word that Nikola had finally chosen his moment to strike. The little fluttering companion chittered urgently about the betrayal that had been uncovered within our ranks. Hesperia hardly wanted to believe it, her face crumpling with denial. She insisted she wanted to lay her own eyes on Sina, declaring that with our fractured world, we could hardly trust anything that we didn't witness with our own eyes.

Hesperia offered us her shortcut so that we could travel faster than conventional means. We protested at first, knowing the risks. We weren't meant to traverse the in-between realm that she controlled. It caused excruciating pain, it pulled at our life roots like thorns.

This time was different. We walked through with surprising peace, our passage smooth as silk. It was as if we all had a voice, or a hand in what the realm was allowed to do to us. It was clear we were all fundamentally different after our visits to the grotto. It was also a transformation that none of us wanted to discuss with each other.

No one asked probing questions. No one exchanged meaningful glances. We moved through Hesperia's void and emerged on the other side in Ashbell, only to find our sanctuary in complete ruin. Nikola had pushed further into what little we had left, destroying everything in his path.

I didn't believe my eyes when I saw Koa fighting desperately against Vespera. I left my sisters, who went to take in the full scope of destruction, too. My feet carried me as fast as they could to Koa's aid.

"She's not herself! Stay back!" Koa shouted, stopping me from moving forward into danger.

"Then let me help!"

"No, I don't want you to get hurt," Koa protested, moving me behind him and stopping her blade with his own. "Look at her eyes!"

I released blood ropes from my palms and willed them to wind around Vespera until she was completely restrained. She squirmed and grunted against the bindings but made no attempt to break free with her own magic.

"See!" I shot back at him triumphantly.

"What if you had been hurt?" he demanded, worry creasing his features.

"What is wrong with her?" I asked, ignoring his concern for my safety.

"Nikola whispered something to her, and she was changed instantly. It was like she only knew me as her enemy," Koa explained with pain in his voice.

"The others? Are they acting like her, too?" I pressed.

The sinister hiss of a viper filled the air instead of his answer. Nikola was back in his true form, massive and serpentine.

I tried to turn back the hands of time so that we would arrive before Nikola could do this damage. It failed completely. It turned back everything but his presence—he remained constant through my manipulation. If I kept turning back the hours, he would instead be placed in the middle of hundreds of unexpected reinforcements.

The situation we faced was the best we could hope for.

I caught sight of Hesperia behind Nikola the viper, and she put all of her effort into raising the already dead warriors again so that they could rejoin the battle with renewed purpose. I blinked and reset time to where it was before I touched it. Our hand wasn't strong, but it was the best it could have been under the circumstances.

Ruri and Sage worked together in perfect harmony to shape a mountain around the viper Nikola. I used my magic to ensure he was held down while they crafted their trap. They had nearly completed an entire stone kingdom around him, a fortress that was nowhere I'd ever want to live, but it made a useful cage.

Nikola's massive tail sliced open the back of the mountain like paper and he weaseled his way out of it with fluid grace. As he escaped, he slammed his tail into both Sage and Ruri with devastating force. It flung them across the rocky ground of Ashbell, and I knew they were seriously injured. They had to be after such an impact.

Koa grabbed me by the arm with urgency. "You shouldn't be so close to him. Come on."

I pulled my arm from his grip and kissed him instead, fierce and desperate. "Where else do we have to be?"

Koa tossed me a claymore with visible apprehension etched on his face.

"If we're going to win, then we need all hands actively fighting against him," I declared with determination.

He placed each of his hands on my face with tender care. "If anyone should die today, let it be me. The universe will exist long after I'm gone, but it should never know a time without you in it."

I wanted to share in the romantic moment that he tried to create, but I only felt crushing guilt for offering his memories as my sacrifice to the entity. Had they already been taken from him? Did he still recall any of our shared history?

I wasn't brave enough to ask in the life-or-death situation that we were facing.

"Then we both make it out alive," I replied with a forced smile.

I left him and charged at Nikola with my weapon raised. He hissed menacingly and swiped at me with his massive tail. The blast knocked the wind completely out of me, my lungs screaming for air. His tail sent me spiraling through the air and crashing into the hard ground with bone-jarring force. He drew his tail back and drove it into my stomach before I could stand from the ground.

I didn't roll fast enough to avoid the strike. The shock radiated through me like a rush of arctic air, numbing and violent. My skin prickled with cold fire and my heart slowed to an irregular rhythm.

I met Koa's horrified face and although his lips moved frantically, I only heard ringing in my ears. I coughed up blood, but it didn't offer me any relief from the agony spreading through my body.

The bright light that suddenly pulsed from Koa offered that relief instead.

I still only heard ringing when he hit his knees and blood began running from his mouth in crimson streams. Nikola removed his tail from my body, and I discovered that I didn't have a single scratch anywhere on my skin.

Koa had taken the wound for me. He hit the ground face-first without a second movement, utterly still.

"Did he not tell you?" Nikola hissed with cruel satisfaction. "They bound their lives to you. If you die, they die instead and offer you a second life."

"You knew about this?" I growled, rage building in my chest.

"While you wallowed in your own pity, some of us placed eyes and ears around the battlefield. We planned strategically. We didn't act as if we could save the world simply because we decided we wanted it really badly," Nikola's voice mocked me with venomous amusement.

CHAPTER FORTY
NO TRUE FRIENDS

HESPERIA

I carried my own sword, and another that I took from the weapons rack before we were thrust into the chaos that had completely engulfed Ashbell. One sword was driven deep into the mouth of a creature who no longer had arms or legs, just a writhing torso. Orange liquid oozed from it like infected blood. The second I plunged into the stomach of what had once been Kyra's mortals, now twisted into something unrecognizable.

Nikola's celestial commanders grabbed at pieces of rock from the sky's farthest reaches and called it down on us like divine judgment. One massive boulder crashed into the side of the castle in the distance, sending up clouds of dust and debris. I took it as a bit of luck—there was nearly nothing on our side the longer this battle raged on.

We were sent to gain more power, and came back to find even more devastating loss. If it hadn't been Mother who sent us on that mission, I would have thought we were deliberately set up. Distracted and pushed away so that Nikola would have an easier time destroying everything we held dear.

I took the head of another creature during my desperate push to get to the ones I knew and loved. I could hardly save everyone—that had never been within my power. To begin with, I never had the ability to create or save lives. The closest I could manage was after all their suffering ended, I could pull their souls back into the realm of the living. It was hardly a kindness. They'd feel the pain of death again and return with full recollection of it burning in their memories.

There were ways to bring them back peacefully, but we hardly had the luxury of time for such gentleness.

My heart sank like a stone when I watched blood splatter into the air from a part of Coy I could not see clearly. When he dropped to his knees, I felt ice water flood my veins.

I took off in a desperate sprint, my lungs burning. I pushed past soldiers and their desperate grabs at empty air. They wanted to stay away from death, but I was the wrong sister for that comfort. The sun caught steel and the flash blinded me momentarily. I only saw that glint and Coy beyond it.

I forced myself to run faster, my legs screaming in protest, but if the flash of steel was aimed for his neck, I'd hardly make it in time to save him.

I had wasted too much time playing by rules that I didn't think still existed in this war. I stopped running and knelt down until my hands touched the blood-soaked ground. We kept treating Nikola as if he were an honest opponent playing by the same moral code. As if he wouldn't do anything and everything he needed to get us out of his way permanently.

We played by rules that helped preserve the mortals and their way of life. We would lose if we continued this naive approach. The mortals hardly had a place left to call home as it was. Much more of what we faced, and there would be nothing at all left to protect. Dragons flew overhead sending lines of fire and acid into the ground, scorching everything they touched.

I wished the sight had brought me hope, but it only brought me grim confirmation. Rules only applied to those that followed them, and we were in a time where no one who followed them would be on the winning side.

I dug my nails into the dirt and ripped open a jagged hole that led to the void realm—the in-between space of life and death. I gave permission and released all of the souls that sat in waiting, trapped for ages. I called to the souls that had been locked away there from times beyond the one we currently lived in. Everyone that Nikola had hurt, or hidden away, was free to leave their prison.

I ripped my nails through the dirt and sent an open slice across the ground all the way to Coy like a lightning strike. It bought me precious time. I got back to my feet and ran to him with renewed urgency.

Relief washed over me like warm water when I saw he was surrounded by blood, and none of it came from his body. He hovered protectively over Mother and Father, his stance defensive.

"I knew this was where you would want me," he declared with quiet conviction.

I allowed myself to cry, if only for a moment of weakness. "I thought you were hurt!"

I pulled him by his collar until he was close enough that I could wrap my arms around his waist, holding him like an anchor.

"I'm all right," he assured me, his hands gentle in my hair.

"We need to get them out of here," I spoke urgently, but I didn't remove myself from his comforting embrace.

"You aren't leaving, and neither are they," Sina announced from behind us, her voice dripping with malice.

Coy grabbed me tighter to keep me from moving toward the threat. "She is with Nikola. She has been for as long as we can determine."

"What?" I pulled away in shock and disbelief.

Even then, I couldn't believe it, couldn't accept the betrayal. She was supposed to be my teacher, my friend, my mentor.

"We don't need to do this. You can die still thinking whatever you'd like about our relationship," Sina spat with venom.

"What could they have possibly offered you to gain from this?" I asked, my voice breaking.

"Your position," she answered with cruel satisfaction. "I kill you, I get to eat your heart and become the new Sister of Fate under Nikola's rule."

"What do you gain from that that you didn't already have? You could have asked for anything from me. I would have done it gladly," I shook my head in confusion.

"I don't want to have to ask!" she screamed with rage.

She grabbed me by the arm and plunged her pointed tail into Coy's chest before I had time to react to the sudden movement.

"I don't want to ask you for anything ever again. I want to take it for myself. Nikola will allow me to do as I please, when I please," Sina continued with growing fury. "Get up!"

She swung her crimson-covered antlers at me with deadly intent.

I could only roll and blink desperately. Crimson blood was my sight, and the sound of steel clashing on antler was my audio. Nothing else ran through my mind while the sun began its descent into the darkening sky. I saw Nikola the viper in the backdrop, ever approaching like death itself.

Father pulled me to my feet with strong hands. "We will take Nikola. Focus on what's in front of you!"

He shook me firmly before he turned me to face Sina directly. I glanced back all the same to see Mother and Father carrying Coy away to safety.

"You're too stupid for the position you hold," Sina spat as she lunged at me with murderous intent. "You don't see anything coming. You learn nothing from your mistakes. It was so easy to do what Nikola wanted right under your nose."

"If trusting you is stupid, then maybe I am," I replied, slicing her scales with my sword and drawing dark blood.

"It is," she hissed. Our weapons met and held us apart in a deadly standoff. "Nikola always knows what you'll do—you're predictable. Coy's heart wasn't preserved simply because he felt bad about what happened. It was preserved so that we could use it now. He's dying, but not before Nikola will take control of Coy and turn him against everyone. Nikola will make Coy kill everyone he's near and then let him die in the middle of their bodies. Your lover will die knowing he killed mommy and daddy, and left you to die, too." Sina laughed with genuine delight at the cruelty.

I called to the souls I had unleashed to come to my aid, and even though our weapons clashed multiple more times before they arrived, sending sparks flying, the souls did respond to my call. They pulled and tugged at her flesh with desperate hunger. They tried their best to cling onto any thread that would get them closer to the living than the dead. I watched her scaly body fight to stay connected to her soul in a haze of supernatural glitches.

I reached into Sina's chest and ripped out her still-beating heart with my bare hands. I gripped it with my nails to ensure that I impaled it and it couldn't fall while I ran. I ran as fast as I could until I found the dragon guardian of Erebus, searching frantically. His small stone frame fought as if he were the biggest of them all, fierce and determined. When Usha saw me approaching, he gazed at me with fear. It was only then that I realized I had been bleeding from multiple places, painting a trail behind me.

I shoved the heart into his mouth and held it closed until he swallowed it completely, the power transferring instantly.

If Nikola wanted to bring Sina back from the dead, if he

thought she was worth anything, so be it. She wouldn't come back as the Goddess of Winter—that title now belonged to Usha.

He lit up the dimming battlefield with a brilliant white burst of power that let me know he had fully assumed her old position, the magic settling into his small frame.

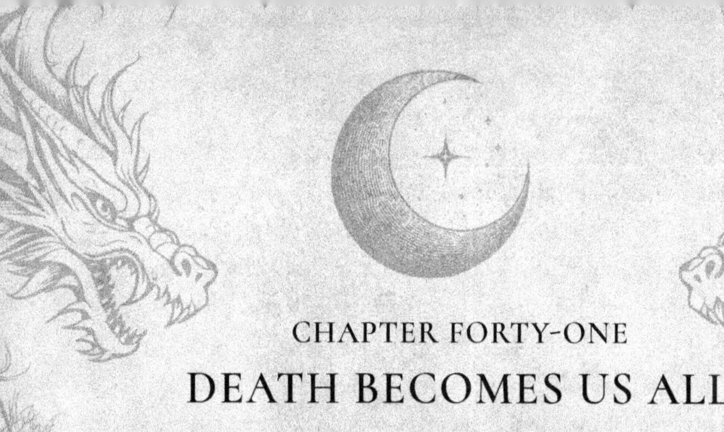

CHAPTER FORTY-ONE

DEATH BECOMES US ALL

RURI

Belladonna, my fearless dragon companion, fought Sahir back with primal fury. Sahir had grown exponentially in strength since the last time I had seen her, her power radiating like heat from a forge. Whatever Nikola had offered her, she had received it in abundance.

Maybe it was the hearts she had consumed, their power flowing through her veins.

It brought a bit of savage joy to me, even in the devastated state the realm was in, to see Sahir still using illusion crystals to hide her true form. She was still covered in the permanent scarring from the poison she was fed, the marks etched into her skin like a map of her suffering. I saw through my own magic, but did Nikola? Did he see the proof written on her skin that we were as weak as he thought we were?

The joy the thought brought was fleeting as smoke. Every plan we made, every upper hand we thought we possessed was crumbling to dust. There was no point in keeping the realm preserved any further because there was nothing, and no one left to save. Angels, Seere, Fae, Dwarf, Man—they all covered the ground in cold flesh and crimson pools.

Buildings burned and collapsed into rubble. The acrid smell of smoke filled the night air, choking and thick. The sun had abandoned us and we fought under the eerie glow of two moons hanging in the darkened sky. It felt as if that's how it should have been all along—a world bathed in death.

Yumi struck me with her whip across my forearm and the pain was hardly something to crumble over. I remembered every other time she had done it to me, each strike carved into my memory. I had built a tolerance to the sensation of the lash over years of abuse. She wore a collar that I recognized with bitter familiarity—I had seen Yumi use the fate chains and collars from Minna so long ago. I could see that she hadn't yet grown used to the sensation of it on her own skin, the way it chafed and burned.

I had. I had long since adjusted to the feeling of her lashing me, my body conditioned to endure.

I called down purple lightning and she rolled away from it with practiced grace. Strike after strike I summoned, and when she was focused on dodging them, I tossed orbs of purple fire at her with deadly precision. They hit one after another in her midsection like meteors. I heard the breath leave her lungs in a sharp gasp. From the shock, or pain, it didn't matter which.

It gave me the distraction I needed to pounce on her like a predator. I wrapped my hands around her throat and squeezed with all my strength.

She clawed at my hands until they ran with blood, her nails like razors.

"Even if you kill me here, I'll come back for Caym," Yumi grunted out between strangled breaths.

She lifted her knee and drove it into my crotch with vicious intent. I cried out from the contact and she wrapped her arm around me to flip us with surprising strength. She straddled me and followed my lead by gripping my throat with iron fingers.

"I should have killed him when I had the chance. Hung him outside of the Chamber of Starlight so everyone could see him every day instead of hiding him away. I could have used his bones for a stool, his skull for a cup. The possibilities are endless for creative torture. It's not too late, still," Yumi leaned her face into mine while she spoke, her breath hot against my skin.

I felt her spit hit my cheeks like acid.

"You're right. It's not too late to plan what we will do with the bodies of the dead," I choked out, defiance burning in my chest. "I think I'll chain yours in the sky for the carrion birds."

I raised my head to hit hers as hard as I could, our skulls colliding with sickening force. We both fell dizzy and blind from the impact to our heads. I only had to recover faster than she did—I could be dizzy, as long as I got to my feet first.

I repeated it to myself like a mantra while I tried to stand, but the words hardly made themselves reality. I puked beside both of us before I felt even a bit stable, my vision swimming. I stumbled to my feet and was met with a sharp, burning pain in my chest.

She had stabbed me. I reached up and grabbed the dagger that protruded from inside of my heart, but when I pulled at it, shock waves were sent through my entire body. I looked up at Yumi with growing horror.

She grabbed my face and turned it to the side where Jeb lay protectively over Caym's body. His skin was already pale as winter and his chest utterly still, no breath stirring his lungs.

"Do you see that? I'm going to stab you again and you'll join him in death. It's that simple. Be still and it's over for you. The two of you can have the peace you wanted so desperately. Doesn't that sound nice?" Yumi whispered with false tenderness.

I took my hand off the blade that stuck out of my chest.

The pain was mysteriously gone, and it slowly removed itself with some kind of magic that had not come from me. The wound was painless, but my heart still ached with unbearable loss.

It did sound nice, like the sweetest mercy. The dagger hurt less than watching him die before my eyes. I lifted my hands in surrender and opened my body to her blade. She could have her pick of how I died—I would only be an empty shell if I remained in this world.

I closed my eyes and held my breath, waiting for the final blow.

"Do it," I pleaded, meaning every word.

Even though it was to be my last breath, the fire still roared around us and steel still rang out in the distance, the world continuing its violent dance.

A bony hand slapped me hard in the face and I shot my eyes open in shock.

"Fool! Selfish!" Jeb roared with righteous anger. "You leave me behind? You leave everyone to die?"

A knot caught in my throat at his accusation. His hurt was palpable, radiating from him like heat, but my answer was yes. I didn't regret the choice that I was about to make, the choice that I still wanted to make with every fiber of my being.

"Enough!" Jeb yelled again, his voice cracking with emotion.

He used his cold, skeletal fingers to turn me around and force me to face my mother. Dahlia stood with Belladonna, and they spoke words that I could not hear over the ringing in my ears. Belladonna bowed to her with solemn reverence.

Dahlia glanced at me with a smile—one that was the calmest I had seen on her face yet, peaceful and resigned.

Belladonna lowered herself and wrapped her massive jaw around Dahlia with infinite gentleness. She simply swallowed, and my mother was gone.

She had eaten my mother whole.

A cluster of stars formed in the sky above us like scattered diamonds. They formed the unmistakable shape of a woman in a flowing gown, but before I could fully process what it meant, Belladonna shot a beam of pure white light from her mouth. It connected with Aero across the battlefield, illuminating him like a beacon.

That's where Dahlia had kept her magic hidden—Aero had held it tight and secret all this time. When the power was fully transferred inside Belladonna, the light dissipated like morning mist, and she was marked with a full moon engraved on her forehead. My dragon had become the Goddess of the Moon.

"You leave behind so many sacrifices?" Jeb pushed me, his voice breaking. "You let so many people die for nothing?" He pushed me again, harder this time. "You leave me to suffer alone?" He shoved me with all his strength. "He would be disappointed in you."

I wiped the tears from my face and did my best to shove down the overwhelming feeling of wanting to fade away into nothingness. Jeb was right about everything, but it still almost meant nothing to me—the pain was too great to bear.

LOOK TO THE EAST

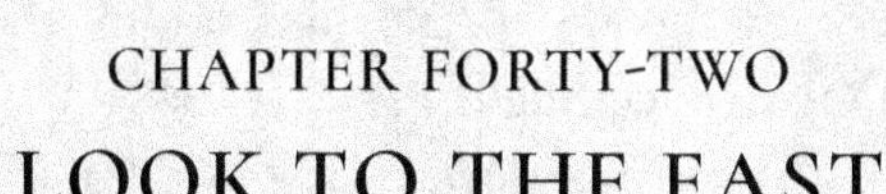

SAGE

Olexei looked to the sky with a peaceful smile, his expression serene despite the chaos around us.

"Those stars look like Dahlia," I observed, staring at the constellation forming above.

"That's because they are your mother," he responded with gentle certainty.

The idea that she had died had never crossed my mind before this moment. The idea that I might die, or Vespera might die, or that the realm would be crushed and we would lose—those thoughts were constantly at the front of all of my anxieties. Getting my mother back just to lose her so quickly had never felt like a real possibility, too cruel to contemplate.

"What do you mean?" I asked, though I didn't know why I said it.

I knew what he meant perfectly well. I understood it with crushing clarity. Still the words fell out of my mouth like water.

"She and I knew when we woke that our time had come to an end. We made peace with the idea that we were handing over the world to you and your sisters long ago. We had hoped to be around to guide you longer, to see you grow into your full power. We will still be able to watch you from the sky," Olexei explained with tranquil acceptance.

"Why are you talking to me like you're about to leave too?" I asked, panic creeping into my voice.

"I know that you look down on yourself harshly, but you should know that I'm so proud of you. Everyone makes mistakes—analyze them, feel them deeply, and learn moving forward. You are everything your mother and I hoped that you'd become," he declared with paternal warmth.

He kissed my forehead with tender affection and then moved past me with purposeful strides. He whistled sharply, and the group of deities turned to look at him with expectant faces. He never lost his smile, even while he gathered them to him for what I sensed was something final.

"It's time," he announced simply.

"Time for what? Fill me in!" I demanded, desperation making my voice crack.

The seasonal deities and Belladonna gathered around Olexei in a tight circle, their faces grave with determination.

Juniper, the Goddess of Wrath, was the last to join the crowd, her expression heavy with sorrow.

"We're going to bring her back. I told him that I needed more time, that I could find another way, but he told me there wasn't one that wouldn't cost us everything. We agreed to a middle ground—if we looked like we would lose, if Dahlia died, we would follow his plans," Juniper explained, moving forward as if I wasn't relevant to their decision, the same dismissive way Olexei had.

Vespera and Ruri fought Sahir and Yumi on one side of us, their battle fierce and desperate. Hesperia and an undead army clashed with Nikola on another side, the sound of steel and magic filling the air.

Was I supposed to leave them to do whatever they pleased

so that I could help my sisters? Would my sisters forgive me if I left Olexei alone to die for their plan?

Olexei tipped back a leather bag and poured the contents into his mouth. It looked as if he were consuming dust and ashes. Inola, the Goddess of Spring, Cyrus, the God of Summer, and Vero, the Goddess of Fall, surrounded Olexei in a protective triangle. Juniper tossed flower petals around them and lit them on fire with her magic. They all chanted words that I could not understand, ancient syllables that made the air itself vibrate.

Olexei's body burst into flames the same as the petals by the time they started their second chant. I watched in horror as I saw his heart fall away and leave only his life root floating in his chest cavity. There was nothing left of him but gleaming bone.

They chanted with increasing intensity until flesh grew back over the bones and the fire died down to embers. A heart formed over the life root and silver hair sprouted from the reformed skull.

Pink eyes looked back at me—familiar, beloved pink eyes.

They really had done it.

They had brought Astra back from the dead.

Meteors and stars came crashing down from the sky like divine rain, lighting up the battlefield with celestial fire.

A second set of stars formed in the sky beside Dahlia's constellation. They were brighter than the other stars by a considerable margin, pulsing with power.

Dahlia and Olexei were giving their lives away to save us all.

Caym's body was the next to convulse and release a beam of brilliant light. It shot inside of Astra's mouth and although I was curious what it meant, it was the same moment I realized with crushing finality that Caym was truly dead.

The seasonal deities rushed to cover Astra's body with

clothes, their movements urgent. She looked disoriented and unsure of anything until I followed her gaze to Kyra.

I knew there would be many more impossible choices to make before the sun rose and our battle was over.

One of those choices was mine to make. Ruri had lost Caym again, and I was standing around uselessly. Again.

I slammed my hands into the ground with violent force and sent vines rumbling toward the group fighting. They reached out and gripped the legs of Sahir and Yumi with crushing strength. They ripped them onto their knees in the dirt, sending up clouds of dust. I sent another wave to wrap around Nikola's massive serpentine form. It wouldn't stop them permanently; it wouldn't be enough to truly hurt them.

It would be enough to give my sisters a brief respite, for them to consider their next step or even take a precious breath.

Belladonna saw what I was doing, and she charged forward with Divala, the dragon guardian of Brontide. He had not followed Kyra when she switched sides—he swore an oath to protect the mortals and Kyra had sent them to be sacrifices. His white head was engraved with the symbol of the sun, gleaming with new power.

Belladonna opened her massive mouth, and instead of using the purple magic that she usually wielded, she released the pure white light of the moon. Divala followed and sent a beam of golden sun after hers, the two lights combining in brilliant harmony.

Olexei had given his position to Divala and Dahlia had given hers to Belladonna. They were the new sun God and moon Goddess, cosmic forces reborn.

It made me realize with stark clarity that although our duties, our sacred jobs, were permanent fixtures of the universe, they were things that had to be tended to by some-one. We didn't have to be the ones to do them forever. We weren't as important, in the end, as the position itself was. We were replaceable in the right situations, our egos meaningless compared to the greater good.

I had one last thing that I could contribute to the fight before I stood beside the rest of the deities grasping at threads. I called to the sprites that I had created in what felt like another lifetime, when the world was simpler.

Vespera had brought them back with Hesperia's help, but I was hardly grateful for it at the time. I had made even less time for them than I made to be thankful for the things that I was surrounded by. I should have seen that fatal flaw before the universe was ending around us.

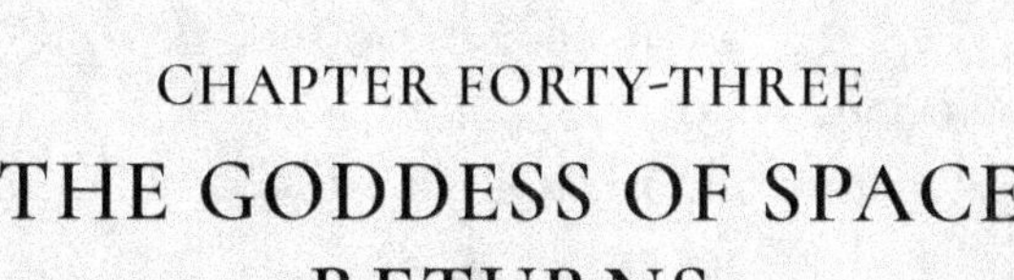

CHAPTER FORTY-THREE
THE GODDESS OF SPACE RETURNS

SAGE

"Do you really think that you can beat me?" Nikola roared, his voice shaking the very foundations of the earth.

He threw his massive head down and crashed his fangs into where I stood, the ground exploding around the impact. I tucked myself and rolled with hardly enough time left to dodge them, feeling the rush of air as death passed inches from my body. Ruri crashed lightning from the sky down into his serpentine form and did her best to pull rock formations from the ground and hurl them into his scaly hide.

We were only a distraction, buying precious time. We tried to pull his attention as best as we could so that Shivani could position herself to bleed him dry. She was getting into position while we tried to slow him down with everything we had. We already knew that just hitting him like we were doing meant nothing against his ancient power.

We also knew that we couldn't kill him—not in any traditional sense.

"I do think that we can beat you!" Hesperia yelled back at him with fierce defiance.

I threw pointed branches into his hide and tried to make him swallow poison leaves, watching him brush me off as if I were hardly pinching him. I attacked as if I believed we would win, but I did not feel the same unwavering confidence that Hesperia projected. I did not believe that we were going to emerge victorious.

Every direction that I could see was covered in blood and broken bodies. I still felt the oppressive heat from the volcano, but I felt nothing else meaningful. Not hope, not enthusiasm for battle. I hadn't even felt dread for the last few hours. I had felt fear days ago, but now there was only numbness.

I felt hopeless when I witnessed my father give his life to bring Astra back from death. I felt crushing sorrow when I learned my mother had died, too. I felt broken when I realized that Vespera was the only guardian left alive among us.

My body and mind could hardly process anything other than the relentless heat from the volcano anymore.

Everything that we had built was gone, reduced to ash and memory. The planet itself was damaged deeper than we had ever touched before. Nikola's celestial commanders had called down enough meteoric rocks from the sky to ensure that destruction was complete. Astra was back, so maybe she could match them on that front and call down her own celestial objects.

"Your mother couldn't succeed in stopping me. She couldn't succeed in making you four without help either," Nikola mused with cruel satisfaction.

"I don't care," I snapped with venom. "You enjoy living in the past, but news flash—that's long gone. Do you think that you can keep using that over us forever? Do you even see either of them here fighting you? Sure they didn't truly defeat you in their time. Maybe that was out of love for who you used to be. Did you consider that? Maybe they didn't want to hurt their brother. I don't have that same connection to you. I hardly have the same kind of connection to the deities that you keep bringing up as the one that you remember."

Shivani laid her hand on Nikola's massive tail with careful precision. When she lifted it, a stream of his ancient blood came with her touch. He yelped and flung himself around in genuine pain, the sound echoing across the battlefield.

I felt my heart jump and a smile wash across my face at the sight. It only held for a brief moment before reality crashed back. I recognized another emotion at the sight of his pain, and it was pure joy. I was happy to see him wither, even if only for a moment. It was only a moment, though. He slapped Shivani hard enough that her body hitting the ground was a blur of violent movement.

She didn't struggle on impact or gasp for breath. She laid utterly still, unnaturally motionless. Hesperia screamed and ran to check on her fallen sister. I knew it wasn't a good result when Hesperia let out a soul-wrenching scream.

"She's gone!" Hesperia cried out, her voice breaking.

My tongue was dry and tasted of ash and defeat. The moonlight mercifully hid Shivani's face from view.

I refused to be saddened over another death, refused to let despair claim me. I was going to take decisive action to get her back. If I were needed to nurture growing life, if Hesperia was in charge of souls before they went to an afterlife, then the two of us should be enough to bring her back.

I grabbed Hesperia's hand and pulled her toward the slice in the earth she had opened earlier. I led us both inside and used vines to search desperately for my sister's soul. Hesperia caught onto what I was trying to accomplish and she joined in the effort with determination.

I was sure that it was only a moment or two, but it felt like centuries that we searched through the void. Ruri, Astra, the dragons, the Nola—they held Nikola back while we pulled Shivani's soul from the depths of whatever the void truly was.

Hesperia shoved her soul back inside of her body with

force, and I held my hands over her eyes until my vines penetrated them, weaving life back into death.

What rules were there to say that we couldn't bring someone back if we wanted to? Dahlia and Olexei were gone and they had left us in charge of everything. Didn't that mean we made the rules now?

Shivani gasped for air and after several desperate gasps she let out unexpected laughter.

"We can do that!" she yelled with amazement. "We could have done something like that this whole time?"

I couldn't help but let out a laugh with her, the sound strange in the midst of destruction. It wasn't funny in any traditional sense. It wasn't a joke by any measure. I'm sure she didn't laugh because she found it truly amusing.

I think we both laughed because it was foolish—how absurd our situation had become. How could someone like Sahir have caused such an insurmountable issue for a group of girls that could raise the dead and deny Nikola his request to take life permanently?

He didn't feel so powerful any longer, his mystique cracking. He didn't seem like such a life-ending primordial being. He seemed like he only had one skill, and it was using others to appear strong.

He opened his mouth and a forked tongue hissed out menacingly. A haunting tune followed and body after body shivered and twitched in unnatural reanimation across the battlefield.

He was starting the cycle again, raising his own army. We needed to end it once and for all.

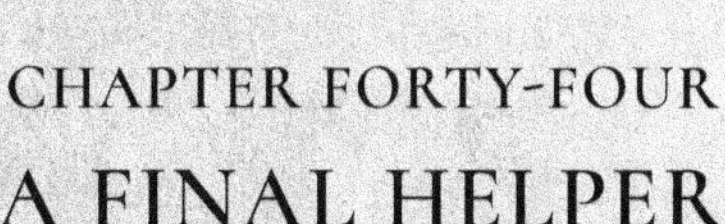

CHAPTER FORTY-FOUR
A FINAL HELPER

RURI

I watched the slice in the ground from Hesperia with wide, unblinking eyes. A man with a weathered beard and white eyes looked back at me from the depths. He tapped the thin layer that kept us apart with patient persistence. I didn't understand why soul after soul climbed through with Hesperia's permission, but he didn't follow them. He waited, he watched with ancient patience. He motioned for me, as if asking permission or perhaps assistance.

He acted as if he needed my help lifting him out of the void, and I wanted to deny him at first, but I wasn't sure that I'd stick with my refusal. He looked harmless enough, frail even. He was thin and pale as parchment. He looked as if he once had the commanding build of a god, a presence that demanded respect. He was just an old man now, diminished by time. He did resemble my mother in his facial features, and that similarity caused the largest part of my hesitation.

No one that resembled my family had turned out to be on the side I also wanted to occupy.

He knocked again on the barrier and waved at me with increasing urgency.

Did it matter anymore? We were either dead soon, or destined to become the most powerful beings left to exist.

What difference would one more ally make?

I lowered my hand past the thin layer that separated our worlds and grabbed onto his arm with firm resolve. There was surprising resistance when I tried to pull him through, as if the void itself didn't want to release him, but Jeb reached in and grabbed my arm and helped me lift. The resistance vanished after that, as if his touch had broken some ancient spell. The two of us lifted him out and he greeted us with a grateful smile.

"Who are you?" I asked, suspicion coloring my voice.

I stuck close to Jeb as if he were my personal guard.

"I am the Blood Weaver," he replied with a respectful bow.

He held one pink eye and a second white, creating an unsettling but somehow familiar gaze. Black hair so long it looked like a curtain framed his ancient face.

"Why were you trapped there?" I demanded.

"Is this the time for lengthy explanations? Maybe we should start with the fact that I can help you get them back," he suggested with urgency.

"Them?" I asked, my heart beginning to race with hope.

"Hold out your hand for me, and the other to his," he instructed, pointing to Jeb.

I did as he asked, because I knew he meant Caym and the others. The weaver reached into the void and used the same blood magic that Shivani wielded. It made my heart skip a beat—I hadn't seen anyone use that magic but Shivani and Helia.

He pulled Coy from the void first, and he emerged whole and breathing. Already in a body and just as shocked to see me as I was to see him alive. Koa was next, and he lay on the ground for a moment before taking the time to look around with wonder and confusion.

My heart raced like a wild thing and I gripped Jeb's hand tighter, anchoring myself to reality.

He pulled Caym last, and my husband rested on his knees for only a few breaths before jumping up and lifting me into the air with joyous strength.

"I thought I lost you forever," I cried against his shoulder.

"I thought that I had to watch you give up on everything," he replied, gripping me as if he didn't believe I was real.

"Now that is an interesting twist," Nikola mused with dark amusement.

I opened my eyes to see the Blood Weaver watching Nikola with a knowing smile. Nikola transformed himself back into human form and walked toward us with predatory grace.

"My big brother took a page from my book. He used the sisters to come back without telling the full truth," Nikola observed, shaking his head in mock amusement.

"I never lied to them. I helped create them, I was banished for my efforts. Now I'm back to help them get rid of you permanently," the Blood Weaver declared with quiet conviction.

"So mighty you believe yourself to be," Nikola taunted, pointing dismissively.

"If he helps us kill you, then I don't care who he is today," I called out with fierce determination.

"How did you manage to return?" Nikola asked with genuine curiosity.

"I tethered myself to Caym with his blood. He acted as an anchor to the living world," the Blood Weaver admitted without shame.

I furrowed my brows, wanting to feel upset by the idea of someone using my husband, but I still had my hands on Caym. He was back, solid and real. I owed the Blood Weaver for that miracle.

"Enough talking," I declared.

I shot a strike of purple lightning into Nikola with vicious intent. Then a second strike for good measure. Sage joined me in the coordinated assault. She gripped Nikola's feet and turned them to solid stone. Shivani pulled blood from his eyes in crimson streams, and Hesperia raised warrior after warrior to attack him in endless waves.

Astra raised herself into the sky and called down flaming rocks like divine judgment. She lit up every star that shook with life and unleashed them upon him. One by one stars hit the dirt and transformed into gods ready for battle.

Sage left Nikola's feet as immobile stone and we all ran from him as molten rocks pounded his flesh mercilessly. His body lay deformed in a crater filled with fire and destruction. Shivani was the one that didn't relent. She kept the blood draining from him even while his flesh melted off the bone like candle wax.

Belladonna and Divala used their combined beams of sun and moonlight to keep Nikola pinned down. Jeb jumped into the hole with fearless determination and laid both hands on him. Nikola screamed and begged with genuine terror. The sound sent shivers down my spine—I didn't understand what Jeb was doing to him, but I hoped it would be something nightmarish.

I jumped into the hole too, and there was nothing left to protect his chest anymore. The heat that surrounded him felt hardly a few degrees warmer than Ashbell's natural temperature. I grabbed his heart and my sisters pulled me out with desperate urgency.

Koa held Yumi on her knees beside Caym who restrained Sahir with iron grip.

"Jeb, do you have any obsidian?" I called out.

He looked up at me and left the smoking hole immediately. He was quick to give me the dark stone, and I was even quicker to shove Nikola's heart and life roots inside it like a prison.

Shivani dropped her arms when there wasn't so much as a drop of blood left to drain from him.

I tossed water from my hands into the crater, and Nikola was no longer there. He was nothing but memory and ash.

"You girls really are stronger than even I had imagined possible," the Blood Weaver observed from behind us, his voice filled with genuine admiration.

CHAPTER FORTY-FIVE

SPLITTING THE END

RURI

There were countless tasks to handle moving forward. The realm looked worse than it had at any time I had seen it in any of the lifetimes I had lived, scarred beyond recognition.

Astra stood alone in front of us all and demonstrated what it truly meant to be the Goddess of Space. She sorted the stars into organized piles in the sky and flung the ones without souls in different directions with casual grace. The sky would be filled and bright when the sun set again, a tapestry of light. She moved celestial bodies around above us as if they were only little pieces of sand to be casually tossed about between her fingers.

When she was confident that she had all of the souls sorted from the stars, she ripped them from their place in the darkness and sent them falling to us like divine rain. They crashed into the ground with tremendous force and sparked golden light on impact. One by one, deities stood from the dust and debris. They were disoriented and dirty, but they were gloriously alive.

As Astra finished her cosmic work, I felt nauseous and

dizzy for a moment. I felt as though the world flipped and spun for only a heartbeat, reality shifting around us.

When the unsettling feeling wore off, I felt at ease for the first time in ages. As if it might be the last time I had to feel awful before we could start fresh.

Caym stood beside me while we watched the new, and biggest constellation dance through the sky. Even with the sun rising to block them out, the two bright forms danced as if they were the happiest they'd ever been.

The Seere that had survived in Ashbell helped guide the newly resurrected deities inside of the temples. They'd have a lot to catch up on after their time among the stars.

"They couldn't have had a better ending," Caym observed with quiet satisfaction.

"Neither could we," I smiled in return, meaning every word.

"I think I could improve on ours. We smell absolutely awful," he laughed, wrinkling his nose.

"We have a few things left to do, but I think we can wash off together afterward," I winked, feeling lighter than I had in months.

I'd never be able to put words to the way I felt moving forward. I'd never allow him to leave my side again, not for any reason. It would also take me a long time to sleep again without seeing his body laid motionless against the rocks, that image burned into my memory.

It would take us all a long time to adjust to peace.

Sahir and Yumi still sat on their knees in the dirt. They were wrapped in every form of magical protection we could think of, layered like armor. They weren't getting free. The fate chains were realistically enough, but the extra support made us feel better about our security.

"I've thought about this moment a lot," I declared, approaching Sahir.

"Please, spare me the self-righteous speech," Sahir replied, rolling her eyes with practiced disdain. "I'd rather endure anything else."

"I went over handfuls of options," I continued slowly, savoring each word. "I considered your daughter and the way you left her chained to the bottom of the ocean. I just know she has to be cold and lonely. I thought to myself, 'what would match that perfectly?' It hit me! Astra is back!"

I moved closer to her and held her chin firmly in my hand. "Hesperia made these just for you."

I threaded the fate hooks through her eyelids as slowly as I could, taking my time. I felt the pinch of skin followed by the release of pressure once the hook was through completely. I used the thread to weave braids in her hair with artistic precision. Sahir was unable to blink now—it would remain that way forever. She tried to convince me with her silence and stoic expression that my efforts were useless.

I didn't believe it because I saw the liquid forming in her eyes, tears she couldn't shed.

Astra took her body into the sky, high enough that if we weren't deities, we wouldn't have been able to see Sahir hooked by the wrists with more fate hooks. We wouldn't have been able to watch while Astra connected massive chains to them and bound her to two separate planets for eternity.

But we could see it all. We saw every detail of her punishment. I was glad for it—it brought me happiness, closure, and a sense of justice served.

Caym handed me a fate box that matched the one Orla, the Goddess of Night, had spent night after night trapped inside.

Yumi struggled violently before I even opened my mouth. Her face spoke of dawning realization and terror.

"I thought that this was the best fate for you. I can't kill you, but I can hand over your position and lock you away forever," I explained, holding open the box.

"Stop!" Yumi struggled and flailed desperately. "I was

being controlled! I never would have hurt anyone if it was up to me! It was Nikola! It was his songs! They made me do terrible things!" She pointed behind me to the Blood Weaver with desperate accusation. "If you don't do the same to him, you'll regret it in time! You'll regret all of this!"

"He helped us bring Caym back," I replied simply, unmoved by her pleas.

I pulled her heart out with steady hands and let the box pull her inside like a vacuum. I locked the chains and her eye pressed itself into the small slot she was given to see through. I handed the box to Caym and gave the heart to Ryujin the dragon to consume. He would become the next God of Starlight, even after he discovered Sina's betrayal. He had remained loyal to Caym.

I was confident in my choice.

The seasonal deities stood in a line waiting for our last bit of business before we could put all of this behind us. Nikola's heart was split into four equal pieces—spring, summer, fall, winter. They would guard the fragments left of him and ensure he could never return to torment anyone.

One by one, they opened their mouths and I fed them the pieces with ceremonial solemnity. My sisters sealed Nikola deep inside of his new prison with layers of protective magic. The dragons seemed to be strong enough to handle the monumental task because they hardly noticed a difference when he was sealed away inside of them.

Our realm would be safe and sound at last. We would finally have a chance at the peace we had wanted so desperately, fought so hard to achieve.

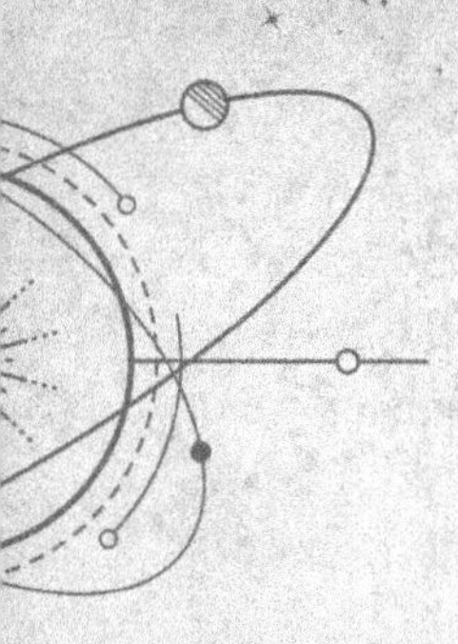

CHAPTER FORTY-SIX

THE PRISONER

ASTRA

I took each step to the dungeon as slowly as I could, my feet heavy with dread. It was hard for me to believe what I was told when I hardly believed what I saw with my own eyes. I didn't take seriously the kind of deep hate that Kyra held in her heart.

I took in every scratch on the obsidian walls, studying the scars of violence. Every nail that sat inside of the wall had nothing hanging from it, empty and purposeless.

I took in anything that I needed to, desperately avoiding the thoughts I had to face once I reached the bottom of the stairwell.

Kyra was already in my sight before I was ready to see her, her presence hitting me like a physical blow. Her dark blue curls were a tangled mess of neglect. She leaned into the wall from the corner of her cell, her posture one of complete defeat. She sat on the cold floor even though she had a bed and a chair to choose from.

She noticed me, but hardly moved in acknowledgment. It was only her eyes that shifted over to me with weary recognition. Bright green eyes sat around sunken lids that spoke of sleepless nights. Kyra was clearly exhausted beyond measure. As tired as she was, she was also obviously hungry because of how much weight she had lost, her frame gaunt and fragile. I wasn't sure how she had picked up a weapon at all during the battle.

She looked as if she had given up entirely on everything. I walked to the bars that separated us and sat down heavily. I didn't want to face her directly, couldn't bear to. I needed to talk without seeing the way she looked, without confronting the physical evidence of her fall. I couldn't believe that she had turned on us as it was. Trying to believe it while seeing her in this broken state was even harder.

"How are you feeling?" she asked, her voice cutting through my thoughts.

Her voice was dry and low, parched from disuse. Another stab to my heart that was already bleeding. Sitting in a space where I felt loyalty to one person that I loved meant betrayal to the other was excruciating.

I knew what she did was wrong, but I couldn't say with certainty what I would have done if the tables had been turned. Would I have had the strength to sit firmly on the side of good without slipping into darkness? I thought that I would have. I held well when I lost Ruri, but who could have predicted my choices if I lost both of them?

Could I truly pass judgment on her when I wasn't sure of my own moral certainty?

"I'm doing all right. It's strange to be back among the living. The afterlife that I was in was dark and empty. Nothing like what Caym runs in Merripen," I replied, indulging her small talk.

"I'm sorry you had to go through that," she murmured with what sounded like genuine regret.

"Why did you do it?" I asked, my voice barely above a whisper. "What made you think it would be worth it?"

"I didn't think clearly," she whispered back. "You don't understand grief until you're drowning in it."

"I don't understand grief?" I spoke out loud but not to her, incredulous at the statement.

"That's not what I meant," Kyra clarified, moving closer to the bars.

The sounds of her chains filled the air with metallic music that made my skin crawl.

"We lost good people, great deities who deserved better. They might have lived if you had stayed on the right side of the fight. Maybe Nikola would have struggled more if you hadn't handed him a race of people that Ruri blessed beyond any other. She did that for you, you know?" I sat straighter, finding strength in my anger.

Maybe this was what I needed to help me see straight through the fog of emotion.

"She may have done that, but I didn't ask for it," Kyra replied, her voice growing firmer with defiance.

"What did you ask for? What would have made you happier? It wasn't me, clearly. It wasn't the idea of our future with Ekron. You never stopped to consider that Ruri needed to hide you for your own protection. That if Yumi knew of you and the potential that could have been inside of you, you would never have been allowed to stay in Brontide safely."

"It should have been my choice to make. She could have explained this to me and let me decide my own fate. That's what I wanted. I wanted your focus to be on me, and not her," Kyra admitted, her hands gripping the bars beside me.

"You wouldn't have been happy until she died," I accused.

"If you had just said that you loved me more than her—"

"Do you think that's fair to me? To make me have to decide that?" I interrupted. "Would you have demanded the same about Ekron? When he took my attention too? We found a way to bring him back, you know. We are so close to the dreams we were supposed to share together. You gave up on them when they were practically on our doorstep." I held back tears that threatened to spill.

"We can still have them, Astra, we can still live those dreams. Let me out of here and I can show you," Kyra pleaded desperately. "Let me out and I'll prove to you that I learned from my mistakes."

"Did you? Will you speak to Ruri with respect? Will you sit down with her and have a real conversation? Can you prove that I should trust you again?" I asked, though I already knew the answer.

Kyra was silent and I knew what her lack of response meant. I stood and brushed my leather pants off before I cleared my throat with finality.

"It doesn't matter, Kyra. I came to say goodbye," I admitted, the words heavy as stones.

"Goodbye?" She scrambled to her feet in panic.

"Yes, goodbye. Even if I wanted to save you, I can't. It's not up to me anymore. I only wanted to find some reasoning or peace in this. I think I have it now. Revenge was the most important thing to you."

"What's going to happen to me?" Her voice trembled the same as my own, fear making us mirror each other.

"The Blood Weaver will be here soon. You were given to him in exchange for assistance in winning against Nikola."

"You're okay with this but not what I chose to do?" she yelled, hysteria creeping into her voice.

"I'm not okay with either situation. Both sides are going to take time to understand and process. I think that yours hurts worse if I'm being honest. You were supposed to be my partner for life. Your shoulder was one that I counted on even when I wasn't around. I was so sure that we shared one mind, one set of morals and goals. Seeing that I was wrong about that..." I paused, gathering my composure. "It's heartbreaking in a way that I hadn't felt yet, and I have felt a lot of pain." I reached for the necklace and ripped the chain with sudden violence. "Here."

I grabbed her hand through the bars and tucked the broken jewelry into her palm. I didn't want it anymore. It was a promise we made to each other that only I had kept.

"I can come back later," Quade announced quietly from the doorway.

"What is he going to do with me, Astra?" Her body and voice shook with uncontrolled panic.

"I haven't asked him," I admitted with painful honesty.

"It will be painless, I can assure you," Quade promised with gentle certainty.

I nodded, unable to speak. I didn't want to see or hear any of what was coming. Quade understood with only a look and he stepped to the side so that I could leave.

I did it at a speed that I didn't have when I entered, my feet moving with urgent purpose. I made it to the top of the stairs when I heard Kyra's screams for forgiveness echoing from below.

Even if I wanted to give it to her, her fate after the forgiveness was out of my hands.

CHAPTER FORTY-SEVEN

REBUILD NOT RELIVE

HESPERIA

"A little to the left," Coy called from far behind me, his voice carrying across the expanse of sky.

I pushed the smaller floating island a bit further, feeling the familiar tingle of magic flow through my fingertips. The waterfall landed perfectly in the sky, its crystal cascade catching the starlight. The shimmering water would eventually help aid in rain for the mortals below.

"Perfect!" Coy shouted, and I could hear the grin in his voice.

Deimos had been missing since Nikola charged on Ashbell. We had sent soldiers to find him, but their searches yielded nothing. None of us trusted him unattended—I certainly didn't. I refused to believe that he had seen the light and become a changed man, not after what I'd witnessed. He had left my realm in shambles. It was a disgusting and barren wasteland when I returned, the very air thick with decay and neglect.

Dark and jagged the islands had become. Nothing like I

had left them. The sight had made my heart clench with a mixture of fury and grief.

But my home was slowly moving back to what I remembered it to be. The sky was painted in deep purples and midnight blues, filled with the shimmer of thousands of stars that twinkled like scattered diamonds. Astra assisted happily, her magic weaving alongside mine. She needed the distractions, and I loved having her around. Her presence brought a warmth that had been absent for too long.

Clouds floated their way between my floating islands, soft and billowing. The islands themselves were now filled with lush shrubbery, and Sage had contributed mushrooms from the Erebus caves—strange, luminescent fungi that pulsed with an otherworldly glow. They had freed Orla, and she quietly moved back to the caves where she belonged.

Other islands held tall trees covered in pink leaves that rustled in the gentle breeze. They were a gift from Ruri and the Garden of Sunlight that still held Emon in Semper, their petals catching the light like silk.

"Are you happy with it?" Coy asked, settling beside me.

"I love it." I smiled, drinking in the beauty of what we had rebuilt together.

Nola held the two of us up with steady grace, and they carried us back to the main islands. Caym had been kind enough to let me keep the dragons I had bonded with while we fought. They had been the greatest blessing to enter Cosima, their loyalty unwavering.

Astra already waited for us on the main island, her silhouette elegant against the twilight. She stood with a smile on the edge of a glittering pond that led to a waterfall, the water's surface reflecting the stars above.

"You finally decided to show up," she teased, though her eyes sparkled with affection.

All four seasonal deities, two gods, and two dragons stood waiting as well. Quade stood with my sisters, and the sound that filled the air was the best I had heard in years. Laughter rang out pure and clear, a melody I had almost forgotten existed.

"Are we ready?" I asked, my heart quickening with anticipation.

"I've been ready for a long time," Astra replied, her voice soft but determined.

Ruri carefully placed a dragon egg in the middle of the water and backed up, her movements reverent. The egg was smooth and pearl-white, emanating a subtle warmth. The rest of us surrounded it, forming a circle, and pushed our magic inside. I felt the power flow from each of us, different yet harmonious, weaving together like threads in a tapestry.

Quade held the broken pieces of Sahir's heart and Ekron's, fragments that still pulsed with residual energy. He pushed them inside the egg with a kind of magic that I did not recognize—something ancient and powerful that made the air itself hum.

We were still learning about him and what his place in everything really was, but he had helped us all so well that we —or at least I—didn't question him much. Trust had to start somewhere.

The egg shook violently and sank into the pond of water with barely a splash. Astra knelt down, her knees pressing into the soft moss at the water's edge, and placed the missing piece of Sin's soul she held in her charm into the water. The fragment glowed briefly before dissolving into the depths. It was Quade who combined them all, his magic binding the disparate pieces into something whole.

He stepped back after, exhaustion evident in the set of his shoulders, and Ruri used her magic to let us see inside the egg. Through the translucent shell, we glimpsed a small baby's shape with a beating heart, strong and steady and alive.

"We really did it," Astra choked out, tears streaming down

her cheeks. She turned and hugged Ruri tightly. "I knew that you'd keep your promise."

Coy wrapped his arms around my waist from behind, and my smile grew until I thought my face might split from joy.

"Are you sure you want to stay in Cosima?" I asked, leaning back against his solid warmth. "You'll be stuck on leaf duty."

"Mm, that does sound awful," he murmured against my ear, his breath tickling my skin. "Maybe I'll ask Koa if I can move in with him instead."

I laughed despite myself. "There's no place I'd rather be than helping you sort souls here. We have an egg to guard, after all. It'll be our responsibility to ensure he grows well for Astra."

"That does sound perfect," I agreed, watching as the others continued to marvel at what we had accomplished.

I couldn't have asked for more. After everything we had endured, everything we had lost, this moment felt like the beginning of something beautiful.

CHAPTER FORTY-EIGHT
THE LAND OF THE DEAD

RURI

Caym handed Jeb a small red ribbon with the widest smile I had ever seen grace his weathered features. Jeb tied it around the wrist of his new wife with trembling fingers, and she mirrored the gesture, her own hands steady and sure.

"The two of you are now bonded for life," Koa announced, his voice carrying across the gathered crowd with warmth and authority.

Applause erupted in a thunderous roar that seemed to shake the very ground beneath us. Malina clapped enthusiastically from my arms, though she only understood that everyone was clapping, so she needed to as well. Her tiny hands created the softest patting sounds. We had been able to bring her back in a dragon egg, and her growth had been swift since she hadn't needed to be pieced together like the others. She was reborn as the Goddess of Joy, and it showed in every giggle and bright-eyed smile.

Caym held Dina's hand, and the two of them stood proudly beside the bride and groom. Dina had been reborn as the Goddess of Fertility, her presence already bringing a subtle bloom to the flowers around her feet. Instead of clapping, she waved at me with unbridled excitement, her green pigtails bouncing with each movement.

She had been the most excited little girl over getting to stand with Uncle Jeb while he married. Malina had been too shy to join her, preferring instead to sit on my rounded belly where Lex grew and kicked. He would be the new God of Storms, and I could already feel the electric energy he carried.

Jeb and his wife walked down the aisle, their steps synchronized and unhurried. Malina slipped from my arms to toss flower petals in front of them, the soft pink blooms creating a fragrant carpet. Her little pink dress dragged behind her while she pranced, completely absorbed in her important task.

We had held their bonding ceremony in Merripen after we built them a new home—a cozy cottage surrounded by gardens that would flourish under Dina's influence.

"I think it went well!" Astra declared from beside me, her voice bright with satisfaction.

"I'm still adjusting to not being on guard," I admitted, my shoulders unconsciously tensing as I scanned the crowd out of habit.

"Me too," she agreed with a rueful laugh. "I think a part of me will always be nervous someone will crash important events."

She paused mid-sentence to wave enthusiastically at Ekron, who waddled behind the wedding party with determined steps. He still clutched the tiny silk pillow where the bonding ribbons had rested during the ceremony, his pink eyes practically glowing with pride at his successful ring-bearing duties.

"He looks just like you," I smiled, noting the way his chin tilted up with the same stubborn dignity Astra carried.

I walked out after the newlyweds and followed the crowd to the long tables groaning under the weight of food. The Nola had ditched their usual dark cloaks for crisp dress vests and tailored pants, and they served drinks with toothless grins that warmed my heart. The sight of their joy was something I would never tire of.

One day, Caym and I would have the same ceremony, and it was my deepest hope that my sisters would be ready to join us. I wanted to wait until we could all celebrate together. We had missed so many milestones as it was—too many years stolen by war and separation.

"Say ahh," Caym murmured as he pushed a perfectly ripe strawberry between my lips, the sweet juice bursting across my tongue.

"These are so good!" Quade mumbled through a mouth full of food as he worked his way down the line of tables, sampling everything with the enthusiasm of someone discovering flavor for the first time.

"You should try them with cake," I suggested, licking strawberry juice from my bottom lip.

"I will!" Quade nodded with eyes as wide as saucers, already reaching for a plate.

Caym took the hint and fed me a bite of vanilla cake before he kissed me, his lips sweet with frosting. Our girls immediately pulled him away by his hands, their matching green ponytails swishing as they dragged him toward the food tables. Ekron followed with boundless enthusiasm, his little legs working overtime to keep up.

"He looks good as a father," Astra observed, her voice soft with something that might have been wistfulness.

I agreed wholeheartedly. It was everything we had always wanted—this peaceful scene, this simple joy. I couldn't recall a time when we'd had to question whether it was possible. A quiet realm filled with children and dragons looked perfect for both of us. The Nola doted on the children even more than we did, though I didn't voice that observation aloud.

A shadow of guilt passed through me as I thought of my selfish choices when it came to Kyra. The only part I truly regretted was how it had affected Astra. I had robbed her of the chance to decide her own future, and the weight of that knowledge sat heavy in my chest. I hated the idea, and I hated even more that my happiness might feel like salt in her wounds.

"You look good as a mother," I offered quietly, hoping she could hear the sincerity in my words.

Her smile brightened, genuine and warm. "It's thanks to all of you."

"How are you doing? Really?" I pressed gently.

Astra maintained her smile as she watched Ekron playfully push against Caym's legs, demanding attention.

"I'm good," she nodded perhaps a few too many times. "Sometimes it's hard, but I'm good. We all had our choices to make, and we have to live with them."

I wasn't entirely sure if she was trying to convince herself or me, but I let the moment settle between us.

"How is Orest?" I shifted the topic to safer ground.

"It's doing wonderfully!" Her happiness became genuine with this subject, her whole posture brightening. "I'm so glad I get to stay there, and I don't have to disguise myself as Thann anymore. The students are thriving, and we'll have another group of dragon guardians arriving soon."

"Kids are fed," Caym announced with a smug smile as he rejoined us, looking slightly disheveled but thoroughly content.

"Dance?" He held out his hand to Astra, and she accepted with a graceful curtsy.

I let out a deep breath of relief, feeling the last knot of tension leave my shoulders, and joined my sisters and our friends in celebration. For the first time in longer than I could remember, the future felt bright and full of possibilities.

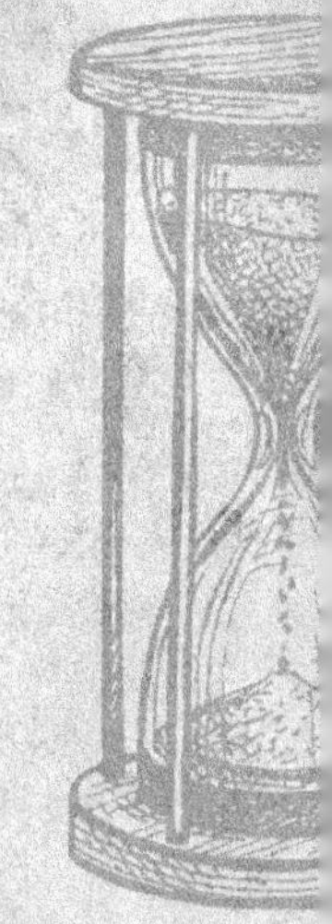

CHAPTER FORTY-NINE

THE RULER OF MORTALS

SHIVANI

"Be honest with us. We are willing to meet any need," Koa encouraged, his voice gentle but firm as he leaned forward across the worn wooden table.

"We need everything if we're being honest," a weathered man replied, his calloused hands fidgeting with the brim of his hat. Dark circles shadowed his eyes, speaking of sleepless nights and endless worry.

"There are a lot of children still, and not a lot of homes. They eat as if they don't understand they don't have anywhere to go back to," another man agreed, his voice thick with the weight of responsibility he carried for the orphaned young ones.

"As they should," I interjected firmly. "If food is what you need, then more food you will have. No child should ever have to ration their meals out of fear."

"I stayed so that none of you would need to eat as if you wouldn't eat again," Koa continued, his voice remaining soft despite the passion behind his words. "I want to see you all thrive. I understand that there is some resentment toward us, and I don't blame you for it. I wish our losses in the battle had been fewer as well. I can't turn back the curse of the shifter either, but I can promise you a rebuilt kingdom. Food, clothing, safety—whatever you need."

The men crowded around the table exchanged silent looks, their weathered faces etched with cautious hope and lingering doubt. They had refused to ask us for any help since we returned, their pride wounded and their trust shattered. We had instead focused on rebuilding the local shops of Sephtis, but even the families that relied on their small stores remained hesitant to accept our aid.

They feared we would eventually ask for their sons or husbands as payment for our generosity. I couldn't blame them for that fear—it was what they had known before. The difference was that I had already gotten back everything I had lost. They weren't so fortunate. Some mortals we had been able to bring back through magic and divine intervention. Others had been too shattered, their souls too fractured, and all we could offer was the guarantee of a peaceful afterlife. It didn't bring them the same comfort as having their loved ones to hold, to hear their laughter echoing through their homes again.

"With my word as the head of Shadows of Justice, I swear that we won't leave until every one of you has a warm bed and a full belly!" Aero proclaimed, rising to his feet with such conviction that his chair scraped loudly against the stone floor.

"Yeah!" Fennic slapped the table enthusiastically and jumped up as well, his energy infectious. "We can build for days! Weeks if we need to!"

Fennic was someone we had been able to bring back, and he hadn't taken two breaths before asking what the next task was. Meeting Aero had changed him for the better, giving him purpose and direction he'd never had before. The two of them had built a second location with us so that the Shadows of Justice had a proper base of operations.

"We will take you at your word then," the first man nodded slowly, some of the tension finally leaving his shoulders.

"We will send food today and gather supplies to start building at first light," I promised, meaning every word.

The group made their way out, their footsteps echoing in the large room. Most of them were still apprehensive, glancing back over their shoulders as if expecting us to change our minds or reveal some hidden agenda.

"We can call on everyone else for help," Aero suggested once we were alone.

"There are several dragons already working on the land," Koa explained, rubbing his temples where a headache was clearly forming. "They've been turning patches of sand into fertile soil we can actually grow crops from. It wouldn't have been possible without Juniper's earth magic guiding the process."

"I think it looks weird, but it's not my place to say," Fennic held his hands up defensively, clearly trying to avoid another debate about aesthetics.

"No one will care what it looks like when they have fresh food on their tables," I interjected with a slight smile.

"Fine, fine. I just think aesthetics matter too," Fennic grumbled as he stood. "People need beauty in their lives, not just sustenance."

Aero murmured something to him as they both headed for the door, probably agreeing to discuss it later when tensions weren't so high.

"I think it looks wonderful," I reassured Koa once we were alone.

"I haven't really thought about what it looks like," Koa admitted with a frown, suddenly self-conscious.

"I know, but in case you worry about it later—it looks good. So will the new housing areas. The market street looks better than it did the first time around, and the people are being taught how to carve in stone as well. It may be moving slowly, but it is moving forward." I leaned across the table to offer him an encouraging smile, hoping to ease some of the burden I could see weighing on his shoulders.

He chuckled, the sound warming something deep in my chest. "I can't believe that now you're the one teaching me to have patience."

"I need to leave you with something to think about while I'm away," I teased gently.

"I'll miss you," he admitted, reaching across the table. I took his outstretched hand, feeling the calluses from sword work and the warmth of his skin.

We were still working on getting closer, still learning how to navigate this new relationship between us. Things between the two of us moved the same way Sephtis was being rebuilt— slow and steady, with careful attention to every detail.

"I'll be back soon," I promised, squeezing his fingers. "The vampires need much less help than even I anticipated. The Queen of Brisa is all too happy to have them join her kingdom. The witches and vampires haven't even needed a single suggestion that I've offered. They know exactly what they want their new kingdom to look like, and I'm just happy to know that they survived to have one."

"Be safe while you travel," he urged, his thumb brushing across my knuckles.

"I will. There's not much to worry about now except maybe a wild animal or two," I laughed, though we both knew the roads held more dangers than I was admitting.

CHAPTER FIFTY

THE REALM OF THE GODS

SAGE

We had changed the throne room entirely, transforming it into something that felt more like home than a place of intimidation. Two thrones of gleaming gold and midnight black velvet sat side by side, their surfaces catching the light that streamed down from above. We had painted the room in different shades of blue—from the deep sapphire of ocean depths to the soft powder blue of morning sky. The most dramatic change was opening the roof by replacing it with crystal-clear glass so that we could watch the ever-changing canvas of the heavens above. It had quickly become one of my favorite rooms in all of Semper.

"How were the visits?" Vesim asked, settling into the chair across from our thrones with the easy familiarity of someone who belonged here.

"The girl I hired for the bookstore absolutely loves her job," Vespera replied with a fond smile. "She has already expanded the place significantly, and if she keeps going at this pace, I may need to hire a second employee."

"Hmm. Imagine what can be accomplished when you

actually try to sell books instead of using the store as a front to read in peace," Vesim teased, her eyes sparkling with mischief.

"She still uses it as an excuse to read half the day, so she's perfect for the job," I chimed in with a grin. "I also found out that the Daughters of Steel are the ones being paid to handle the deliveries."

"How are they adjusting to the new order of things?" Vesim inquired, her expression growing more serious.

"I think they're having a harder time believing I'm actually a Goddess than they are with the change in ranks," I admitted with a rueful laugh. "We never really cared about hierarchies anyway—we were more concerned with getting the job done."

Vesim listened carefully, but I could tell she was eager to share what had transpired while Vespera and I were away. She had done an amazing job maintaining order in Semper, and the fact that she was the only mortal living in the realm of the gods spoke to how much we trusted her judgment.

"The last of the displaced deities have been settled into their new quarters," she reported with obvious satisfaction. "We've finished rebuilding all of the damage that was done during the conflict. Juniper was kind enough to spread some of the soil from her garden throughout the Garden of Sunlight, and it worked wonders—the golden fruits have come back to life, more vibrant than ever."

"It seems we're finally done with the major reconstruction then," I smiled, feeling a weight lift from my shoulders.

"There's one more thing," Vesim continued, her expression darkening slightly. "Quade has requested access to the Sunlight Garden. He didn't elaborate on his reasons."

I glanced toward Vespera, but she only offered a confused shrug, clearly as puzzled as I was.

"What do you think about his request?" I asked Vesim, trusting her instincts.

"I'm not sure it's a wise choice," she replied carefully. She paused, as if wrestling with whether to continue, then seemed to come to a decision. "When he was here before, he caused the fruits he could touch from outside the garden to wither and die."

"It could be a symptom of who he is, like what happens with Caym's presence," Vespera offered, though her tone suggested she was trying to convince herself as much as us.

"It could be," Vesim agreed, though her voice lacked conviction.

"Thank you for being honest with us," I murmured, reaching over to pat her shoulder. "Your perspective is invaluable."

I seemed to be the only one who felt truly uncomfortable with Quade's presence. Everyone else appeared convinced that he was helpful and genuinely grateful to be free again. I wanted to hope for the best, but something about the sheer number of secrets he insisted on keeping made unease coil in my stomach like a serpent.

I tried not to dwell on my concerns for too long. If none of my sisters were worried, perhaps I was being overly cautious. Still, the feeling persisted, a nagging voice in the back of my mind that refused to be silenced.

"So, my queen of the gods," Vespera drawled playfully as she reached for my hand, her fingers intertwining with mine, "what's left on our agenda for today?"

"We need to check on the rebuilding progress, meet with the newly arrived deities, then we have a meeting with our siblings. There's also a blessing ceremony to perform at Orest," I counted off on my free fingers, the list feeling manageable for once.

"Is there time for a kiss anywhere in that busy schedule?" Vespera fluttered her lashes at me with exaggerated flirtation.

"I think I can make time for one," I smiled, my heart warming at her playful expression.

Vespera leaned in to kiss me, but the moment our lips were

about to meet, a strange zap of electricity shot through me like lightning. The sensation was wrong—foreign and cold—and it sent my stomach plummeting toward my feet. I opened my eyes, expecting to see that she had felt it too, but instead she appeared as a haze. Her form blurred and glitched for a terrifying moment, like a reflection in disturbed water, before everything felt like it rewound itself.

"Is there time for a kiss anywhere in that busy schedule?" Vespera fluttered her lashes at me with the exact same expression, the exact same tone.

Hadn't she just asked me that? My heart began to race as confusion clouded my thoughts.

I blinked hard, trying to clear my vision, and told myself I must need more rest. But deep down, a chill was spreading through my bones that had nothing to do with fatigue.

CHAPTER FIFTY-ONE

THE GLITCH

RURI

I paced the garden of our cabin in Merripen, my bare feet wearing a path in the soft earth between the flower beds. Caym had taken the children to help the Nola for a little while, and they had left chattering excitedly about their important task. Meanwhile, I was here biting my nails—something I had never done before in my entire existence. My stomach churned with acidic worry as dark thoughts swirled around my mind like storm clouds.

I picked absently at the rose bushes that surrounded the porch, their thorns pricking my fingertips without my notice.

I had called Hesperia to visit because she was the only one who had experienced something like what I thought I was feeling. The only one who might understand the creeping dread that had settled in my bones.

"Hi!" Hesperia called out cheerfully as she materialized, waving with genuine enthusiasm.

It was painful to watch the happiness drain from her face as she took in my appearance.

"What's wrong?" Hesperia asked immediately, her voice softening with concern. "I can see it written all over you."

"Have you noticed anything… strange lately?" I asked, my voice barely above a whisper.

"Strange how?" She shook her head, confusion flickering across her features.

"When I sleep, I hear these voices calling out in the darkness," I began, the words tumbling out like water from a broken dam. "They call for 'the seed water clock death'—it feels urgent, desperate, like they need our help more than anything in the world. Then, when I'm awake, I see our world… change. Sometimes people's faces shift or distort for just a moment, like reality is glitching. It's like I'm the only one who can see it happening. Like I'm going insane."

The confession left me feeling hollow and exposed, as if I had torn open my chest and shown her my bleeding heart.

"I have been getting terrible headaches lately," Hesperia admitted slowly, her hand moving unconsciously to her temple. "We do have other realms, you know. Other worlds we created and helped look after in the early days. We left them with a key to call on us if they were ever in desperate need—a specific incantation: 'I call upon the sisters of Seed, Water, Clock, and Death.' It wasn't taught to everyone, only to those we trusted most. But I don't understand why it would alter our world like this."

I bit my nail again, tasting copper from where I'd worried the skin raw. I was falling apart inside at the terrifying possibility that I had built a life after unspeakable tragedy that was so utterly perfect, I couldn't have imagined it any better myself. I had never been happier, never felt more complete. The only thing missing was my other children—but even that pain had dulled to a manageable ache.

"Hesperia," I ran a trembling hand across my eyebrows, feeling the dampness of cold sweat. "When you were trapped in the locket that Nikola and Deimos created, did it feel real the first time? How did you finally realize it wasn't what you thought it was?"

Hesperia's eyebrows drew together in concentration. "I realized something was wrong when I was speaking to one of you about a shared memory, and you didn't remember something we had supposedly done together. Once I noticed that inconsistency, the entire illusion began to unravel like a poorly woven tapestry."

She guided me up the porch steps with gentle hands and settled me into the rocking chair that had been carved for me so long ago, its familiar embrace offering little comfort.

"Now that I'm thinking about it," she continued, settling into the chair beside me, "it was remarkably easy to defeat Deimos and rebuild everything afterward. It felt like it took almost nothing to piece the entire world back together, as if the universe itself was eager to comply with our wishes."

She paused, her expression growing distant. "I kept the soul blade that I used to break out of the locket's prison."

"Do you think we can use it to test this reality?" I sat up straighter, hope and terror warring in my chest.

"If it will bring you peace of mind, I think we should try," Hesperia replied without hesitation. "We've fixed the realm, set the mortals back on the right track. But more than that, I want to start rebuilding our relationship as sisters. I miss the three of you more than I can express."

My head hung lower than usual, shame weighing on my shoulders like a heavy cloak. I had been avoiding them on purpose because I didn't know how to bridge the vast chasm that had opened between us. So many lifetimes had passed since we were just young girls playing in gardens and learning magic, laughing without the weight of worlds on our shoulders.

"It feels like we're all so fundamentally different now," I admitted, my voice thick with unshed tears.

"I don't think so," Hesperia replied gently. "Do you

remember when Sage first started practicing her nature magic and she accidentally turned Cyrus into a walking stick bug? It took weeks for him to be turned back, and while he was trapped in that tiny form, the weather was completely out of control because of how furious he was. Sage still seems to enjoy growing things from people—that's a similarity that spans millennia."

Her expression was so completely serious, so matter-of-fact, that I couldn't help but laugh despite my anxiety.

Hesperia nodded with satisfaction. "You used to laugh at exactly these kinds of things back then, too. See? Things aren't as different at their core as you think."

"Can we test your blade first, before we move forward with anything else?" I asked, needing to know the truth even as part of me feared it.

I understood what she was doing—trying to reconnect us, to build bridges back to who we used to be. I wanted that too, desperately. I just couldn't shake the feeling that something fundamental was wrong with our reality. As Hesperia watched me with that gentle, understanding smile, I saw the cabin behind us shift colors, turning grey and lifeless before snapping back to vibrant normalcy.

Hesperia lifted her skirt without hesitation and unbuckled the knife from her thigh, the blade gleaming wickedly in the afternoon light. She held it out for me to take, and I accepted it without a moment's pause.

"Pick a spot and strike it," she instructed calmly. "It doesn't matter where—just do it and see what happens."

I looked down at the blade, then back to Hesperia's encouraging face. A wave of pure terror ran through my body as the full weight of what I was about to do hit me. I was suddenly, overwhelmingly aware of how afraid I felt at the idea that I might shatter my own perfect reality in a single stroke.

I was nearly prepared to live with the lie, as long as it remained this beautiful.

I stood on unsteady legs and walked to the side of the cabin, my heart hammering against my ribs. I raised the blade with a shaking arm, took a deep breath that did nothing to calm my nerves, and drove it into the wooden wall with all my strength.

Nothing. Nothing happened to the wall, or to our world, or to the perfect life I had built.

But something did happen to me. I felt a sense of relief so profound it nearly brought me to my knees—the kind of release that comes after holding your breath for far too long.

I stabbed at the cabin again, and again, and again. I stabbed until my arm felt like lead and dropped to my side, until the blade bent and warped from the force of my desperate strikes. Hesperia stood beside me in complete silence, without the smallest hint of judgment on her face, letting me work through whatever madness had taken hold of me.

I knew I must look utterly foolish, but there was a part of me that still needed to release the crushing weight of losing Caym over and over again, of losing Kyra, my parents, everyone I had ever loved.

Maybe I was simply letting my mind play cruel tricks on me. Maybe this peace was real, and I was the one who was broken.

CHAPTER FIFTY-TWO
THE DOUBLE DATE

SAGE

Vespera sat close beside me, her warmth a comfort against my side, while Shivani and Koa sat across from us at the polished wooden table. We had positioned ourselves in the center of the library, surrounded by towering shelves that stretched toward the vaulted ceiling. The library was closed for the day so that we could have our double date in peace—it was supposed to be fun, a chance for bonding and laughter. We were supposed to be enjoying ourselves, creating new memories to replace the painful ones, but no matter how beautiful the idea had played out in our heads, the air of new beginnings felt stale and forced most days.

"Before Dahlia left for the stars, she mentioned that she had hidden a piece of her power somewhere," Shivani began, her fingers drumming nervously against her teacup. "A piece of herself that she split four ways, apparently. I haven't been able to stop thinking about it since she told us. Do you think it means that there's actually a box or something hidden somewhere with literal pieces of her in it? Please tell me we're not going to discover we have to eat body parts again."

She shivered visibly at the thought, her face paling.

"I sincerely hope not," I replied, my stomach turning at the memory. "I don't know how I managed to choke down those hearts as it was."

"Watching you all do it was terrible enough," Koa admitted with a grimace. "I couldn't imagine what it must have actually tasted like."

We laughed at his expression, but the sound felt hollow and uncomfortable to my ears. I only felt a fleeting moment of peace before the familiar weight settled back on my chest. The world around us was perfect, we were all supposedly perfect, but the crushing burden of my guilt remained too heavy to bear. Every smile I managed to hold was only genuine for a heartbeat until I remembered what I truly was—someone who was only good for betrayal and poor choices.

There would come another time, another crucial moment where I would make the wrong decision again. It was only a matter of time before I let them all down once more, just like I always did.

How could I have even begun to apologize for the magnitude of my past mistakes?

How could I possibly do something significant enough to make up for the damage I had caused?

I lay awake most nights, every night, replaying every wrong choice I had ever made like a cruel slideshow behind my closed eyelids. The guilt ate at me from the inside, a constant gnawing that no amount of happiness could silence.

Vespera leaned over and pressed a gentle kiss to my cheek, her lips soft and warm against my skin. When I turned to give her a grateful smile, Nikola's cruel face was looking back at me instead. His cold eyes bored into mine with malicious satisfaction. My body jolted violently, and when I blinked hard, it was Vespera's concerned face again, her eyebrows drawn together in worry.

I looked frantically around the room, but no one else

seemed to have witnessed what I had seen. They were still talking casually to each other, their voices creating a gentle murmur that felt like it was coming from very far away.

They continued their conversation as if they existed in a completely separate world from mine. I stood up abruptly, my chair scraping against the floor, but they never stopped talking, never acknowledged my movement.

The books on the shelves began to mold before my eyes, their pages turning brown and crumbling, then dissolving into fine dust that drifted through the air like ash. The library's beautiful wooden beams were suddenly riddled with holes, eaten through by hundreds of tiny insects that swarmed and writhed in the rotting timber. The entire view in front of me began to move at a speed beyond human comprehension, blurring and shifting until everything dissolved into nothing but barren dirt and empty space.

Yet the group still sat at their table, still talked and laughed as if nothing had changed, as if the world wasn't crumbling around them.

I blinked again, and suddenly I was back at the table. Vespera's hand rested warmly on my thigh, her thumb tracing small, comforting circles through the fabric of my dress. Nothing had moved. No one had seen what had happened. The library was pristine again, the books whole and beautiful on their shelves.

I was losing my mind, and there was no one I could tell without sounding completely insane.

CHAPTER FIFTY-THREE

A MEETING, AGAIN

RURI

"I called everyone to the cabin so that we can talk about some strange things that have been happening," I began, my voice already trembling with the weight of what I was about to confess. "I've been seeing glitches in our reality." I cleared my throat, trying to steady myself. "I was pregnant—I am pregnant—but when I woke up this morning, I wasn't anymore. I wasn't even in our world; I was just lying in a black abyss surrounded by flames that never consumed me."

Koa and Coy both looked down at the ground, their silence speaking volumes. It was a polite and quiet way of telling me that they thought I was losing my mind. I knew that's exactly what their downcast eyes meant, and the knowledge cut through me like a blade. Vespera kept her hand protectively on Sage's lower back, but her lips pressed into a thin line of concern.

"I've seen it too," Sage whispered, her voice barely audible above the creak of the cabin's wooden beams. "It's nearly impossible to explain, but it's as if the world is melting like wax and then being hastily put back together again. As if reality itself ran out of power for a moment."

Her words made my heart skip a beat, relief and terror warring in my chest. I wasn't alone in this madness.

"I think we need to seriously consider that if we keep looking for something to go wrong, if we keep expecting things to revert back to the way they were before, they will," Shivani interjected, her voice carrying the weight of hard-earned wisdom. "We're all so accustomed to things falling apart around us that chaos is the only constant we know anymore. Maybe we're creating problems where none exist."

Silence hung between all of us like a suffocating blanket, stretching for what felt like an eternity before anyone dared to speak again.

"We did test my soul blade," Hesperia offered quietly. "It worked before when we were trapped in a false realm created by that cursed locket. Maybe Shivani has a point. Maybe we just need to sit down and really communicate with each other. I thought that once we reached this point of peace, we would all be speaking more openly about our fears and doubts. It feels like the only cage we're trapped in now is the one we're maintaining around ourselves through silence."

My breathing grew labored, each inhale feeling like I was drowning in thick air. I knew with every fiber of my being that I wasn't crazy. I knew that something fundamental was wrong with our reality. But sitting here, listening to them dismiss my concerns or explain them away, I felt like I was being mocked, ignored, gaslit into questioning my own sanity.

Caym moved closer to me and took both of my hands into his calloused palms, his touch warm and familiar. "If you're struggling with something, please talk to me. I'm here for you, always."

I was as heartbroken by the possibility that I might inadvertently ruin our perfect world together—this place where all of our dreams had finally come true—as I was devastated to think that even he only wanted to half-listen to my desperate warnings.

I pulled my hands free from Caym's gentle grip and bolted from the cabin, my bare feet pounding against the wooden porch. I needed fresh air, needed space to think and reevaluate what was happening to me. Maybe they were right. Maybe I was the problem.

A thunderous fist pounded against the sky above me. Once, twice, before it burst through like glass, and the clouds came cascading down over me like torrential rain mixed with fragments of heaven itself. Deimos stepped through the gaping hole in the sky before shrinking down to normal human proportions, his presence making the air around him shimmer with dark energy.

"Ruri," Deimos whispered urgently, his voice carrying desperate relief. "I thought I'd never manage to break through. I've been trying to reach you for months."

"Months?" I stammered, my mind reeling from the implications.

The world around us began to slide and distort like wet paint running down a canvas, everything dissolving into streams of color that fell like impossible rain.

"He's still alive, isn't he?" I whispered, my voice barely a breath as the horrible truth crystallized.

"Nikola is still alive," Deimos confirmed grimly.

My knees nearly buckled beneath me before Deimos caught my arm, steadying me against the revelation that shattered everything I thought I knew.

"How much of this life is fake?" I asked, my voice breaking. My thoughts immediately went to the most precious parts of my existence. Caym? My children? My breath came in ragged gasps.

"I'm going to get you out of here," Deimos declared with fierce determination.

"Why?" I demanded, jerking away from his touch. "Why would you help me now?"

He had never been on our side before. He had used me, lied to me, manipulated me at every turn. I wouldn't—couldn't—forgive him for what he had put us through.

"I was wrong about everything, but I do care about you," Deimos admitted, his voice heavy with what sounded like genuine regret. "I always have."

I pushed him away from me and ran toward the cabin that was now visibly melting like ice in summer heat.

"Caym!" I screamed his name like a prayer, like a lifeline.

He came running outside immediately, but the look on his face—a mixture of profound sadness and resignation—sent terror coursing through my veins like ice water.

"Where are the children?" I pleaded desperately, grabbing at his shirt. "You have to get them. You have to help me get them out of here!"

Caym reached up and gently cupped both sides of my face with his strong hands. "I can't save them, my love. They're not real. They're all part of the elaborate dream that Deimos created to trap you."

Before my eyes, Caym began to dissolve, melting into clear liquid like snow in spring. The water that had been his hands dripped down my cheeks and onto my shirt, while the rest of him soaked into dirt that was rapidly turning to ash beneath my feet.

I collapsed to my knees, my hands clawing at the disintegrating ground where he had been. I wasn't pregnant anymore—my rounded belly was gone, my children were gone, my husband was gone. Everything that had given my existence meaning had been nothing but an illusion.

Deimos wrapped his arms around me from behind, and my body temperature spiked rapidly as rage consumed me. I struggled violently against his grip, every muscle in my body screaming in protest. It was all his fault. He had orchestrated this elaborate torture. He had taken everything from me and then failed to maintain the dream convincingly enough for me to remain blissfully unaware.

The rest of the world that hadn't yet melted into puddles of false reality became engulfed in a blinding white light that seared my retinas. I pressed both hands over my eyes until the blazing illumination finally stopped.

When I opened my eyes, I was sitting in gray ash that still held traces of warmth. Endless fires burned all around me, their flames reaching toward a blood-red sky. I was back in Ashbell, but the volcano oozed molten rock and everything that had once been beautiful now burned in eternal torment. Nikola had turned everything in the realm to ash and suffering.

Deimos grabbed my wrist without warning and sliced it open with a blade that appeared from nowhere. I tried to protest, but he was already filling his cupped hands with my blood before his own body started to glitch and pixelate like a broken image. He chanted something under his breath in a language I didn't recognize, and then he began to fade in and out of existence, his form becoming unstable.

Parts of his body fractured into small squares of distorted images, like a shattered mirror reflecting fragments of different realities. A brilliant ray of light burst from his mouth just before a scream of pure agony tore from his lips, the sound echoing across the burning wasteland.

Deimos exploded into hundreds of blue butterflies, their wings catching the firelight like stained glass. On their delicate wings, I could see glowing souls trapped within the gossamer membranes. The butterflies landed gently in my outstretched hands, and I heard the voices of my children calling for me from within their luminous forms, their cries both heart-breaking and filled with hope.

CHAPTER FIFTY-FOUR

THE FINAL CHANGE

SAGE

My sisters were scattered across the ashy ground like broken dolls, their bodies sprawled at unnatural angles. The look of shock etched into their faces had to have matched my own as the full scope of our situation crashed over us like a tidal wave. Nikola slithered toward us with predatory grace, his massive serpentine form cutting through the smoky air. He hadn't abandoned his snake form, but I could still see the cruel satisfaction twisting his reptilian features into something resembling a grin.

His forked tongue flicked out to taste our despair before he spoke, his voice a sibilant whisper that seemed to come from everywhere at once.

"I didn't count on Deimos being the reason the four of you finally escaped my little paradise," Nikola mused, his tone dripping with dark amusement. "Still, I did have more than enough time to accomplish a few crucial things while you were all playing house." His eyes glittered with malicious pleasure. "I'm sure you're all feeling very disoriented right now. Yumi is trapped in the box where she belongs, Sahir is nothing but stardust scattered across the sky. The guardians are dead—well, all except for dear Vespera. It truly was laughably easy to manipulate you all into doing exactly what I wanted when you thought you were acting for yourselves. Dahlia and Olexei are lost among the stars now. My path to ultimate power cleared itself beautifully, really."

Ruri scrambled to her feet with desperate urgency, her hands shaking as she clawed at the ground. "Caym!" she screamed, the sound tearing from her throat like a physical wound.

Her anguished cries pierced through a part of my soul that I didn't know existed, awakening a pain so raw and profound that it felt like being flayed alive. It was a scream of loss that transcended anything I had ever experienced, the sound of a heart being ripped from a living chest. Ruri dug frantically through mounds of gray ash, her fingernails breaking and bleeding as she pulled out Caym's unnaturally still body. Koa rolled out from beneath him, gasping and alive but barely conscious.

Caym appeared preserved by some cruel magic, but Koa and Coy were already showing signs of decay, their skin taking on a sickly pallor that spoke of creeping death.

Nikola's massive tail whipped through the air and slammed into Ruri with bone-crushing force, sending her flying through the smoky air like a ragdoll before she crashed into the burning wreckage of what had once been a beautiful building. Hesperia rushed after her without hesitation, but Shivani only fell to her knees and gripped the ash-covered dirt with her fingernails until they bled, crawling desperately toward Koa's deteriorating body.

Maybe Nikola was right about everything. If Dahlia—with all her wisdom and power—couldn't defeat him, then who were we to even attempt it? Who were we to think that we could succeed where she had failed so completely?

But as I watched my sisters suffer, as I saw the destruction

Nikola had wrought upon everyone we loved, something crystallized inside me. I got to my feet slowly, deliberately, and gained Nikola's full attention. He slithered toward me with inhuman speed, his massive form casting shadows that seemed to devour the light around us.

I didn't move. I didn't try to run or defend myself. I knew exactly what I wanted to do, and the thought had barely entered my mind before I had already made peace with the inevitable cost. Nikola's jaws opened wide, revealing rows of fangs like obsidian daggers, and he slammed his enormous head down over me.

I allowed his jaw to close around my body, feeling the heat of his breath and the crushing pressure of his bite. As his head lifted with me trapped inside, I placed both of my hands against the roof of his mouth and closed my eyes in concentration.

I released vines directly into his skull, feeling them burst forth from my palms like green lightning. I wrapped the thorny tendrils around his eyes and tightened them with all the fury and grief I carried, squeezing until I felt the sickening squish and pop of his eyeballs bursting. The satisfying crack of bone told me he now had nothing but hollow, bleeding sockets where his eyes had been.

From my feet, I released more vines through his lower jaw, these ones sprouting razor-sharp thorns that impaled him from within. The thorns grew longer and sharper, piercing through muscle and sinew like nature's own torture device.

The vines continued to spread and grow, sprouting flowers with snapping jaws of their own. These carnivorous blooms took savage bites out of his scaled flesh, leaving behind patches of festering rot that spread down his massive tail like a plague. The smell of decay filled the air, mixing with the sulfur from the volcano.

I felt my strength ebbing away like water through a broken dam. I was pushing my abilities far beyond what I had to give, drawing on reserves of power I didn't even know I possessed. In my mind, I reached out for Astra, thinking of her with desperate fondness. I had always admired her strength and grace. I remembered watching her in the golden city and thinking that I had never seen someone look so naturally collected and born for leadership as she was.

My left arm gave out first, the connection to my vines severing as my muscles failed. But the plants had taken on a life of their own now, continuing to grow and wrap tighter around Nikola's thrashing form without my direct control. My right arm followed shortly after, going limp and useless at my side. Every attempt to draw breath sent shards of agony through my chest, as if my ribs were made of broken glass.

I felt Nikola's massive body crash to the ground with a thunderous impact, and his jaw opened just enough that I could see the mesmerizing flow of orange and red magma streaming from Ashbell's volcano in the distance. Even in this moment of approaching death, it was strangely beautiful—like liquid fire painting the sky.

For a brief moment, I allowed myself to imagine what might have been. I would have enjoyed being able to build a peaceful home there with Vespera, somewhere far from all this violence and pain.

Using the very last dregs of my strength, I unleashed one final surge of rot and strangling vines into Nikola's dying body. Then, with my final conscious act, I gathered all of my remaining power and sent it surging across the realm to Astra —my gift to the sister I had always looked up to.

I felt my heart beat once, and the space between that beat and the next felt like an eternity stretching out before me. I felt light as air, weightless and free, before I finally entered the welcoming darkness that had been calling my name.

CHAPTER FIFTY-FIVE
THE FINAL STAND

HESPERIA

Nikola squirmed and hissed beneath the mass of vines that had wrapped themselves so tightly around his massive form that they pierced clean through his scaled skin. Dark blood oozed around the thorny bindings as his flesh protruded grotesquely between the green restraints.

The landscape stretched endlessly in every direction—nothing but gray ash and the skeletal remains of what had once been a thriving realm. The light was dim and sickly, filtered through smoke and despair, but every desperate writhe that came from Nikola's dying body brought its own flickering light of hope to our hearts.

Astra descended from the smoke-filled sky like an avenging angel, and with her arrival came a scent that nearly brought me to my knees. Wet grass after spring rain and fresh lavender —the unmistakable essence of my beloved sister Sage. The fragrance clung to Astra like a ghostly embrace, and I knew with crushing certainty that Sage was gone forever. In that moment, I understood why Nikola wasn't simply shaking off the vines and rising again like he had so many times before.

He was being slowly crushed under the overwhelming weight of every ounce of power that Sage had poured into her final, desperate gambit.

She had given her life to secure our victory, and now Astra carried her legacy as our fourth sister. The responsibility and grief were written in every line of Astra's face.

I refused to waste a single second of the precious time Sage had bought us with her blood. I would not allow her sacrifice—or the sacrifice of nearly all of our friends—to be in vain. Shivani read the determination in my mind from where she knelt beside Koa's deteriorating body, understanding my plan without need for words.

She whipped crimson blood from her fingertips like liquid lightning, the scarlet streams lashing at Nikola every time he managed to lift his enormous head even a few inches above the ash-covered ground. Each strike left burning welts across his scales, and his pained hisses filled the air like a symphony of justice.

I pulled out my soul blade, its familiar weight comforting in my trembling hands, and drove it deep into Nikola's exposed chest. The blade sliced through scale and muscle like they were parchment. I dug with frenzied desperation, my hands becoming slick with his dark blood, until I finally saw his still-beating heart—black and twisted, pulsing with malevolent energy.

With grim satisfaction, I formed glowing red fate chains in my free hand, the magical bonds materializing from pure will and determination. I used them to slice his corrupted heart into four equal pieces, each one writhing with its own terrible life. This was our plan—the one thing that could finally end his reign of terror forever.

I wrapped each of the four pieces of Nikola's severed heart in separate fate chains, the red bonds pulsing with binding magic that would hold even beyond death.

Ruri finally joined our circle, moving with mechanical

precision despite the emptiness that haunted her eyes—the hollow look of someone who had lost everything that mattered. But even in her grief, she finished the magical cage around his heart with elemental magic, her power weaving ice and fire and earth into an impenetrable prison.

Shivani pressed a lock made of her own crystallized blood onto the chains, the crimson seal glowing with the power of her life force. Then Astra, without speaking a word to any of us about how she had gained such an ability, twisted the lock's keyhole completely away from existence itself, ensuring that no key of any size or origin could ever fit inside to free the monster's heart.

The massive serpent body of Nikola finally went completely still and lifeless, his reign of terror ended at last by our combined efforts and Sage's ultimate sacrifice.

But as we stood over his corpse, the true scope of the destruction around us became impossible to ignore. It wasn't just extensive—it was complete and total. Every corner in every direction we could see was utterly barren, reduced to nothing but ash and shadow. Nikola had systematically turned the entire realm into a lifeless abyss, and in all this desolation, I hadn't laid eyes on a single familiar face beyond our small group.

Only the four of us remained. Only we four sisters and one guardian had survived to bear witness to the end.

Only the four of us and one guardian were left to put everything back together again, knowing that no matter how hard we tried, nothing would ever feel the same as it had before we lost so much.

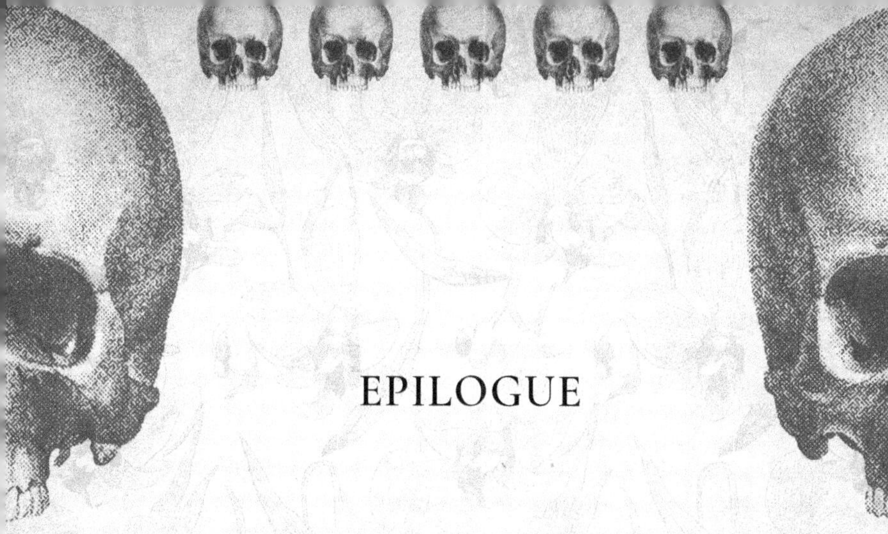

EPILOGUE

CAYM

I stood before the abyssal mirror that the Blood Weaver had left behind, its surface rippling like liquid shadow despite being solid as stone. Through its dark depths, I watched the sisters of fate methodically cage the four pieces of Nikola inside dragons—four ancient dragons for four pieces of his severed heart, just as the plan had always dictated.

I watched the hollow emptiness that haunted their eyes as they sat in the ash-covered ruins, staring at the devastation with no clear idea of where to even begin rebuilding their shattered world.

I watched the terrible cost they paid trying to bring back what little they could from the ashes of everything they had loved.

"I'm glad to see you again, old friend," Quade murmured from somewhere beside me in the consuming darkness.

"I cannot say the same," I answered, my voice echoing strangely in this place between worlds.

He drew a deep breath that he released just as heavily, the sound carrying the weight of eons. "I know it must be agony to watch and feel so helpless, but you did make a deal. A trade of hearts for thirty days so that you could help them when they needed it most—and help you did. They wouldn't have made it nearly as far as they did without everyone's efforts, especially yours."

Time moved differently in the dark abyss where we stood suspended between existence and void. What felt like mere heartbeats for us translated to days and weeks in the mirror's reflection, watching them move at an accelerated pace through their grief and reconstruction. Ruri built a magnificent tomb of gleaming obsidian and golden citrine with her own hands, each stone placed with reverent care. They laid my body inside it beside Coy and Koa, and I watched my children weep at my feet.

But they had come back—all of them, even the two we had lost during Ruri's mortal life were with her again, their small forms alive and vibrant. The sight brought a smile to my face even through the crushing agony that pressed against my chest like a physical weight. I couldn't be with them, couldn't hold them or comfort their tears, but at least she had a piece of what she had always wanted most.

"Is there truly no other deal we can make?" I asked, though I still couldn't bring myself to look at him.

I already knew the answer before he spoke it.

"Not today, Caym. Perhaps another time, when the cosmic balance shifts again," Quade responded with what might have been genuine regret.

Even if I had wanted to break my word and fight against this fate, there was nothing within my power to do. I was trapped in a strange state of existence that I barely understood—neither fully alive nor completely dead, suspended in this liminal space where time had no meaning.

I watched through the abyssal mirror day after endless day, night after starless night. I watched until I began to feel myself becoming part of the abyss itself, as if the darkness was slowly claiming me piece by piece. My feet became covered and held down by creeping shadows that felt almost alive. The darkness blanketed my knees like a suffocating embrace, as if trying to lull me into eternal sleep.

My mind grew blank and empty as I watched them rebuild Cylla one painstaking day at a time, their progress maddeningly slow but undeniably steady.

I knew only the sound of my own heart beating in the silence and the memory of my lover's eyes—those were the only things that kept me tethered to who I had been.

I had forgotten how to move my limbs, forgotten the feeling of breath in my lungs, but I hadn't forgotten the distinctive buzz of Nikola's presence. I hadn't forgotten the oppressive weight he cast over everyone when he was near, that suffocating aura of malevolence that made the very air feel thick and poisonous.

I felt him becoming restless in his prison, stirring like a caged beast. I felt him tug and pull at his magical chains with increasing desperation. The mirror showed me the disturbing evidence—seasons growing wildly erratic across the rebuilt world. Snow fell in the middle of summer, and lakes froze solid beneath blazing suns.

"You've felt it too, I see," Quade observed from somewhere in the enveloping darkness. "I hadn't seen you blink for so long that I thought you had been lost to the void entirely."

"Cylla is becoming erratic again," I whispered, my voice barely more than a breath.

"There's an entire universe becoming erratic," the Blood Weaver corrected me, his tone heavy with implications I didn't want to consider. "And this is only the beginning."

REFERENCE GUIDE

DRAGONS

Ryujin—Second in Command of the Armies from the Age of Moonlight, in dragon form.
Sina—Winter Goddess in dragon form
Vero—Fall Goddess in dragon form
Cyrus—Summer God in dragon form
Belladonna—Ruri Dragon
Usha—Erebus Guardian
Divala—Brontide Guardian
Kaida—Onyx Dragon

TIMELINE

Age of Moonlight—Dahlia's rule, the beginning of time
Age of Starlight—Yumi's rule, the middle of time
Age of Darkness—Nikola's rule, the destruction

Temple Leaders

Dominic—High Priest of vampires
Dimitri—Lower Priest of vampires
Inola—High Priestess of the Order of the Arcane Tome

TEMPLES

Temple of Magic
Temple of Rebirth
Temple of Vampires
Temple of Healing
Temple of Water

Realms

Semper—Realm of the Gods
Cylla—Realm of the Mortals
Cosima—Realm of Dreaming Souls
Merripen—Realm of the Dead

ORIGINAL DEITIES

Yumi—Goddess of Starlight
Dahlia—Goddess of the Moon
Olexei—God of the Sun
Nikola—God of Insanity

Seasonal Deities

Sina—Goddess of Winter
Vero—Goddess of Fall
Cyrus—God of Summer
Inola—Goddess of Spring

SISTERS OF FATE

Sage—Goddess of Nature
Ruri—Goddess of Magic
Shivani—Goddess of Time
Hesperia—Goddess of Fate

Deity-led kingdoms
Ruri—Ashbell
Kyrell—Solaris
Thann—Orest
Astra—Edur
Kyra—Brontide
Orla/Sage—Erebus
Izaria—Daxon

Titles and role changes after the Age of Darkness
Malina—Ruri and Caym's daughter
Lex—Ruri and Caym's son, God of Storms
Divala—New Sun God
Belladonna—New Moon Goddess
Ryujin—New God of Starlight

Usha—New God of Winter

Astra—New Goddess of Nature and Sister of Fate

OTHER NOTABLE INHABITANTS

Lui—Leader of the Timekeepers.

Fiia—A small fluttering creature made of starlight that helps send messages back and forth.

Jeb—Commander of the Nola.

Nola—Keepers of the underworld, helpers to the God of Death.

Vina—Cave protectors

Seere—Clerics of Ashbell, created by Ruri. They are covered in black scales with magma-colored veins, orange eyes, and black hair. They commonly wear masks to avoid breathing in the excess ash on their land.

Mita—Nearly transparent skin. Golden eyes and tinted skin. Black hair. Their golden veins pulse with the thunder magic they wield.

Angels—Guardians created to protect Yumi and the realm of the Gods.

Timekeepers—Collectors and protectors of knowledge from the Age of Moonlight.

Blood Guards—The Second created guardians of Semper. Made by blood from Helia, the Goddess of Time.

False deities—Deities created in the likeness of powerful originals in order to take their place. Helia, Minna, Thann, Kyrell.

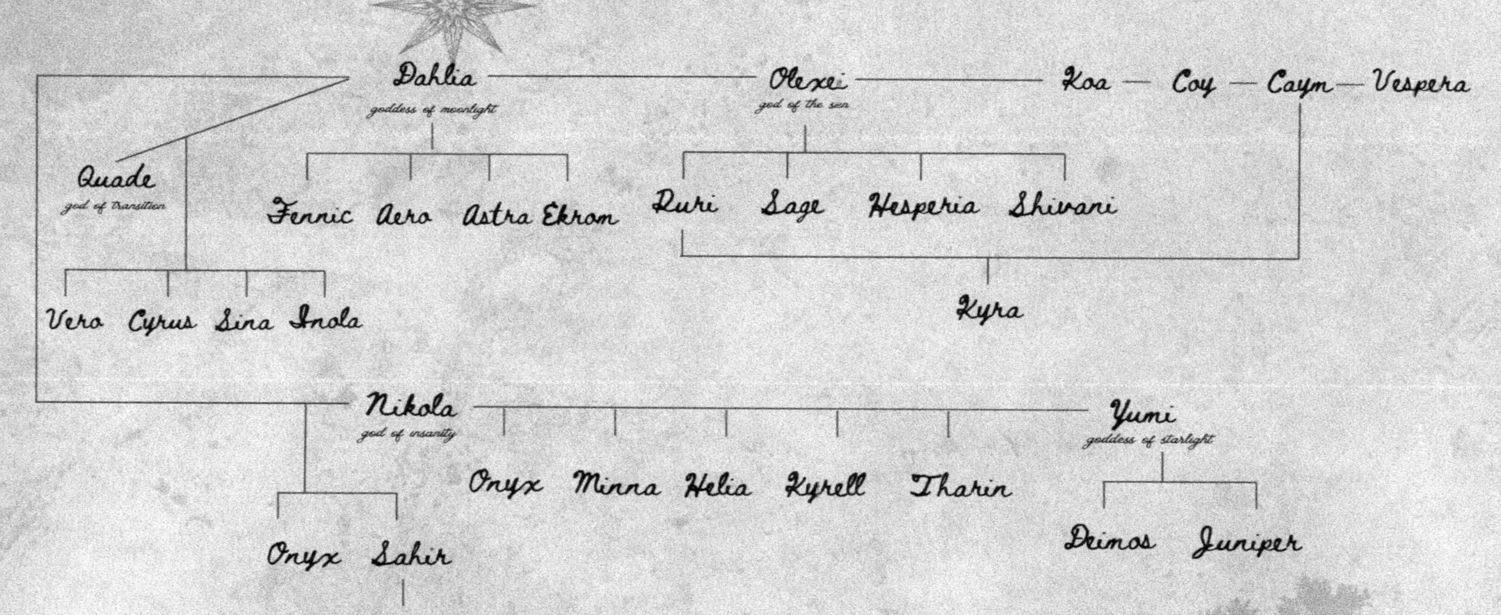

Dahlia
goddess of moonlight
Olexei
god of the sea
Koa — Coy — Caym — Vespera
Quade
god of transition
Fennic Aero Astra Ekrom
Ruri Sage Hesperia Shivani
Vero Cyrus Sina Inola
Kyra
Nikola
god of insanity
Yumi
goddess of starlight
Onyx Minna Helia Kyrell Tharin
Onyx Sahir
Deimos Juniper
Izaria

COMING SOON...

The Bloodborn Inheritance

Hourglass of Blood, Book Two

Shadow of the Last Born, Book Three

The Bonebound Court

The Hollow Crown, Book One

Bound By Bone, Book Two

Midnight Oath, Book Three

The Origins of Cylla

The Serpent's Vengeance

Keep up to date with the latest news and release dates by following on social media.

Find Harleigh Rose Knight on all platforms.

www.ingramcontent.com/pod-product-compliance
Lightning Source LLC
Chambersburg PA
CBHW070605300726

48975CB00006B/1719